WHIPHAND

Margaret pointed wordlessly to the belt. Richard picked it up and fitted it around his waist, handcuffs to the front.

'Hands behind you,' she ordered.

He loosened the buckles and turned the belt.

'Tighter,' Margaret ordered in her could-do-better voice.

'Help me, then,' Richard said, turning to face her.

With a resigned sigh she pulled the buckles tighter, nipping his waist in. She locked the handcuffs on his wrists and stowed the key away.

'Now sit down at my feet,' she commanded. 'My feet and toes may require some attention later. You will like that, won't you, Pamela?'

WHIPHAND

G. C. Scott

This book is a work of fiction.
In real life, make sure you practise safe sex.

First published in 2002 by
Nexus
Thames Wharf Studios
Rainville Road
London W6 9HA

www.nexus-books.co.uk

Typeset by TW Typesetting, Plymouth, Devon

Printed and bound by
Clays Ltd, St Ives PLC

ISBN 0 352 33694 3

1

The German Visitor

Richard came home early on a Wednesday afternoon in October. There was a chill in the air, a foretaste of autumn and the long winter, even though the sky was a high washed blue and the westering sun shone brightly on the leaves of the oak tree down by the river. The wind rushed through the pine woods across the stream, tossing the branches wildly. But inside, with the door closed, Richard was conscious of the contrasting silence of the house. Helena hadn't said anything about going out, but she might well have decided to go shopping, or to call on one of her clients. He called her name, ending on a question: 'Helena?'

When there was no reply he went through into the kitchen. The breakfast dishes were stacked in the draining board and the kettle was cold on the range. So she was away. Nevertheless he went all through the ground floor, looking for a note or for some clue that would tell him where she was or when she might be back. There was nothing. He wondered once again if perhaps her aunt Margaret had returned to take Helena back to Germany as she had threatened to do, leaving him no choice but to follow and try to get her back. Margaret, he knew, would like very much to have them both in her power again, turning him and Helena into her slaves. The same thought came to him whenever he came home to an empty house.

He pushed the thought aside. There was always the danger that Margaret would once more seek to interfere in their lives, but he didn't think she would return so soon to the scene of her latest defeat. She was not one to take defeat lightly, and she would not relish the thought of another one. So she would bide her time and make better plans before trying again.

Richard went to his study to work on the plans for the new houses he was building near Walcott. He had bought the land at a good price with the backing of Walter Jennings, who had admired the house Richard had built for him, and who enjoyed his own liaison with Helena. Richard was building three houses which he hoped would sell at good prices. As his own architect, he also enjoyed seeing the plans on paper taking actual shape in bricks and mortar. He worked for nearly three hours and there was still no sign of Helena.

The sun was sinking behind the treetops across the river when he stood up from the draughting table to stretch himself. He went along the hallway to the bathroom for a shower. Drying himself with a large towel, he made his way to the bedroom. Unusually, the door was closed. He turned the knob and pushed it open. The curtains were drawn so that the room was in semi-darkness, but it was still light enough to let Richard see at once the woman bound to the bed.

He dropped the towel in surprise. He felt his stomach muscles contract and his cock stir with excitement. It is not every day that a man comes home to find an attractive woman spread-eagled on her back on his bed. He knew at once that it was not Helena. The woman whose wrists and ankles were bound to the opposite bedposts were both heavier and somehow more mature-looking than his lover. Her breasts, heavy, fuller than Helena's, rose and fell to her quiet breathing. Her thick pubic hair was dark where Helena's was blonde. She wore a form-fitting helmet which completely enclosed her head, buckled tightly so that her features were outlined beneath the smooth black latex. As well as concealing her identity, he guessed that the helmet served as both gag and blindfold. Yes, there was the small hole for inflating the gag and, as he looked more closely, he saw that the woman's jaws were held apart and her cheeks slightly distended by it.

Probably there were earplugs as well. If so, that would explain why she had made neither sound nor movement when he entered the room. He moved quietly to the bed and stood looking down at the stranger. The rope which held her wrists and ankles so tightly to the bedposts was the same as the rope he and Helena used to tie each other in their own sex games.

Richard felt himself growing erect. Someone who knew just which buttons to push had left this woman for him to discover. Suddenly he knew it must have been Helena who had arranged this surprise for him, and with that knowledge came recognition of the captive woman: Ingrid, Helena's foster-mother, who had helped transform him into a female and with whom he had shared a brief but torrid encounter in the process. He had last seen her like this: bound to her bed, gagged and blindfolded, waiting for her lover to come for her. Then, as now, Ingrid had worn only stockings and suspenders. When he left her for her lover, she had promised that one day he would come home to find her tied to his bed and waiting for *him*.

As he looked down at Ingrid, Richard saw once again the full, ripe body of the woman he had met and loved almost a year ago. Strange, he thought, how soon he had forgotten the tiny dimples on either side of her buttocks, the wide flare of her hips, the long taper of her legs, the solidity of her thighs. And strange, too, how quickly it all came back when he saw her again. He drew a deep shuddery breath as he took in her beauty. Ingrid's long chestnut hair, escaping from the back of

3

the mask, lay on her shoulders and trailed almost to her breasts.

He kneeled beside the bed to touch her hair, tangling his fingers in it. Ingrid, aware that she was no longer alone, twisted her head towards him. Beneath the tight rubber Richard saw her mouth move as she tried to speak. 'Ihhharrrrr?' she grunted, the sound of his name choked back and distorted by the gag.

'Yes, it's me, Ingrid,' he replied. He bent his head to hers and kissed her lips through the mask, feeling her mouth trying to respond to his through the tight rubber. Richard slid his hands beneath her shoulders, then raised her head and turning her face towards him as he held the kiss. He buried his hands in her long silky hair, twisting it round his fingers as he held her head to his lips.

Ingrid sighed. Her body strained towards him, her wrists and ankles pulling against the ropes as the muscles in her arms and legs stood out beneath the fine texture of her skin. Richard felt the cords in her neck tighten as she raised her head. Richard drew back his head, breaking the long kiss.

Ingrid moaned, the sound coming from deep in her throat.

He shifted so that he could lie alongside her in the bed, throwing his right leg over her thighs and straightening his left leg. As he moved he felt the sheer nylon of her stockings on his own flesh. The sensation electrified him. His cock was erect, pushing against the outer curve of Ingrid's hip. He tugged it until it lay against her, pressed between their bodies. When he looked back at Ingrid, he saw that her nipples were erect too, taut and crinkly with her excitement. As he shifted his thigh into her crotch, he was aware of the heat coming from her cunt.

Briefly, he wondered why she was so aroused. He didn't remember this wildness in her. She had been eager. Passionate, too, once she believed that he really

4

wanted her. But never this eager. He wondered if her German lover had deprived her of sex.

Ingrid was raising then lowering her hips beneath him, thrusting against his leg and making little sideways movements against his cock. Restrained by her bonds, Ingrid could only make small, tight movements, but he knew from her moans that she was fully aroused and ready for him.

Richard raised himself until he was kneeling between her outstretched legs, looking down at her full breasts with their taut erect nipples. He would have liked to caress them, to caress her whole body in fact, to reacquaint himself with all its secret places. But Ingrid's urgency forbade it. He grasped his cock and guided it into her cunt. When the tip of it touched her labia, Ingrid raised herself to allow him to penetrate her, and as he slid inside the tight wet sheath of her sex she moaned as loudly as the gag permitted.

When he was fully inside her, Ingrid began to make tiny, satisfied noises deep in her throat, almost like a cat purring, while her vaginal muscles clamped tightly around his cock. She arched her back and thrust with her hips, eager to take all of him inside her.

Richard lay still and rode her as she bucked beneath him. He could see the muscles in her arms straining and taut as she pulled against the ropes on her wrists. Her hands were clenched into fists and the ropes were digging into her flesh but Ingrid seemed oblivious to the pain. He could feel her legs straining tautly even though he could not see them. His own arms were around her shoulders, supporting her head. Ingrid's breasts were flattened against his chest, and she was trying to press her nipples ever harder to him.

As he raised Ingrid's face once more to kiss her through the tight rubber mask, she began to thrash wildly, moaning loudly as she came. Her hips thrust wildly and her imprisoned arms and legs became rigid with the intensity of her pleasure. The orgasm seemed to last forever, Ingrid's moans loud in his ears. He pressed his lips over hers, feeling them working through the tight rubber. Her breath was loud in his ears as she drew air through the breathing holes in her mask. Her faint perfume mingled with the scent of the rubber and her own body odours in an intoxicating fragrance that enveloped him and made him dizzy.

Richard marvelled at Ingrid's frenzy. She was out of control, her body racked by spasms of pleasure that passed like waves. He imagined himself riding out a storm at sea as she heaved and strained beneath him. He was so absorbed in her orgasm that his own took him by surprise, the rippling spasms almost lost in Ingrid's wilder motions. But he groaned with the intensity of it as he spent himself inside her. It felt as if he were emptying himself of a fiery stream, pouring himself into the raging storm that was Ingrid. And the effect on her was dramatic. She stiffened, each separate muscle seemingly as taut as a bowstring. Ingrid gave a deep muffled cry and then her body went slack beneath him.

He was reluctant to get up, but he thought he had better make the attempt, if only to allow Ingrid to catch her breath without his weight on her.

But as he shifted his weight Ingrid stirred. She seemed to sense that he was going to withdraw from her, for she made a dissenting noise at once. At the same time she made small thrusting movements with her hips, as if encouraging him to ride her once more. Richard felt himself growing erect again, to his surprise and pleasure.

Ingrid felt it too. She sighed and opened her legs as widely as she could.

Richard slid fully into her, probing her depths, feeling her grow warm and tight around him. He lay still for a while, enjoying the sensation of being so deeply inside her, and Ingrid too relaxed and lay back to savour her complete penetration and her utter helplessness. She sighed in satisfaction.

Richard could feel the growing excitement in Ingrid's body. Her nipples were growing hard against his chest, but most revealing was the increasing warmth of her cunt. He could feel it in his own cock. Soon her vaginal muscles began to clench around him and her breath began to rasp in his ear as she became more and more aroused. Once more Ingrid was tugging unconsciously at the ropes that bound her, savouring her helplessness and her complete domination and the thorough fucking that was sure to come.

Richard lifted his hips, withdrawing and then pushing slowly back into her. Slowly, he told himself. This was something to be enjoyed leisurely. Rushing would spoil it. He only hoped he could keep to his resolution.

As soon as Ingrid felt him sliding out and then back into her she sighed again, a long sound of pleasure. Her hands, he could see, were once again clenched into fists, the cords in her wrists standing out, the muscles of her arms tense. Ingrid's legs moved slightly under him, the smooth nylon of her stockings brushing his flesh with the familiar electrifying effect as she shifted on the bed and pulled at the ropes that bound her ankles to the bedposts.

Ingrid rocked her hips, making tiny thrusting movements in time with Richard's slow withdrawal and return. He saw a flush spreading down her neck, seeming to flow out from under the tight rubber mask that covered her face and head and to spread over her breasts. And she was beginning to moan as her arousal proceeded, a recurrent sound of pleasure. Richard thought he could detect tiny tremors in her vaginal muscles, the forerunners of the climax she was holding back, teasing them both by postponing the moment when she would lose control. They both knew that her orgasm would be more intense the longer she could wait. And so would his. So they both played the game

7

of holding on while trying to drive the other over the edge.

As they rocked slowly together Richard raised himself on his arms and looked down along their joined bodies. He looked at Ingrid's smooth flat stomach and at the tops of her thighs. Her stockings were long, reaching almost to her crotch, but he could see the place where they ended, and he was excited by the contrasting textures of flesh and nylon. He looked at himself going slowly in and out of Ingrid's tight wet cunt, and at the slow thrusting of her hips, rising and then falling in time to his own thrusts.

Then he raised his eyes to Ingrid's breasts. The nipples were taut with her excitement. He lowered himself once again, shifting until he could take one of them into his mouth. Ingrid gasped with delight as his lips closed over the pink bud of her nipple. Richard kissed it, flicking the sensitive flesh with his tongue. Ingrid cried out deep in her throat, her delight muffled by the gag but obvious to him as she tried to push her upper body against him, to allow him to take more of her breast into his mouth.

Richard bit her suddenly, a sharp nip that drew a shudder and a cry from her. The shudder went on and on, the cry rising louder as Ingrid began to come. She thrashed wildly beneath him as the pleasure washed through her straining body. He guessed Ingrid would have gone wild if she had not been tied. As it was, she could only express her passion by the clenching of her muscles and the unconscious movements of her head. She twisted it from side to side, the tight rubber giving off sudden highlights in the subdued light. The mask made her impersonal, preventing any of her natural features from showing, and Richard found this exciting. She could be *anyone*, one of his fantasy lovers, a complete stranger whom he compelled to respond to him with this wild pleasure.

And did Ingrid, too, derive more pleasure because of the mask, and from her inability to see who was actually lying on top of her, whose cock was inside her, who it was that was actually forcing her body to respond? Perhaps so. Richard knew that he responded more fully when Helena put the mask on him.

Ingrid was losing control. The interval between her orgasms was becoming shorter and shorter. Richard worried her nipple between his teeth while Ingrid thrashed wildly and came again, until finally, as before, her frenzy sent him over the edge.

He could tell from the sweat running down her body that she was exhausted. He waited for a few moments, allowing Ingrid to catch her breath, before he rose from the bed and began to remove the rubber mask. When he lifted it away from her face, he bent down and kissed her lips. Ingrid sighed with pleasure and returned the kiss softly.

'I am so glad to be here,' she said as he began to untie the ropes that held her.

'And I am so glad you came,' he replied. 'Pun intended,' Richard added with a smile as he helped Ingrid to sit up. He sat on the bed beside her and took her in his arms, inhaling the mingled fragrance of her and the sharp odour of her cunt.

Ingrid laid her head on his shoulder and closed her eyes. 'I have dreamed of seeing you again almost every day since you went away. It was worth the wait.'

Helena had always said that she didn't mind what Richard and her foster-mother did as long as it made them happy, but he wondered what she would say if she came back at that moment and saw him holding Ingrid among the disordered bedclothes. Professing tolerance was not the same thing as practising it.

'Helena told me she would be away for four days, and that you were not to worry about being with me. She said to tell you not to feel guilty. She also said that she would swap tales with you when she came back,' Ingrid added.

Richard smiled at the thought. He guessed that Helena would not spend the time alone, and he hoped that she and whoever she was with would find pleasure together. When she came back, they would be able to arouse one another by comparing notes.

Ingrid rose unsteadily to her feet. 'Bathroom,' she said. 'After all that fucking I have to pee. I must.'

Richard sat on the bed until she came back. He was glad to see that she had not removed her stockings and suspenders. He looked steadily at her legs as she approached him.

Seeing the direction of his gaze, Ingrid smiled. She stood still for a moment so that he could admire her before pirouetting slowly before him. She ended up facing him, still smiling. When he remained silent, her smile faded slowly, to be replaced by a worried expression. 'Richard, what is the matter? Are you thinking I am not a young woman like your Helena?'

Richard came back to the present with a visible start. He opened his arms and Ingrid came hurriedly to him. She stood close to him as he closed his arms around her waist and held her to him, his cheek against her stomach. He stroked the marvellous length of her legs and fondled her bottom. 'I want you the way you are. Please don't talk about that again or I will have to spank you.' He spoke half jokingly, and Ingrid's body lost some of the tension as he continued to hold and stroke her.

'Would you really spank me?' she asked him, attempting to lighten the atmosphere.

Richard looked up at her face and saw there a mixture of relief and curiosity. 'If you keep talking about being too old I will take you over my knee and use a hairbrush on your luscious bottom. That's a promise.'

Ingrid drew in a sharp breath and laughed. 'I believe you would. Helena says you enjoy whipping her.'

'Does she also say that she enjoys it?' As he spoke he wondered how Ingrid would respond to the lash – or the hairbrush. Would she enjoy it as much as her foster-daughter? Richard felt his cock stir as he contemplated Ingrid strung up under the whip.

'Yes, but I still do not understand how,' Ingrid told him with a catch in her voice.

'Then one day soon I'll show you,' Richard said.

'Oh, no. It would be too painful!' Ingrid looked flushed and hectic.

He dropped the subject abruptly, standing up and embracing her. 'Let's get something to eat. I'm hungry after all that sex.' He led the way down the stairs and to the kitchen. As Ingrid followed him, he heard the silken whisper of her nylon-sheathed thighs rubbing together. The sound aroused him as it always did.

They took coffee and toast through into the sitting room. Richard lit the log fire in the fireplace and drew the couch up before it. They sat together watching the flames flicker and enjoying the warmth. Richard unfolded the blanket he and Helena used on chilly evenings and made Ingrid lie down on the couch. Then he lay down beside her and drew the blanket up to their chins. Beneath it he held her close as the firelight made moving shadows in the darkening room. The thick mane of her hair was silky beneath his stroking fingers, and as he gently rubbed her scalp and neck Ingrid relaxed with a sigh and snuggled against him. Soon they slept, entwined on the couch.

Richard woke some time later. Ingrid slept on. The fire had burned down to a bed of glowing embers and the room was quite dark. Outside the wind had got up and was now moaning around the eaves. He extricated himself slowly from Ingrid and strode over to the hearth to make up the fire. The room had become colder with

11

the change in the weather. He threw two more logs on the fire and waited to make sure they would burn before going back to the sofa. This time Ingrid made a small protesting noise as he lay down, but she didn't wake. In the growing light from the fireplace he studied her features closely, finding her as attractive as ever.

He worked his way slowly back into position on the couch, and Ingrid fitted her body to his. He slipped into a dream of making love to his lover's foster-mother.

Some time still later he woke again. Ingrid was the reason. She was sitting astride him and was in the act of guiding his erect cock into her. Richard shifted to allow himself to be guided without letting her know he was awake. Ingrid completed her own penetration and called softly to him, 'Richard, wake up.'

He opened his eyes and feigned surprise at finding himself inside her.

Ingrid was delighted. 'Is this not a fine way to wake up? Do not struggle. I have you just where I want you.' She laughed triumphantly and rocked her hips.

Richard held still as she moved on his cock. 'Yes,' he replied. 'There's no better way.'

Ingrid was kneeling astride his hips, her knees bent and her thighs spread wide to allow him all the way inside her. Her full round breasts hung above him, and he reached up to caress them. Ingrid sighed with pleasure as he fondled her breasts. Her eyes closed and her face went slack as the double stimulation – cunt and breasts – drove her to the first orgasm. Her mouth opened in a soundless scream as she came, thrusting herself down on to his cock and moving her hips to grind her clitoris against Richard's pubic bones.

The firelight glowed on her skin. Moving highlights and shadows gave her the look of a wild animal moving through a dappled shade. Richard watched in fascination as she took her pleasure, her body shuddering as she came. He released Ingrid's breasts and thrust his hands into the thick mane of her hair, pulling her face down to his. He covered her lips with his own, forcing them open then darting his tongue into Ingrid's mouth. She groaned deep in her throat, their breaths mingling as their bodies writhed in the dance of desire and pleasure.

The blanket slipped to the floor, revealing Ingrid's entire body in the firelight. The red glow of the flames showed the hollows and rounded fullnesses of her, gleaming on the sheer nylon of her stockings, the muscles sliding smoothly beneath the shiny nylon and the smooth skin of her legs as she raised and lowered herself on Richard's cock. Richard was so taken with the sight that he could hold back no longer. His own orgasm mingled with Ingrid's ongoing ecstasy. Their mingled cries of release rose in the dark room, low growls of pleasure and groans of satisfaction.

Ingrid collapsed against him, moaning softly as the storm subsided. Her cheek lay beside his, her long thick hair spread over his face so that he could inhale the soft fragrance of it. She pressed herself against his body, trying to make herself touch him all over. Richard stayed hard inside her. And thus they drifted off to sleep once more, and woke from time to time to move against one another, enjoying the prolonged coupling without the need to begin again.

Ingrid woke towards dawn to see Richard looking at her.

'Penny for 'em,' he said with a slow smile.

'What?' Ingrid's grasp of English idiom was patchy. It was one of the things he loved about her. Helena too had lacked the fluency she was now developing. He sometimes regretted the change. Ingrid's precise, often stilted English was a pleasant contrast to her abandoned body language.

'What are you thinking about?' he asked.

13

'Gretchen is falling in love with you, even if she won't admit it.'

He looked puzzled. 'Who?'

'Margaret. Gretchen is a nickname, one she doesn't like. Literally, it means "little Margaret". I call her that to tease her, though it is also a way to show fondness. Which she also dislikes. But I do it anyway. Elder sisters often do that.'

Richard was incredulous. 'You must be mistaken. When I sent her back to Soltau on her own, she was spitting mad. Didn't she tell you?'

'Of course not, although I guessed it,' Ingrid replied. 'She would never admit defeat. Or to any deep feelings. But she is thinking about you all the time.'

Richard thought back to Margaret's visits to the house. On the second occasion he, too, thought he had broken through her defences. But she had resumed her mask of dominance and hardness soon after the tenderer moments, as if she regretted the momentary softness and surrender. She had certainly been angry at his and Helena's refusal to return with her to resume their role as her slaves.

'She *is* falling in love with you,' Ingrid repeated as his silence continued.

Richard, like almost any man, was flattered by the idea that a beautiful woman like Margaret might fall in love with him. It was especially flattering to think that someone who had held herself aloof from others had let down her defences for him. The dominatrix in love with her slave was an exciting idea. So while he continued to deny it to Ingrid, the notion of Margaret pining for him was pleasant. With an inner smile he imagined himself calling her 'Gretchen'. She would probably get angry.

Yet the idea of Margaret going all soft and yielding was somehow dismaying. One of the most exciting things about her was the way she had dealt with him

14

both in Soltau and here in his own house. It was not possible or desirable to return to her as a slave, but the fantasy of a dominant woman waiting to discipline him, to tease and arouse him, was not an easy one to give up. He needed Margaret to be what she had always been, even if he only encountered her occasionally.

Ingrid tensed. 'I felt you jab me,' she said with a smile. 'Was that because you want *me* again, or because you are thinking of Margaret?'

'Both,' he said as he pulled her down on top of him.

The next day Richard worked on his drawings while Ingrid borrowed his car to drive into Norwich. Shopping, she said. Hating the very idea of a trawl around the shops at the best of times, he left her to it and put in the time more usefully on his drawings. As he worked he paused from time to time as random memories of last afternoon and evening came to him. Despite Helena's assurances to the contrary, he still felt enough guilt to make the interlude with Ingrid more memorable. Other women he had known would have been speechless (or screaming) with rage, shock or jealousy (or all three) if he had embarked on a simultaneous affair with any of their mothers. Helena was one in a million, he told himself.

Richard considered Ingrid's revelations about Margaret in the light of this new liaison. If Margaret was furious at his choice of Helena, she would be raging if she discovered that he was having the foster-mother as well. Was Margaret really falling in love with him? It was hard to think of her yielding to any softer emotions. And would she try again to recapture him and Helena? Probably, he thought, resolving not to relax his vigilance even as he regretted the need for it. For his part he would rather be on good terms with Margaret (as in bedfellows, he reflected wryly) than not, but it only required one to open hostilities, or to sustain them.

By the time Ingrid returned to Bacton it was late afternoon and Richard had worked up a nice head of steam, what with one thing and another. Absence, he reflected, made the heart fonder and the cock stiffer. At the sound of the returning shopper he left his workplace and went to greet her in the hall.

Ingrid came in with only a moderate number of new acquisitions, considering that she had spent nearly the entire day in town. Today she wore a light green full-skirted dress that ended at her knees. Richard was pleased to see that she had worn tights (or stockings and suspenders, he thought with lifting spirits) and high heels. Ingrid had once said that her fashion ideas were out of date, but if this was evidence of them he approved. Her long hair shone warmly in the sunlight coming through the nearby window.

She set her parcels down in the entryway and held her arms out to Richard with a smile. 'I am back,' she said happily, stating the obvious and lifting his spirits with her presence. 'Did you miss me?' Without waiting for his reply she embraced him and lifted her laughing mouth for a kiss. Her lips opened to him and her tongue darted into his mouth. Then, laughing still, she broke away from him and reached down to touch his cock, itself becoming more obvious beneath his trousers. 'You *did* miss me!' she exclaimed delightedly.

She led him by the hand into the kitchen. 'Come, make coffee and sandwiches which we can eat before the fire. I will help you.' They carried the food into the front sitting room and Richard set about laying the log fire in the stone fireplace. As he worked Ingrid folded the blanket that had covered them during their night on the couch.

'Shopping is not so easy when you reach my age,' Ingrid said. Richard looked quickly at her, and judged she was testing the waters again with the older-woman question. Instead of replying, he reached for her hand

and, when she gave it to him, jerked her suddenly off balance so that she landed across his lap. He turned her over and pulled her skirt up around her hips. As he did so he was pleased to see that she was indeed wearing stockings and suspenders. And no pants.

Richard arranged Ingrid face down on his lap. By the time she had recovered from the initial surprise he had put his leg between hers and spread them apart, his free arm pressing her down as she struggled.

'Richard!' she cried in alarm. 'What are you doing? Oh!'

Her cry coincided with the slap of his hand on her bare bottom.

'I thought that would be obvious,' he replied as he raised his hand for the next slap. There was a red mark on the fair skin of her bottom where the first had landed. Ingrid squealed when he struck her again, twisting as she tried to escape.

'Oh! Richard. Don't do this. Please!' She looked wildly up at him, an expression of dismay on her lovely face.

Richard ignored her cries and her ineffectual attempts to escape as he rained a series of steady slaps across her bottom and the backs of her thighs. The flesh was beginning to glow a dull red all across the target area. He felt himself growing excited as he continued to spank her.

Ingrid made ineffectual attempts to stop him, but she was at a distinct disadvantage, having to reach around behind her back without being able to see where the next slap would land. She was protesting indignantly as she squirmed on his lap. 'Stop! Please do not do this to me! Oh!'

But Richard did not stop. Her squirming body was having a pronounced effect on his cock.

Which Ingrid must have realised soon afterwards. Her protests became less indignant, her movements less frantic and more, well, more acquiescing, as Richard

17

put it later. The spanking went on, and as it did Ingrid's attempts to escape became more erotic. Her taut body relaxed, seeming to flow against him. She thrust her hips up as if inviting the next slap, and at the same time she felt his erect cock pressing against her stomach.

Ingrid looked wildly at him. Suddenly she moaned, surprising them both. The sound was remarkably like those she had made during their lovemaking on the previous evening. She began to shudder as he struck her, thrusting up and down with her hips against his cock. And her cries gradually became cries of pleasure.

'Oh!' she gasped. 'Oh, God! Don't stop. Please don't stop!'

Richard noted wryly, even as he continued to spank her, that Ingrid's command of English had extended itself under stress. It had taken Helena a lot longer than this to begin using contractions, even when she had been strung up under the whip. She had cried (quaintly but excitingly, to Richard's ears), 'Please do not stop!' even when on the verge of orgasm.

Ingrid was grinding her hips against his legs, seeking to bring her clitoris into contact with anything even moderately hard enough to bring her to orgasm. Her cries of pleasure were unmistakable now.

Judging the right moment, Richard suddenly stopped spanking Ingrid and arranged her more comfortably on the sofa. He slid out from under her and placed her chest on the seat, leaving her kneeling on the floor with her bottom sticking up in the air invitingly. As he settled himself behind Ingrid, between her calves, he couldn't resist striking the reddened skin several more times. Ingrid made guttural sounds of pleasure as the blows landed.

But when he suddenly thrust a finger into her crotch, seeking her cunt, she gasped in pleasure and spread her legs to assist him. She moaned loudly when his insistent finger slid inside her.

She was wet and parted and eager, her flesh hot against his hand as he probed her depths. He slid the finger in and out, and Ingrid's hips began to rock backwards and forwards in time with the finger inside her. Her little gasps and moans of pleasure rose and fell to the same rhythm as she succumbed to the arousal. Richard turned his wrist slightly so that his knuckle came into contact with her clitoris.

Ingrid stiffened at once. 'Yes! Harder!' she urged him. She thrust wildly with her hips, seeking the touch that would bring release. Her reddened bottom moved frantically before his gaze.

Struck by a sudden inspiration, Richard withdrew his finger abruptly from Ingrid's cunt. At once she wailed in dismay: 'Don't stop!' He didn't intend to. He thrust the still-wet finger insistently into her anus, feeling her resistance to that penetration at once. The lubrication was necessary.

'No!' she cried once, weakly, looking wide-eyed at him over her shoulder. She tried ineffectually to push his hand away.

But Richard thrust his other index finger into her cunt, teasing her clitoris with his thumb. Ingrid's body, faced with dual penetration, abruptly ceased all resistance. The finger in her cunt distracted her so that she allowed her anal sphincter to relax. Richard's finger slid into that tight sheath to the knuckle.

Ingrid gave one more wild glance over her shoulder before she submitted to the double penetration. Her hips bucked wildly at the double stimulation, her excitement heightened by the unexpected, illicit anal probe. He felt her sphincter clamp down spasmodically around the invading finger, and she sighed with pleasure from the finger in her cunt. When Richard began to move both fingers in rhythm, Ingrid went wild. Richard watched his lover's foster-mother's face closely as she slipped over the edge into a raging, all-consuming orgasm, her body heaving, her breath coming in gasps, her inarticulate cries of pleasure filling the room. Then she screamed aloud, a full-throated cry of animal release and ecstasy.

Margaret, he remembered, had screamed like that on her last visit. Ingrid was completely wild, out of control, bucking and moaning as he thrust his fingers into her twin orifices. Her vaginal and anal muscles clenched and loosened in time with the repeated orgasms that shook her body.

Ingrid lost her last reservations as she experienced the wild pleasure of her dual penetration. When finally she begged him to stop, her voice was barely above a whisper. The words seemed torn from somewhere deep inside her. 'Please stop now. I can't stop if you go on. It will kill me.'

Richard slowly withdrew the two fingers and Ingrid's taut body relaxed. Her head hung down between her forearms and her legs spread loosely, as if there were no more strength in them. For long minutes he let her lie bent over the sofa. Then he raised her and helped her to lie on the seat.

Ingrid lay with her eyes closed and her breasts heaving as she tried to catch her breath. There were dark patches of sweat on the dress under her breasts and across her stomach. Similar dark patches marked the sheer nylon of her stockings where the sweat had run down her thighs. Her body still shook with small tremors, the aftershocks of the earthquake that had racked her.

Richard sat on the floor and laid his head on her stomach. Ingrid tiredly moved one hand to rest it on his cheek, stroking softly. They lay quiet for a long time.

It was growing dark when Richard rose from the floor, quietly so as not to waken Ingrid. He stretched stiff muscles. His hand still stung dully from the spanking. Ingrid was deeply asleep, her breathing slow and even and her body completely relaxed. The sleep of the just thoroughly fucked, he thought with an inner smile. She lay as before, her skirt pulled up to her waist and her thighs slightly apart. The sweat had dried from her dress and stockings, he saw. The sight of her déshabillé was both exciting and comforting: two people at ease with one another needed no false modesty.

The fire caught easily, the logs crackling softly, the heat and light spreading through the by-now dark and chilly room. Just like last night, Richard thought. A remarkable woman. He covered her with the light blanket she had earlier folded so carefully and went to the kitchen to make fresh coffee to go with the uneaten sandwiches. This time, with more leisure, he added hot chicken soup to the menu. Cherry pie and more coffee for afters, he decided.

When he came back with the laden tray, Ingrid was awake. She was smiling softly as at some inner pleasure.

The smile transferred to him as he came closer. Ingrid put out a hand to touch his leg while he drew the coffee table nearer.

'Eat,' he said simply, and Ingrid rose to a sitting position. The blanket fell to the floor but she made no effort to cover herself. From waist to toes she was completely bare. The firelight made shifting highlights on her long full legs and the sheer material of her stockings.

Ingrid smiled more broadly when she saw the direction of his gaze. 'Like what you see?' she asked teasingly.

Richard nodded wordlessly.

She patted the sofa beside her. He sat. She looked at him searchingly for long silent moments before she bent to kiss him softly on the mouth. 'Thank you,' she breathed. She took his hand and laid it on her thigh, at the point where smooth stocking ended and smooth flesh began. A sign of trust and peace and a promise for the future.

They ate in contented silence in the firelight.

Ingrid seemed subdued but happy, examining quietly what they had done. At length she spoke wonderingly, 'I did not know such pleasure existed. It was ... overwhelming.' She was staring at the fire as she spoke. She sounded far away, reliving the experience. Then she looked up into Richard's eyes and said with a teasing smile, 'You should not surprise me that way. The shock is bad for the heart.'

There it was again, the older-woman question beneath the lightness, as if something impelled her to bring up the subject once more. It was hard to tell in the shifting firelight, but he thought she might be blushing. 'Are you asking for another spanking?' he asked suddenly.

Ingrid's confusion became more pronounced. 'What ... do you mean?' Her voice shook slightly.

'I think you know very well what I mean. Yesterday I told you that you'd get a spanking if you brought up the age-difference subject again. But you did it anyway – when you came back from Norwich. It got you a spanking. Do you want another?'

'No ... not ... another.' The hesitation suddenly gave way. 'Not now, anyway,' she said in a rush.

This time there was no mistaking her agitation. Her hand went to her throat as if she were choking. Her fingers trembled.

'You *do* want another spanking,' he said smilingly. 'You just don't want to admit it, do you?'

Ingrid went red all over. He could feel the flush under his hand where it rested on her thigh. She looked distressed at being found out. He took her into his arms and leaned close to her ear. 'Dearest Ingrid, don't be embarrassed with me. You have kept Pamela's secret for me. Surely you should know I'll keep yours. And help you enjoy your fantasies, if that's what you want. Just tell me what you want me to do whenever you get the urge.'

She remained silent, but he felt the tension leave her body. After a time she turned her face to him and kissed him softly on the mouth. 'I was . . . afraid you would think me . . . strange . . . if I told you that.'

'Don't be silly. Beside Helena's unholy joy in the whip, your obsession is small potatoes. But I'll tell you something else that may make you feel better. Margaret introduced me to the whip in Soltau. She was rather too vigorous for my taste at first, but I grew to like it. Helena sometimes lashes me now. It's a pleasant variation. And of course there's the little matter of Pamela. So you're among fellow perverts. We won't give you away. You might say flagellation is in the English blood. That's why it's called the English disease. But I'm very glad to know several Germans who suffer from it as well. We all need our fantasies. Sure you don't want a bit more now?'

Ingrid shook her head. 'Later. But I *do* feel much better now that you know about me. But now I would like to give you some of the pleasure you gave me. I know that you did not come, while I was . . . climbing the walls, as you say. What can I do for you? I have told you what I like. Now tell me what you would like.'

'Don't keep thinking in terms of repayment and keeping score. If you enjoyed the spanking as much as you appeared to, that's enough for me.'

Ingrid looked softly up at him. 'Helena is a very lucky woman. So am I.'

The silence grew. At length Richard felt he had to fill it. 'Anyway,' he said, 'I enjoyed spanking you. Watching you squirm as your bottom turned red excited me. You have the most exquisite bottom and legs. I love to look at them.'

'Dearest Richard, look as much as you like. Do you want me to take my clothes off now?'

'Later. What I can see is good enough for now.' He stroked her legs softly, running his hand back and forth over the smooth nylon of her stockings and resting it from time to time over her cunt.

With a contented sigh, Ingrid snuggled closer to him and the silence grew around them once again.

When they went upstairs to bed, Ingrid made a point of leaving her stockings and suspenders on when she took off the rest of her clothes. Richard smiled at her, thanking her for the gift.

At breakfast Ingrid showed renewed signs of agitation. She appeared several times to be on the verge of saying something to Richard but each time she drew back. Her hands made little nervous, awkward motions whenever she was not using them to smooth her hair or her dress. All the signs of a woman in heat, Richard thought, wondering how she was going to broach the subject. He wondered how long it would take her to admit her desire to herself. Perhaps it was cruel, but he enjoyed her agitation, her almost-admission of her desires. And, rationalising his refusal to acknowledge the signs he observed, he thought that it would be better for her to come out with it in her own time.

He rose from the table and went into his workroom, where he busied himself with the drawings he was working on. He heard Ingrid go out as he worked. And, some time later, he heard her come back. The sound of her high heels tap-tapping around the house came to him, sounding nervous, unsettled. There was nothing she had to do around the house; nevertheless, she found something to do.

Eventually she came into the workroom and sat down on a spare draughting stool, regarding him silently as he worked then hurriedly looking away whenever he looked up. He saw that her face was flushed and damp with sweat. She watched him with increasing agitation for a time, and just as he felt she was about to speak he looked up at her. 'Do you want me to fuck you now?' he asked with a smile.

His directness took her by surprise. Her reply was not immediately forthcoming and, when she finally spoke, she did so hesitantly. 'I was thinking ... I mean ... Would you like to put ... your cock ... where you put your finger yesterday?'

'How would *you* like it, is the real question.'

'I would ... l-like it ... very m-much, I think,' she stammered, the red tide rushing to her cheeks and spreading down her neck. She averted her gaze in embarrassment.

He rose to stand beside her, taking her hands and drawing her to her feet. She trembled as he took her in his arms, still not looking at him, fixing her gaze on the carpet in the far corner of the room as if mesmerised by what she saw there. He raised her face with a hand beneath her chin, until he could look directly into her clear grey eyes. He saw there both desire and eagerness and a troubled embarrassment.

'Dearest Ingrid, there's no need to be embarrassed with me. Not after the last few days.'

'It is just that ... I feel as if I am asking for something ... something ... well, *wicked*. I mean, a woman of my age asking a man to shove his cock into her backside. I never knew I would ... like it ... so much.' Suddenly she blurted out, 'Oh, I didn't mean ...'

'It doesn't matter. You still said the magic word.'

Ingrid flushed more deeply. He could feel her trembling in his arms. But it wasn't just fear, he saw as he continued to hold her troubled gaze. It was anticipation too. Richard wondered how accidental her reference to age had been. She wasn't a calculating woman, he knew. But sometimes she just didn't know how to face what she wanted – what her body demanded of her. Modesty, that was it. She had been brought up to speak and act modestly, while her body demanded the opposite of her. He decided to give her everything she wanted without further discussion – to give her no chance to waver or change her mind. It wasn't all that hard a decision. His cock had already made it for him.

Richard led her by the hand up the stairs and into the bedroom he shared with Helena. 'Stand still,' he commanded, releasing her hand.

Ingrid stood by the window, looking out into the afternoon sunlight on the trees across the river. She seemed afraid to face him – or the strength of her own needs. She caught a momentary glimpse of herself in the mirror and looked hurriedly, almost guiltily, away. She made no objection as Richard began to undress her. She was as still as if it were all happening to someone else – except for the small uncontrollable tremors that shook her body from time to time as his hands touched her flesh.

The dress fell at her feet, and Richard slid the straps of her slip down her arms as they hung at her sides. The lacy slip joined her dress on the floor, so that Ingrid looked as if she were standing in a pool of silk.

Today she wore smooth grey stockings. The high-heeled shoes made her ankles appear slimmer and her calves fuller. The muscles of her thighs played softly beneath the sheer nylon as she shifted her weight minutely. The sight of her legs excited Richard, as it always did.

Ingrid wore no pants. Had she been expecting this to happen, and had she made her preparations beforehand? He suspected so. He saw her nipples erect under the sheer material of her bra as he undid the clasp behind her back. Her heavy rounded breasts sprang free as he eased the bra down her arms and dropped it to the floor. Her nipples erected fully as he watched.

When he covered them with the palms of his hands, Ingrid shuddered. 'Oh!' she said, startled and aroused. She made no attempt to cover herself or to draw away from his touch. 'What do . . . you . . . want me to do . . . now?' she asked with a tremor in her voice. Her breasts heaved slightly with her agitated breathing. Her eyes

26

were wide open, rounded half in fear and half in anticipation as she looked at him briefly and then away again at the sunlit trees.

'Stand still while I look at you,' he commanded.

Unconsciously, Ingrid shifted her stance, moving one leg forward and resting more of her weight on it. Her hips tilted into that classic feminine pose, showing off her slender waist and the length of her legs while her breasts jutted proudly. In an unconscious gesture she lifted her arm to smooth her long gleaming chestnut hair back over her shoulder. The pose accentuated her breasts. She essayed a smile. It emerged tremulous, shy. The flush in her cheeks spread to her breasts as she stood expectantly beneath his gaze.

Richard looked at her for long moments, savouring the look of her and the knowledge that she was doing this for him. He was reluctant to break the tableau. Ingrid naked in this quiet room, the bed a mere step away, took his breath away. His cock stirred restlessly, becoming fully erect as he took in the glory of her body.

Ingrid continued to avert her gaze from him and from the mirror. She was in a world apart, a woman who had asked to be buggered and spanked, and who was about to have her wish granted, savouring the last moments before she was summoned to ecstasy – savouring the milder ecstasy of anticipation before the main event.

'Where is the rubber mask?' he asked her, his voice seeming loud in the quiet room.

'Oh,' she said, startled. She was silent for a moment, as if in thought. Then, 'Under the bed,' she said finally, pointing.

'Get it,' he commanded, watching her as she stooped for it. Her rounded bottom seemed to be begging for his hand. 'Stand still,' he told her peremptorily.

Ingrid remained bent over, but she couldn't stop herself from glancing up towards him. She had to know what was going to happen.

Richard struck her with his open hand, the blow sounding loud in the afternoon silence. A red hand-print appeared on her bottom, and Ingrid closed her eyes momentarily as if to savour the sting. He struck her again. This time she made a small 'oh' of pleasure. As he continued to spank her, she closed her eyes completely, surrendering herself to the hand that chastised her. He stopped abruptly. 'Get the mask,' he told her, standing back once more to admire her body. She straightened up and laid the rubber mask on the bed and he saw that she was excited by the spanking and by the knowledge of what was still to come.

Ingrid looked up at him, meeting his gaze directly. 'I bought . . . a paddle . . . today,' she said softly. 'When I went out,' she added. She looked both eager and embarrassed at once.

'Where is it?' he asked her.

This time Ingrid's voice was steadier. 'In the bureau. There.' She pointed to the bureau where he and Helena stored the rope they used in their bondage games.

'Get it,' he said tersely. 'And enough rope to tie you with.'

Ingrid extracted a table tennis paddle from the drawer, and then rummaged deeper to get the rope. As she did so, a large rubber dildo fell to the floor. She looked at it in fascinated silence for a long moment.

'Pick it up,' he ordered her.

She did so, holding the long shaft awkwardly in one hand.

'There's another in the drawer. Get it out as well.'

Trembling, Ingrid brought out a slimmer dildo. Looking at the two of them, she suddenly blushed furiously. 'They are . . . there is . . . one . . . for each hole,' she said. 'For a woman's two holes.' She continued to stare at the dildoes in silence, her breasts heaving as she drew air deeply into her lungs. 'This one –' holding out the thicker of the two '– is for her – my

28

– cunt.' Ingrid seemed to find it hard to use the word in reference to herself. 'And this one, she said even more hesitantly, 'this one must be for my . . . other place.'

'Your arsehole,' Richard told her bluntly, and she trembled again. 'The ring in the blunt end is to hold them inside you and to keep them from sliding too far in and getting lost. We run a rope through the ring so we can pull your plugs at any time. Slip them in, if you like,' he invited. 'See how they fit.'

Ingrid blushed redly once again. 'I would rather you did it for me,' she said in a faint voice. 'After I am tied up. It will feel . . . I will feel . . . more like a captive. Someone who has no choice,' she finished in a rush, as if relieved to have the words out. She laid the dildoes on the bureau and looked steadily at Richard, all desires known, waiting for him to take command of her body.

And command it to ecstasy, Richard thought. But what he said was, 'Leave your stockings and suspenders. It excites me – as you know very well.'

'Dear Richard, I will do anything that excites you. I want you to take pleasure too. Pleasure in my body, in all of me.'

'I see where Helena got her nature from,' he said with a smile as he began to remove his clothes.

Ingrid watched him closely as he did so. When he took off his pants, his rigid cock drew a gasp from her. 'For me?' she asked. 'You got that just thinking of putting these into my . . . my cunt and arsehole?'

'Well, that wasn't the only thing I had in mind,' he said. 'I was looking forward to touching your body – all over. I was thinking of kissing you, and of feeling your tits against my chest. And I wanted to tease your nipples and stroke your bottom. And of course I was thinking about stuffing you full of me and the dildoes.'

Ingrid trembled with excitement when he picked up the rubber mask and approached her. Shaped plugs of foam rubber went into her ears. She stood still while he fitted the rubber helmet over her head and ensured that the inflatable gag went into her mouth. Richard fitted the nosepiece carefully so that the openings allowed her to breathe through her nostrils and the eye-pads fitted snugly against her eyes. Then he buckled the mask tightly behind her head and around her neck. He fitted the heavy leather collar that held the bottom of the mask in place around her throat. Finally he inserted the needle that allowed the gag to be inflated in the wearer's mouth.

With a bicycle tyre pump he inflated the gag, forcing her jaws apart and filling her mouth. Richard knew from his own experience that she was unable to hear, see or speak inside the tight helmet. Ingrid shivered with excitement in her dark, silent world as he had when Helena had done this to him.

Richard tied Ingrid's hands behind her back with the smooth braided nylon rope from the bureau. When she was secured, he paused to touch her cunt. He felt the warmth even before his finger penetrated her. She was wet and parted, ready. A small moan escaped her as he probed inside her, grazing the hard button of her engorged clitoris with his knuckle. Ingrid's knees buckled slightly and she had to fight to remain standing as he aroused her. She was whimpering steadily behind her gag when he again paused. A small sound of dismay followed his withdrawal.

Selecting the larger of the dildoes, Richard spread her labia and slid it slowly into her cunt. As she was penetrated Ingrid stiffened and groaned loudly. But he was not finished with her. Greasing the slimmer dildo with hand-cream, he spread her arse-cheeks until the small pink rosebud of her anus was visible. Slowly he slid the dildo into her anus, pushing against the resistance of her sphincter until the whole length of it was inside her. Only the ring on the base of the dildo was visible from outside. Ingrid's hips bucked spasmodically in reaction to her double penetration.

Richard tied a piece of rope around her waist, taking it down between her legs and through the rings in the dildoes' bases. He took the end up between her arse-cheeks at the back, pulling it tightly into her central groove so that it became a saddle strap. The free end was secured to the rope around her waist at the back. Ingrid, her wrists bound, could not now remove the two plugs that closed her twin orifices, either directly or by pushing them out with her internal muscles.

As she recognised her predicament Ingrid moaned with pleasure. She rocked her hips to move the dildoes inside her, and the reaction was strong enough to make her knees buckle. Richard caught her as she toppled and laid her on the bed, where she thrust up and down and ground her hips into the mattress to make the dildoes move within her cunt and arsehole. Ingrid seemed to have forgotten all about him as she explored these novel sensations.

Richard stood beside the bed and watched her writhe and buck and twist her body, arousing herself. Her auto-eroticism excited him too. To watch a helpless woman realise that her very helplessness was a turn-on always excited him. He remembered his own futile attempts to escape when Helena had left him bound and gagged while she went out. He decided to allow Ingrid to experience the same sensations for a time. It would be interesting to see how she took to being left bound.

He made her stop while he tied her ankles tightly together with another length of rope. Ingrid, naked save for the sheer stockings and the silky suspender-belt, squirmed helplessly on the bed as she waited for him to allow her to continue. Her movements became frenzied as soon as he took his hand away. The muffled sounds becoming more frantic as she fought the rope and the gag and her twin penetrations.

While Ingrid heaved and struggled and moaned, Richard picked up the table tennis paddle she had bought. The flat part was covered in green rubber, with a diamond pattern that would probably imprint itself on her flesh when he struck her. Which he did, suddenly, the flat smack loud in the room.

Ingrid's body went rigid at the blow, and he heard her muffled whimper. He struck her again, leaving a second reddening imprint on the smooth flesh of her bottom. Ingrid held herself still for several seconds as if waiting. When the third blow landed she moaned and began to buck and writhe once more on the bed, thrusting frenziedly with her hips, grinding her pelvis into the mattress, straining against her bonds and the maddening pressure of the dildoes and the shocks from her assaulted bottom.

Her inarticulate moans indicated the onset of orgasm. She went wild as the waves of pleasure flooded through her. Heaving and bucking and twisting, Ingrid came and came and came again. Her hips jerked in time with the spasms in her cunt and anus and belly. She made a maddened humming sound through her gag, interrupted only when she was forced to draw breath.

He lost track of time as Ingrid lost herself in the perverse pleasures of bondage and spanking and auto-eroticism. His arm grew tired at length, and he stopped spanking her to watch the spectacle of her frenzy. Ingrid continued to writhe and buck and heave, straining her muscles as she fought her bonds and the dildoes inside her. Richard wondered if she would ever stop.

At length she did, subsiding suddenly, almost in a collapse. Sweat ran down her ribs and darkened the stockings at the backs of her knees and between her thighs. When he stroked her legs, Richard felt the stockings clinging damply to them. Ingrid was moaning softly to herself, panting as she strove to recover breath and strength. Her long hair, spread wildly across her shoulders, was damp from her exertions.

Richard sat on the bed beside her, turned her over then lifted her helpless body to a sitting position on his lap. He held her against himself, feeling her stiffen as her position forced the dildo deeper into her anus. She moaned loudly, and he thought she would have another orgasm just from that. But Ingrid was evidently exhausted, and as he held her he could feel the stiffness leave her body as she relaxed. She lay against him for a long time, and he became aware that she had fallen asleep in his arms when he heard strangled, muffled snores through her gag.

After a considerable time, Ingrid still sleeping, Richard eased her to the bed and brought a light blanket from the closet. Although it was still a sunny afternoon, the sun was getting lower in the sky, and there was a chill in the room. He knew that Ingrid, naked and bound as she was, would grow cold if left uncovered on the bed. He lay down beside her and covered them both with the blanket. He turned towards her and took her in his arms, holding her body against his own and listening to her quiet breathing and the small moans that came through her gag.

Even though Ingrid was exhausted by her climaxes, he was too excited to sleep himself. His cock remained stiff even as he drowsed. Holding a bound, naked woman in his arms did not happen all that often – not nearly often enough for him. The certainty of having sex with her when she recovered from her own sexual exercise was not conducive to sleep either. So he lay half-asleep, fondling Ingrid's breasts and stroking her taut stomach and the fine skin of her legs through the sheer nylon of her stockings. Eventually, she woke. Dusk was gathering under the trees across the river when he felt Ingrid stir. She moaned through her gag, a questioning noise, and she struggled to sit up before apparently realising that she was bound and gagged. She became aware that she was being held against a man. The stiff cock prodding her bottom was hard to mistake. She relaxed once more, and then, stretching like a cat, she pressed her body against him.

33

Richard cupped her breasts, teasing her nipples with his fingers, feeling them become taut and erect. He could feel her body tense as the signals from her breasts spread to her cunt, and reminded her again of her double penetration. Ingrid moaned deep in her throat, her hips moving backwards and forwards as she felt the dildoes moving inside her once again. This time, however, Richard didn't want to be the spectator to her orgasm. He had been terribly excited earlier on, but this time he was going to take part in it.

Richard moved one hand down to her belly, pressing the dildo into her cunt and drawing a deep groan from her. It was time to change tactics. He let the blanket fall to the floor, looking once more at her body as she lay bound beside him: the long legs; the stockings and suspenders; the full round breasts and the slender waist; the ropes binding her wrists and ankles; the rubber mask that concealed her features. He was half-reluctant to break the tableau. But he sat up and untied her ankles. Standing up, he drew Ingrid to her feet and untied the rope that ran between her legs and held the two dildoes inside her. He plucked the slim one from her anus.

He forced Ingrid to her knees beside the bed, arranging her with her chest on the mattress and her legs spread. He kneeled behind her, between her calves, pushing them aside to open her more fully. But before he entered her there was something more to do – something to heighten her pleasure and his own.

Richard did not use the paddle this time to spank Ingrid. His hand was best for this, he decided, as he struck her bottom and the backs of her thighs. Ingrid moaned as he struck her, grinding her pelvis against the edge of the mattress and thrusting the dildo into her cunt. Richard moved slightly so that he could strike the insides of her thighs as well, the spanking moving closer to her cunt as she bucked against the side of the bed.

Only when he was certain of her renewed arousal did he stop the spanking. Using more hand-cream to lubricate his cock, he pushed the head against her anus. This time he felt her resistance even more acutely. His cock was thicker than the dildo she had taken earlier, but he pushed slowly and steadily, gaining a little bit each time she relaxed. When he was finally inside her anus he held still, feeling her sphincter tight around his cock and enjoying the feel of the dildo in her cunt through the thin membrane between her two passages.

Ingrid seemed to be having second thoughts, her bound hands making futile attempts to push him away and her hips straining forwards in an attempt to lose the anal penetration. But that was why Richard had placed her as he had: the bed prevented any escape. He leaned forwards, his chest against Ingrid's bent back, trapping her bound hands between their bodies. He held himself still, allowing Ingrid to become used to the anal penetration.

After a few minutes he reached round to tease her clitoris with his fingers, and as he did he felt a sudden yielding, her muscles holding him instead of trying to expel him. A sudden flash of heat accompanied her surrender, as the blood rushed to her cunt and arsehole with the beginning of her arousal. Ingrid moaned, a long-drawn sound from deep in her throat as she submitted to her pleasure.

And still he did not move, relishing the tight grip of her muscles around his cock and the heat coming from deep inside her. His fingers continued to tease her clitoris and to push the dildo deeper into her cunt. Ingrid could hold back no longer. He felt the beginning of her first orgasm as a tightening of her sphincter and a ripple of movement from inside her, and then Ingrid was bucking frantically beneath him, her hips thrusting backwards and forwards, forcing him to move with her, to slide in and out of her arsehole as she came.

Her moan of release was curiously high-pitched, not at all like her earlier noises. Richard held on to her as she bucked and jerked in her release, one climax coming on the heels of the one before it. Ingrid went on and on, as if she had not been wrung almost dry in the first session. She seemed demented, unable to control herself, her body in complete charge, intent on the racking pleasure that swept through her.

Richard rode with her for as long as he could, but when she showed no sign of stopping he could hold back no longer. In a series of hot, jerking spasms he emptied himself into her while her anal sphincter clutched him tightly, seeming to milk every drop from him. And as he came Ingrid went mad, racked by her climaxes, completely out of control, moaning and thrashing beneath him.

When the storm subsided at last he lay on top of her, listening to the pounding of his own heart as well as hers. Her face was turned to one side on the mattress, her long hair spread wildly down her back. Beneath the tight rubber of the mask Richard could see her features working, her nostrils flaring as she drew in air through the breathing holes. Once again the sweat ran across her back and down her ribs, making dark patches on the bedspread.

When he felt some of the tension leave her body, Richard tried to withdraw from her. But her arsehole refused to let him go. From behind her gag Ingrid made a sound that sounded curiously like denial. Richard stayed inside her, marvelling at her stamina and the strength of her desire. They kneeled beside the bed, joined together, for what seemed like hours.

Richard's knees were beginning to hurt from the kneeling. He put both arms around Ingrid's waist and held her to him as he rolled over to land in a sitting position on the floor, Ingrid in his lap with her legs spread out widely and his cock still inside her anus. She settled against him with a sigh of pleasure, and he felt her interior muscles grasp him firmly once more: no retreat. Nor much desire for retreat.

Once again hours seemed to pass. The darkness grew outside as the sun set, and still they sat joined on the floor. Ingrid's bound wrists were still trapped between them as she leaned against him, but she seemed not to notice. The tight rubber mask concealed her features, the gag stifled her speech, she could neither see nor hear inside the helmet that confined her head. But she could feel – feel the dildo in her cunt, the stiffening cock inside her anus, the ropes tight around her wrists, the man joined to her. And she wanted to keep on feeling these things for ever, never to let the moment of her ultimate submission and pleasure pass.

Richard felt her tighten herself again, shifting her weight at the same time, attempting to raise her hips to thrust against him. But, bound, with only limited scope for movement, she could not manage what she wanted to do. Another moan, a protest, an expression of frustration escaped from her throat.

He was pinned to the floor beneath her weight, but his hands were free. He reached once more for Ingrid's breasts, teasing her nipples with the fingers of one hand while he slipped the other between her thighs. He grasped the dildo in her cunt and began to thrust with it – in and out, slowly at first and then gradually more quickly as she responded. Her nipple between his fingers grew hard, the button of her clitoris making itself felt against his hand as he thrust in and out, in and out with the dildo.

Through the membrane between Ingrid's cunt and arsehole he felt the dildo sliding up and down his own cock, a strangely disturbing sensation. He grew erect once more within the tight sheath of her anus. Ingrid was beginning to make the enraptured sound he had heard earlier, and he knew she was on the verge of another orgasm, and then, incredibly, she was in the throes of her climax once more, her body jerking spasmodically as she came, her interior muscles squeezing and relaxing, squeezing and relaxing around him. This time when he came he had only to hold still as he spent himself once more inside her. Ingrid's body went rigid as she felt him come. She made a strangled groan as she came with him.

This time, when it was over, she seemed to have no more strength for holding him. He felt her anal sphincter relax but still he could not withdraw from her until he had rolled on to his side and laid her on the floor. Ingrid lay inert, her long legs in the sheer stockings drawn up almost into the foetal position, her bound wrists resting limply on the floor behind her back. She seemed worn out by her many climaxes, unable to move.

At last Richard stirred himself. He moved closer to Ingrid and began to unbuckle the straps that held the mask in place. As they fell away the cool air circulating around her face seemed to revive her somewhat. The inflated gag could not come out past her teeth. Richard had to find the needle and fit it into the valve, allowing the air to escape before pulling the limp rubber bag from her mouth.

Ingrid worked her jaws and tongue, cramped after such long confinement. But when he made to untie her wrists, she managed to croak, 'N – no. Leave . . . me tied.'

Richard grunted his assent and sat down beside her, taking her head in his lap. He could feel the warmth of her breath on his stomach and cock.

Ingrid seemed to breathe deeply, inhaling the aroma of his musk and her own arsehole with relish. She blew gently on his cock, ruffling his pubic hair. 'There may be better ways to die, but I cannot think of any at the moment,' she said almost in a whisper. Then she lay quiet for a while. Later: 'I hate to get up. Indeed, I do not know that I can get up. But I will have to go to the toilet soon or have a nasty accident here. Help me, please, Richard.'

He stood and helped Ingrid to her feet. Once more he made as if to untie her wrists.

She shook her head again. 'Please leave your wild woman tied up. She is enjoying her captivity.' With a smile she continued, 'But could you please take her to the toilet?'

Richard led her across the landing and into the toilet, where he helped her squat on the pan. She peed loudly and long, and with evident relief. 'Like a small orgasm,' she said at the end. 'That's the first time I've ever peed with such a great long shaft inside me. It's a new experience,' she said thoughtfully. 'Exciting.'

He wiped her dry, making her gasp when his hand touched the dildo.

'Downstairs, please,' Ingrid said. 'I am hungry and thirsty after those bedroom calisthenics. But you'll have to help me. My legs aren't working so well, and I wouldn't like to fall with my hands tied.'

Richard again helped Ingrid to her feet and steered her down the stairs with his arm around her waist. She only stumbled once, and he wondered if that might not be just to feel his grip tighten. Ingrid seemed to like leaning against him. He didn't mind.

'How hungry are you?' he asked. 'Soup-hungry or sandwich-hungry or hot food-hungry? I mean, how long are you prepared to wait?

'I think sandwich-hungry,' Ingrid said. 'I would have taken the *soup du jour*, except I don't feel like waiting that long.'

Richard returned her grin and set about making ham sandwiches for them both. When they were ready, Ingrid indicated her bound wrists with a shrug and a look over one shoulder. 'Would you mind feeding me?'

So he did, holding the sandwich while Ingrid took hearty bites, and then eating his own.

Afterwards she said, 'I am tired now. Would you please take me upstairs again and put me to bed?' Halfway up the stairs she added hesitantly, 'And would you mind tying my ankles again, and putting the mask back on me? And the other dildo too. I think it would be very exciting to sleep so beside you. And, who knows, in the morning I may be ready again.'

He led her into the bedroom and tied her ankles and put the mask and gag back in place, and secured the two dildoes inside her as before. Then he rolled Ingrid on to the bed, turned out the light and climbed in beside her. He covered them both with a blanket and pulled her helpless and unresisting body against his own. Through the mask he kissed her on the lips, feeling hers working beneath the tight rubber as she returned the kiss. He laid her head on his shoulder, her dark hair soft against his skin, and listened while her breathing grew soft and even and she slept.

Richard was woken at some time during the night by Ingrid's moans. Half-asleep, he could feel her twisting and writhing in his arms. He realised that she was fighting her bonds and gag as she brought herself to orgasm. He turned her squirming body away from him and reached round to cup her tits, helping her as she fought her way to the edge of orgasm. He guessed she was using the plugs inside her to arouse herself, since her hips began to thrust forwards and back soon after he took her in hand.

His cock grew erect as his own excitement grew to match hers. Auto-eroticism in a woman was always exciting to him, Ingrid's even more so because he could hold her and help her to climax. The fact that she was bound and gagged also excited him. He imagined a captive woman struggling to free herself as Ingrid bucked and jerked in his arms.

At some point his erect cock slid between her thighs, and he felt her clamp down on him, the sheer smooth nylon of her stockings making a delicious friction as she bucked and thrust. Ingrid's breath was coming in gasps and her moans were torn from somewhere deep inside her, choked back by the gag but unmistakable. He freed one hand to reach down to her cunt, pushing the dildo deeper into her and teasing her swollen clitoris as he did so. When she came her body went wild in his arms, shaking and jerking, her back arching, her hips pumping, making his cock slide against her stockings. Richard came then too, the semen spurting out in jerking spasms to run down her thighs and between them.

Ingrid subsided and soon she drowsed again, her body shaken by tiny tremors and her breath catching now and again on a gasp. He wondered if she had been fully awake for her apparently shattering climax. Perhaps she had dreamed of struggling to free herself, and had found instead an orgasm. Richard checked her bonds and the helmet she wore. All secure. She was still his captive beauty. He would ask her in the morning if she had been awake or dreaming. Then he too slept.

Richard woke soon after daybreak. Ingrid, still bound and gagged, still slept in his arms. Gently he extricated himself from her and slid out of bed. As he drew the covers over her lovely, helpless body he caught a glimpse of the patch on her stockings where his semen had dried. There were still sticky blobs on and between her thighs, where she had clamped him during her nocturnal orgasm. He remembered he wanted to ask her about her dreams.

Today Helena would be back. She had not said exactly when. Certainly not with the dawn, but not too late either. She seemed addicted to early rising, as if it were a virtue. Her foster-mother slept on, doubtless

41

worn out by their frantic sex during last afternoon and evening. And night. He decided to let Ingrid sleep a bit longer, though he did not want Helena to come home and find her lovely foster-mother bound and gagged and smelling of sex in their bed.

Helena had said many times that she did not mind what Richard and Ingrid did, as long as they made one another happy. But now the time had come to put aside theory in favour of practice. It might not be such an easy task for any of them. He felt some guilt for the thorough shagging of Ingrid. He tried to ignore it, but it kept nagging. In engineering, triangles were considered advantageous, lending rigidity to structures. In love affairs, they often had the opposite effect. He would have to wait and see.

Richard shaved and showered before returning to the bedroom. He found Ingrid wriggling in the bed, and he guessed she was awake. She moaned when he touched her. He helped her sit up and swing her bound legs on to the floor before he set about removing the tight rubber helmet. Her face, when it finally emerged, looked red and hot and damp. She tossed her matted hair, trying to throw it back from her face.

Richard brushed her hair back before he untied her ankles and removed the dildoes. When her hands were free, Ingrid rearranged her own hair and then lifted her face to be kissed.

'Mmm,' she said. 'Good morning. You smell wonderful. I still smell of sex. May I take a shower before breakfast?'

He dressed while she made her toilette. When Ingrid came back to the bedroom she began to dress wordlessly, acknowledging the end of their solitary idyll. Richard was glad to see her select a suspender-belt and another pair of stockings: shiny dark blue today. No knickers. Bra to match her stockings and suspenders, a slip, a figure-flattering dress with tight skirt.

Ingrid had washed her long chestnut hair, and wore it up in a turban. When she was dressed, she began to dry and style it. Richard knew from long experience that she would need a considerable time with it. He stripped the bed, remade it and took the sheets to the laundry room. Removing the guilty traces, as he put it to himself. At length Ingrid came down, looking lovely and well groomed once more.

The weather had held fine during their tryst, lending a Prelapsarian air to the interlude. Today it was grey and threatening rain. Richard hoped it was not an omen. Nature, he believed, abhorred a vacuum, but it abhorred perfect happiness even more. Things had been too good for far too long. The time of reckoning seemed to be coming. By changing the bedclothes he was not exactly kicking Ingrid out of their bed. Nor was she exactly fleeing in the face of her foster-daughter's returning wrath. Nevertheless there was an air of things ending, in an air of vague worry, and without any assurance of something else equally good.

Helena arrived in the early afternoon, dashing through the front door and calling for them both: 'Richard! *Mutti! Ich bin hier!*' She sounded happy enough. They embraced one another in the hallway, Helena trying to kiss them both at once. Richard felt relieved. Helena looked and sounded like her old self. Ingrid beamed at her lovely foster-daughter.

Looking closely at them both, Helena asked, 'Richard, did she make you happy? *Mutti*, are you glad you came?'

When neither replied immediately, she persisted. 'I expected you to have happy times together. So did you?'

Richard finally nodded. Ingrid said, 'Yes, very good.'

Helena said, 'Then stop looking so guilty, the pair of you. I don't look guilty, do I?' she demanded, trying to.

Richard studied the familiar face, seeing signs of recent happiness there. He felt a pang of jealousy. 'Did you enjoy yourself with . . . whoever it was?'

'Very much,' she replied. 'And, no, I am not going to say anything until I hear what you have been doing while the cat was away. But not now. Help me with my things. I'm starving.'

Richard embraced her fiercely, his jealousy evaporating along with the residual guilt.

'You are not starving, whatever else you may be,' Ingrid told her. 'You look indecently sated. I am dying to hear about it, so Richard and I can try the same thing.'

Ingrid's sally banished the incipient tension. Together they helped Helena move her impedimenta from the car into the house. In the kitchen he watched with a sense of growing happiness as the two women prepared a meal and chatted with one another: very much a reunion. There was no sign of offended territoriality as they moved about the room regarded by most women as theirs alone.

They prepared a late lunch of tuna salad and toast. Despite earlier vows to reveal all about their sexual activities, the talk around the table was quite ordinary. Helena and Ingrid caught up on family and business matters while Richard mostly listened, left out but not feeling so. Naturally the matter of Margaret came up. Richard listened to that with greater interest, saying nothing of Ingrid's remarks about her changing feelings towards him. Margaret, Ingrid said, was planning another trip to England soon.

Helena looked alarmed. Facing her domineering aunt was never easy for her, even though she claimed she felt better about it since coming to live with Richard.

Richard, too, had his doubts about his ability to handle the leopardess of Soltau, despite the most recent success.

'Your aunt hasn't spoken of her last trip. I only know what you have told me. I expected a towering Wagnerian rage. No one has ever sent her away against her will. But she has been more ... distracted ... than angry.

44

There is a curious absence in her manner at times. As you would say –' looking at Richard '– she sometimes seems miles away.'

'In a brown study,' he replied. Seeing Ingrid's puzzled expression, he added, 'Distracted. Absent, as you said.'

'Yes, I suppose so. But why a brown study? Why not a green one, or a red?'

'I don't know,' he said. 'It's just one of those English idioms which the English take for granted and the foreign visitor always asks about.'

'Well,' Ingrid continued, 'in any case, she doesn't seem to have any immediate plans for another attempt at coercion or abduction. She seems somehow . . . softer . . . as well. She smiles secretively for no apparent reason, and these smiles do not appear malevolent. I don't know exactly what she hopes to accomplish by another visit,' she said, with a direct look at Richard.

Richard, who could guess well enough, immediately began to fantasise about Margaret arriving on the doorstep out of the blue, bedroom in her eyes, much as Ingrid must have done. Three women in his bed? And such women! His mind boggled, his cock stirred restlessly, fortunately, safely out of sight below the table. He strove to keep his expression mildly interested.

'*I* know what she wants,' Helena said immediately, 'even if you don't and Richard doesn't want to say. Or maybe you *do* know,' she said to her mother, 'and don't like to say.

So much for delicacy and subterfuge, Richard thought, with a glance at Ingrid. There seemed to be no point in playing innocent, but he decided to let Helena approach the subject. It would be interesting to see if she repeated her earlier position in the presence of her foster-mother.

It turned out that Helena had no qualms about speaking out in company. 'Aunt Margaret wants to get into bed with Richard. I saw that clearly on her last

45

visit, when they actually did get into bed, and I suspected it from what Richard told me about her earlier visits. She may even be falling in love with him, whatever that means to her, and however odd it sounds to anyone who knows her. But I suppose even she is not wholly immune to him. Heaven knows you aren't. Even I sometimes find him attractive.'

Richard flushed, at once guilty, pleased and embarrassed. Helena smiled at him with an overtone of worry. Most flattering.

Studying her closely, he saw that she had no real objection to the new state of affairs. 'Should I build a bigger bed?' he asked.

'Wait until the fish is landed,' Helena replied. 'Isn't it enough to have two women at a time?'

Ingrid flushed with pleasure, smiling at them both.

'How did you ever bring Helena up to be so ... civilised?' he asked.

Ingrid shrugged. 'She was always a rewarding child,' she said. 'Sometimes she even did as I asked her. It was always Gretchen who caused the problems in our family. She simply could not stop trying to bully and enslave people. Even as she was growing up she insisted on having her own way. I guess our father indulged her too often. I know I did. But she was always so beautiful, all blue eyes and golden hair. She looked like an angel but she had the will of a ... a ... well, devil seems too strong a word. But she has a will of iron, that's for sure.'

'Did Helena get her low taste for being whipped from her aunt?' Richard asked.

'Partly,' Ingrid said. 'But she also got – gets – it from her father. For him it was a matter of duty. It may be partly genetic as well, but his ... vocation ... encouraged flagellation.'

Both looked at Ingrid in surprised curiosity.

'I do not mean your foster-father, Helena. Claus was as uncomplicated as anyone can be. Kind and patient and hard-working. He had all the bourgeois virtues anyone could ask. And he loved you.'

Helena nodded, waiting for more.

'I am speaking of your real – or at least your genetic – father, if you prefer. I have never told you much about him, but I suppose now is as good a time as any.' Ingrid paused to smile at them both. 'Since Richard is now one of the family, I can tell you both at once. Kill two birds with one stone, as the English say. Not even Gretchen knows what I am speaking about now. It is not that there is any shame in it. She just never showed any interest. She was too busy getting her own way with everyone when she was young. And too busy trying to enslave everyone when she grew up.' Ingrid's smile took some of the censure out of the expression.

'His name is Hartmann, Father Gregor Hartmann, a Roman Catholic priest.' She watched for their reactions before continuing.

Richard was surprised but not shocked. Putting on a cassock and vowing to be celibate was no protection from what the Catholic Church itself was fond of calling the world, the flesh and the devil. Helena appeared mildly shocked. As she had said, the matter of religion was of no interest to her. Perhaps her shock stemmed from her earliest teachings, those tenets which are almost impossible to shed entirely – and against which she had rebelled, she said, as soon as she knew how to. And largely succeeded, Richard thought. His lover was nothing like what any religion he had ever heard of expected a woman to be. *Kinder*, *Kuche und Kirche* was a foreign concept to her.

Helena spoke into the silence that followed Ingrid's little bombshell. 'I remember nuns,' she said. 'Is that why?'

Ingrid nodded. 'Probably. Your mother was a nun, though she only became one after you were born. Her name was Johanna Witt. We were friends for years and

47

years – schoolgirls together in the same village. Even though she was nearly three years older than me, we were best friends. We went to the same schools, met the same sort of boys – shared the same lover, though I didn't know it at the time. I never told Johanna about my priest-lover. And she never told me about her own affair with him, probably for the same reasons. The world was not nearly so accepting of that sort of thing all those years ago.

'I only found out she was sleeping with him when she knew she was pregnant. She came to me in tears and poured it all out. I listened and tried to think of some way to help her out. The matter of abortion never came up,' Ingrid said. 'In those days it was almost unheard of. Anyway, Johanna wanted you. It was just the scandal she couldn't deal with. We didn't know what to do. She was only nineteen and I was sixteen.

'Johanna had spoken about becoming a nun, but then we all did. The good sisters – and the priests – all doubled as recruiters for the angel factories. The girls were told night and day about the glory of becoming a Bride of Christ. Johanna knows all about that now. The boys were offered the distant and sexless worship of the Virgin Mary as their reward. I have always preferred a more . . . earthly . . . form of love.'

'Lucky for me,' Richard interjected, and was rewarded by a smile from Ingrid.

'Anyway,' she continued, 'Johanna decided to become a nun after you were born. Maybe it was her way of doing penance – a big item in the bad old days – for what she had done. She is now Sister Johanna of the Order of the Sacred Heart. We still correspond. I tell her how you're getting on, and she tells me tales from one or another of the safe Catholic countries of Latin America. She is working as a nurse in Venezuela now.

'When she took the veil, the Mother Superior allowed her to keep you in the convent for a time. She was a kindly woman in her way, and she did not like to part mother and child until it became necessary – about the time you were ready to enter school. So you probably remember the nuns from that time. Your mother came to me and asked me if I would look after you. She was posted abroad soon afterwards. You know the rest.'

There was silence all round the table at the end of the tale. Helena looked thoughtful, Ingrid faintly relieved.

Richard said the first thing that came into his head to lighten the atmosphere. 'You don't happen to have a nun's uniform – habit, I mean, do you? I've always had this fantasy . . .'

'Can't you think of anything but sex?' Ingrid asked, but she was smiling at them both.

'Is there anything else to think of?' He left them at the table to continue their discussion if they wished. If Helena or Ingrid wanted to tell him anything further, they would no doubt do so.

Helena came to him in the workroom some time later. 'Ingrid's gone for a walk into the village,' she announced. 'What have you two been doing in my absence? Whatever it was, she seems very happy about it.'

'Didn't she say anything about it?'

'Only that you had spanked her. She seemed to be ashamed. Guilty might be a better word. Guilty about enjoying it too much, or maybe guilty at admitting it to me. She had a hang-up about it, I know. Did you know that she once tried to make me stop resorting to the whip, as she put it? She thought it was a perversion forced on me by Aunt Margaret, or a hold-over from my days in the convent, where the nuns practised flagellation. Once I convinced her I liked it, she let me alone, but she always worried about me. Now I wonder if it's something I got from my father, too – if one can inherit a taste for sexual torture.'

'Isn't that a bit like cutting the tails off mice and then expecting them to produce tailless offspring?' Richard asked. 'I imagine it was the examples more than anything else – the nuns and the priests at first, and then most importantly dear Aunt Margaret.'

'But I *like* it so much.' Helena seemed puzzled by her reaction.

'All the better for us both,' he retorted. 'It keeps us harmlessly occupied. And I like it, too, you know – thanks largely to you and Margaret. We have a lot to thank her for.'

'That's pretty much what I told Ingrid. It seemed to make her feel less embarrassed by her own enjoyment. But what exactly did you do to her?' Helena asked.

Richard told her about the spankings, and that Ingrid had gone out to buy a paddle. 'She enjoyed the bondage, too, but you must have known about that already. It was you who tied her to the bed.'

'I was surprised when she asked me to leave her tied up. But it seemed important to her. She said something about a promise she had made to you, and she was terribly excited at the prospect of being there waiting for you. Did she really enjoy it so much?'

'Evidently,' Richard said. 'It didn't seem like acting.' He tried not to seem too self-satisfied as he spoke of Ingrid's response.

They were having a drink in the front room when Ingrid returned from her walk. With a faint flush she asked them what they were talking about. She must have suspected they had been talking about her.

Helena made room for her on the sofa with them, insisting that Richard sat between them. 'Now hold us both while we talk,' she ordered him. 'And, *Mutti*, you must stop feeling embarrassed. We both want you here. We want you to enjoy the visit. So you will be sleeping in our bed with us. No one wants to make you sleep alone just because I am home again. And if I happen to wake up in the night and find Richard, how shall I put it politely, fucking you, I shall lead the applause. Or join you. Three in a bed is good fun.'

Ingrid smiled tenuously. Richard felt the tension leave her body as he hugged her closely. 'I feel better too,' he told her. 'Got any more at home like Helena?'

They talked then of the last few days, Richard feeling less guilty about his own enjoyment as he learned that Helena had spent the time happily with Walter Jennings and Edwina and Lindsay. He gathered that three (or four) in a bed had been her rule during the interlude.

Ingrid's description of Margaret's strange behaviour had alarmed Helena more than she liked to admit. If her aunt had gone all soft and dreamy about Richard, might she not make yet another attempt to get him to go back to Soltau, or at least try to separate them, even if for quite different reasons?

Richard took the news with more equanimity, mainly because he had had more time to digest it. He was gratified at her concern. Even the most modest of men – not that he was one – would be happy to see that his lover was worried about losing him. 'Don't worry,' he said to them. 'I want to keep you both happy.'

Helena punched him in the ribs when she saw his grin. 'Aunt Margaret would make short work of you once she had you back home. She would not be the dream-lover you think she will be.'

'*Pardus maculas non deponit*?' he asked. 'But don't you think she might make such a change for me?'

Helena punched him again in the ribs.

'All right, all right. I get the point. But what are we going to do if Margaret turns up on the doorstep, ostensibly swooning with desire for my fair bod? Turn her out into the cold? I couldn't do that.'

'I don't suppose *you* could turn her away. You'd be too busy getting out your cock if Aunt Margaret asked you please to fuck her,' Helena said acidly. 'No doubt

51

she would be dressed to kill and ready to undress again for you – the first time. But the steel is never far from the surface. You know that. No. You will be chained in the closet upstairs. I will deal with her.'

'Oh, and *you'll* turn her away, then? Like you did last time?' Helena looked angrily at him, but she had to admit that he was right. When Margaret said, 'Frog,' she usually jumped – not least because she could rely on Margaret to lash her unmercifully, until she screamed and begged for more, and came and came. Margaret understood Helena very well. Helena knew that her aunt could control her as easily as she could control Richard. That had always been the problem: how to say no to the woman who would accept no refusal, and who knew how to give such wild pleasure to them both.

'I think you're both overreacting to Margaret,' Ingrid broke in. 'I have known her longer than both of you, and I have never seen her like this. In her present mood I believe she would like most to take Richard back to Germany with her – leaving you out of the picture entirely. But I also think she would take you both back with her – or stay here with you – if Richard made it clear that he would not leave you. And I think he would refuse to leave you.'

Richard nodded slowly. He had made the choice between Helena and her aunt long ago, and there was no reason to change his mind now. Helena – and now Ingrid – had made him as happy as he could ever remember. Nevertheless he wondered if Margaret could be persuaded to join their *ménage à trois*. If two women were nice, how much nicer might three be? Margaret's urge to dominate was a powerful aphrodisiac for almost anyone who came into contact with her. Even Ingrid might not be immune now that she had developed a taste for sexual torture, however mild compared to what her half-sister regularly inflicted. Having access to her blonde beauty on a regular basis was terribly exciting.

So was the possibility of being subjected to bondage and slavery, domination and sexual torture at any moment. If Margaret came to stay with them – or even to visit on a regular basis – that would all be available. He knew that Helena would respond. She had spent many years responding to her aunt. The atmosphere in the old house would become electric.

But he didn't say this. Far better to wait and see how things developed.

That night, it was Helena who woke him by climbing astride and guiding him into her warm and slippery cunt, Helena who rode them both to a shattering climax. But it was Ingrid who provided, not the applause (though, she said, the performance was impressive), but something very much like a benediction. 'I'm glad you two manage to enjoy one another so much. It makes me very happy.'

'Tomorrow,' Richard promised her, 'I will spank you until you're even happier.'

2

Margaret Descends

One Friday some five or six weeks after Ingrid's departure Richard came home to an empty house. He called Helena's name but there was no response. In the kitchen everything was tidy, and there was a note on the kitchen table. He guessed that she was going to be late. But the note was from Margaret, short and to the point in her usual style: 'I have taken Helena. She is safe for now. If you want to see her again, tell Pamela that I will telephone her at 1700 hours today.' The military style of time-keeping was typical of her too. It was just past three-thirty (1530, as Margaret would have said). Even if he began immediately, he would not have much time to get ready.

Nevertheless, he went through the house, checking. If Margaret said she had taken Helena, then she probably had done. But he had to know for sure. When he was certain that Helena was not there, he set about obeying Margaret's instructions. He went first to their bedroom to get out the Pamela-clothes. On the bureau he found another note, together with several Polaroid colour photos.

In the first, Helena was pictured in wide-eyed dismay in the front hallway. The photograph had been taken through the open front door at the moment she had opened it and recognised her visitor. The next shot, from the side, was of Helena being hustled out to a waiting automobile. Her wrists were bound behind her back and she wore a bit and bridle by which she was being pulled along. Her eyes were still wide in dismay: this can't be happening to me, not in my own house. But of course it was. In the third picture she was seated in the back seat and a man (Bruno, Margaret's chauffeur, Richard saw) was tying her ankles together. The last shot showed Helena blindfolded in the seat with the door closing.

In the note, Margaret had said, 'Just in case you thought this was a joke ...'

Laying the photos aside, Richard went ahead with the job in hand. In the bathroom he shaved carefully, both face and legs. Margaret had not said anything specific about how he should prepare himself, but he knew she would expect him to look the part down to the tiniest detail. These small but essential Pamela-rituals increased his excitement, despite the photos. Or maybe because of them. He dried himself off and applied perfumed talc to his body. Ladies should smell like ladies, Margaret had told him, while she was teaching him how to behave like one.

Back in the bedroom he chose a new pair of shiny grey tights (Margaret's most frequent choice, and the one he found most arousing). Like all those in his special drawer, these had been altered by Ingrid. The carefully sewn opening in the gusset that accommodated his cock-chain would not be needed this time, because there was no one to lock the ring on to him. Helena would have done it for him, knowing he was going to meet her aunt, but Helena was gone – where he did not know, but he would find out.

The resolve to get Helena back steadied him, made him concentrate on the details of the preparations. He carefully put on the tights and corselet, slid the false breasts into the cups, got into the black satin slip. He sat down at the dressing table to apply make-up before choosing a dress and getting into it.

As he applied the foundation and blusher, the eye-shadow and eye-liner, he took care not to get any on the slip. Margaret was sure to notice if things got that far (and, again despite the situation, he hoped they would), as she noticed all details. On one memorable day in Soltau she had compelled him to undress so that she could inspect his underwear. Finding a smear of foundation on his slip, she had tied him to the bed and lashed him with a riding crop before ordering him to dress again: 'And this time be more careful,' she had said.

The mascara and eyebrow pencil and lipstick were also carefully applied, for the same reason. Today he did not have that much time before Margaret's call.

The make-up done, he went to the closet to select the dress. There was the original French maid's outfit, but that would not be appropriate for this meeting. There was also the tailor-made black silk and lace dress that Ingrid had made for him on Margaret's orders. Margaret had admired it, but wearing it again might not be such a good idea: she might think he was not making a real effort.

Margaret had not seen the one that Helena had selected for him during one of her shopping expeditions. He normally hated shopping, but on this occasion she had let him know that they would be getting something for Pamela. 'Perhaps you should wear a panty-girdle to conceal your erection,' she said when she saw his excitement. 'You're as excited about clothes as any woman I know.'

'You know it's not just the clothes,' he had said.

And she had nodded, smiling. 'But you *do* get excited about shopping for Pamela, don't you?'

So they had gone to Norwich, but had found nothing they both liked. There had been some near-misses, and he had felt a little flutter of excitement as he imagined himself wearing *that* dress, but in each case Helena had vetoed it. Several others had been interesting, but their short sleeves had ruled them out. He had to have long sleeves, unless he wanted to begin shaving his arms as well as his legs. They had finally found a suitable dress in King's Lynn, having driven over on a glorious day that simply would not allow one to remain indoors.

The chosen dress was tight-fitting ('No point in wearing a tent,' Helena had said), blue instead of basic black as the others were, but dark enough to allow him to follow Ingrid's advice about emulating the thrush rather than the peacock.

When Helena had finished the alterations the dress fitted him very well. The unobtrusive padding Helena had added to the hips gave him a more feminine figure. Most men who wear women's clothing, she had said, look like men because they don't have the right width of hip. 'You will be able to pass anywhere except in the toilet. Just don't forget to go to the room used by setters rather than the one set aside for pointers – and be sure to lock the cubicle door.'

Richard chose the new dress now. He stepped into the bottom half, wriggling as he pulled it over his hips. The wig came next, carefully brushed and styled. He decided on a French twist, a style he had always liked despite the dictates of fashion. It only took him three attempts before he achieved a satisfactory result. Then the high-heeled shoes and a last inspection before going downstairs to await Margaret's orders. A strange woman looked back at him from the mirror: make-up all in place, hips flaring widely, glossy tights throwing off fugitive gleams as they caught the light.

He was only just in time, he saw, glancing at the clock in the front room. It was nearly four-fifty p.m. – 1650, as Margaret would have said. Excited, worried and slightly flustered, he sat by the telephone in the hallway to await his mistress's voice.

It came promptly at 1700 – the well-remembered voice that always made him tingle with excitement. 'Pamela.' Abrupt, commanding. No greeting.

'Yes, Margaret,' he said, a tremor in his voice. He tried again. 'Yes.' Better. Firmer.

'Listen,' she said.

'Richard?' Helena's voice sounded frightened. 'Richard, she is going to ship me away ... to Hong Kong, she says. Unless ... you do as she says. Oh, please help me. I have never seen Aunt Margaret like this before.'

The tearful voice was silenced abruptly. He didn't like to think how.

Margaret came back on the line. 'Go to the front gate. I have left a package there for you. Inside you will find instructions for our meeting. Follow them exactly. I will arrive in exactly one hour. Be sure to leave the front door unlocked.' She hung up.

Richard stared worriedly at the silent telephone before replacing the receiver. He would have to do as she wished. He got up to look out of the front window, instinctively checking for passers-by before going out. No one in sight. He opened the door and stepped out into the gravelled driveway, the stones crunching under his high heels as he made his way to the gate. A small cool breeze brushed his legs. He felt his thighs rubbing together, the smooth nylon making its characteristic exciting whisper.

Margaret's package lay in the middle of the drive, not against the gate post or near the hedge. He would have to step into the open to pick it up, doubtless as Margaret had intended. Plucking up his courage, he made a lunge for the brown-paper parcel. Clutching it tightly, he was about to make his way back to the safety of the house when he heard a car approaching. Richard almost dived behind the hedge.

The car stopped across the road. Christine, the woman who lived a few houses away and into whose pants he would like to get, got out. Instead of going to her own house, she leaned against the car to speak to the driver.

Silently he willed her to go away, to go home, to let him escape into the house. At the same time he was aware of the clock running. One hour, Margaret had said. She would not be late. He had to be ready, and he couldn't move. Crossing the lawn, he would be in full view of Christine and the woman driving the car.

The car drove off at last, and Christine's footsteps receded towards her own house. Richard was limp with relief. He waited until he could no longer hear her steps before practically running back to the house. When he stood behind the closed door at last, his breath was sawing in his throat and his mouth was dry.

His hands shook as he tore the paper away from Margaret's package. Only when his heart stopped pounding did he notice that the package was too heavy to contain only instructions. There was something much more substantial and, knowing Margaret, he guessed it was some kind of bondage gear.

It was.

A wide leather waist belt with a pair of handcuffs dangling from a stout metal ring, opposite the buckles. The handcuffs were open, and there was no key. There were also two leather straps, one longer than the other. And of course Margaret's note, addressed to 'Pamela'.

'Pamela,' he read, 'buckle the wide belt around your waist, the buckles behind your back and the handcuffs in front. Use the two narrower ones to bind your legs at knees and ankles. I imagine you can figure out which strap goes where. Pull all the straps as tight as you can. I will check when I arrive, and I will punish any slackness severely. Put the handcuffs on when you are buckled up. Wait for me.'

Richard examined the waist belt. It was quite strong – much too strong to break, with two stout buckles. By making him do the immobilising she was preparing him to submit in advance. Shrugging mentally while tingling physically, he fitted the belt around his waist as directed. He pulled it as tight as he could, and found that it nipped his waist in, giving him an almost hourglass shape.

He pulled the ankle strap tight, the leather biting into his flesh and indenting the glossy tights. The knee strap came next. Richard hesitated before putting on the handcuffs. Once they were on, he would be helpless, doubtless as Margaret intended. But he knew that he was going to do it. Her hold over his will and his imagination was as strong as ever.

He closed the handcuffs around his wrists. The click as they locked sounded fateful in his imagination. He was committed now. No going back. No escape. With his hands held close to his waist by the belt, there was no way he could now reach the buckles on his knee and ankle straps. And of course the buckle on the waist belt was out of reach behind him. Even if he managed to slip the belt around, his hands would always be on the side opposite the buckles. But it was too tight to slip in any case.

According to the note she should arrive in about fifteen minutes. Not a long wait.

But at five p.m. (1700) she had not come. Nor at 1800.

Suppose she did not come at all? he thought, relishing the prospect at the same time as he began to worry about his predicament. His cock stirred under the tight elastic as he contemplated being abandoned and helpless.

When she had not arrived by seven-thirty, Richard began to wonder if he should try to stand and hop into the kitchen for a sharp knife to cut through the waist belt. With extreme difficulty he managed to get to his feet, where he stood swaying for a moment before losing his balance. He fell jarringly to the floor, where he lay winded. He sat up. Tried to stand. Failed again.

In the end he could only manage to clamber back on to the sofa on his belly, turning laboriously on to his back and getting his feet to the floor.

There, he paused to consider his options. Suppose he somehow managed to get to the kitchen and somehow managed to cut away the waist belt and free his legs. Then, although still in handcuffs, he would be free to go . . . where? The thought of Pamela in handcuffs knocking on Christine's door was unthinkable.

Call the police? Just as bad. 'And just what were we doing, sir, when the intruders burst in, forced you into women's clothing and left you in handcuffs? Was anything taken? Any doors or windows forced?' Worse. Infinitely so.

He was sweating in panic when headlights swept into the driveway and a car pulled up outside the house. It had to be Margaret. This had all been part of her plan to make him imagine the consequences of her non-arrival, to make him grateful to her for finally coming to the rescue, no matter that she had put him into this predicament, no matter what she did to him and Helena afterwards.

But – his sense of fair play coming back – *he* had dressed as Pamela, *he* had strapped his own legs together, handcuffed his own wrists, rendered himself helpless so that Margaret could do whatever she wished with him. Her influence on him was growing. Would he never be free of her? Did he *want* to be free of her?

Margaret switched on the lights, flooding the room with brightness. Richard's eyes were dazzled after the long dark. And by Margaret as well. She removed her coat, striding into the room as if she owned the place and him. Under the coat, Margaret wore a skintight leather panty corselet that nipped in her already slender waist and emphasised two other assets that needed no further emphasis. The garment was cut high on her thighs, allowing him to take in her stunning legs from crotch to ankle.

Glorious, Richard thought as he stared at her. Margaret posed for a moment, fully conscious of the impact her costume had on him. Doubtless she had chosen it with that in mind. The tight leather outlined her figure, emphasised her breasts and legs, made her look both beautiful and dangerous. He felt a strong urge to get down on his knees and kiss her high-heeled shoes and the sheer gunmetal-grey tights that clung to her legs. Only the small matter of the straps and handcuffs prevented him.

Margaret's glance swept over him, taking in the new dress, the make-up and hairstyle, the tights and the bondage. She gave a small nod of approval. 'Well done, Pamela. Are you well?

'Is Helena well?' he retorted. 'I want to see her. Where have you taken her?'

'All in good time, Pamela. You should have learned more patience during your time with me. I can see that you will need a good deal more instruction.'

He noticed with a thrill of fear that she carried a riding crop. She casually flicked her calves with it. He could almost feel the sting of it on his flesh. Margaret was the type of woman who made punishment a desirable necessity. Simply staring at her made him feel both subjugated and exhilarated.

Which Margaret could see, for she posed once more, drawing herself up to full height and pushing her breasts out proudly. 'Are you glad to see me, Pamela?' she asked, moving closer.

Her perfume and her female scent made him dizzy.

Margaret reached down to his cock, taut and stiff beneath the dress and the corselet. 'Yes, I can tell you are. That is the highest compliment a man can offer a woman.'

'Are *you* glad to see me?' he asked daringly. He caught the warning in her glance. Clearly the leopardess was not in the mood to discuss her own feelings. But she had gone to considerable trouble to be here, with him in her power, and with Helena safely out of the way.

Taking another tack, he asked her if she had come alone.

Yes, she said. Her business tonight was with him only. She did not ask him about his reaction. No need, from her viewpoint. She had commanded him to prepare himself, and he had followed her orders exactly.

Margaret studied him silently, making up her mind about what to reveal, what to conceal. Finally she said, 'I am going to ship Helena to a man I know in Hong Kong. For her own good, of course.' She spoke without irony. 'She needs to be taught obedience. My friend will do that. Even now she is being crated for shipping. The journey will not be the most comfortable in the world, but that will prepare her for her reception on the other end. She won't be coming back.' Margaret looked triumphantly at him as she made this last pronouncement.

'You can't ship people around the world like so much freight.'

Her cheeks burning red, Margaret suddenly raised the crop and struck him a swift, stinging blow across the tops of his thighs. Under the sheer nylon of his tights an angry red weal appeared at once.

Margaret struck him again, the blow making a whistling crack and producing another stripe on his legs. She seemed on the point of losing control. She was furious. Her breath hissed between her clenched teeth as she drew back to strike him again. She struck him indiscriminately, on his exposed thighs, on his calves, across the stomach.

At first he managed to keep silent, but the savage punishment gradually wore down his control. At first he groaned softly, but soon he was begging her to stop, in a way he would never have thought possible. His entire lower body was on fire with pain. When a blow landed on his stiff cock he screamed. A mistake. Margaret began lashing it repeatedly.

He tried to cover himself with his hands, but the belt held them closely against his waist. Margaret was relentless. And eventually he became aware of a growing urgency in his burning flesh. To his surprise (and to Margaret's chagrined anger), he suddenly came, his body jerking with the spasms and the semen wetting his crotch and tights and dress. The smell of male orgasm was suddenly strong in the room.

Margaret looked at him wildly. Her rage was frightening. She struggled for control, her anger gradually turning to contempt. 'I see that you have learned a thing or two from little Helena during her time here,' she sneered.

Richard ignored the sarcasm. 'And from you,' he said, hoping to calm her down. Few women, he thought, could resist flattery.

Margaret could. She struck him again across the thighs. 'You are a mess! You have lost all self-control, forgotten all I ever taught you!' Two red spots of anger burned on her cheeks.

'If you send Helena to Hong Kong – or anywhere – you will have to deal with me,' he said quietly.

Margaret was momentarily disconcerted by his defiance, but she recovered quickly. She gestured contemptuously, taking in the Pamela-clothes, the handcuffs and straps, the wet patch in his crotch. 'And just how do you intend to stop me? You can't move unless I decide to allow you.'

'You can't keep me in chains forever. If you send Helena away you'll have to do something like that. One day you'll make a mistake, and I'll be waiting. Then, after I've dealt with you, I'll go find Helena.'

'You want her that badly?' Margaret asked, and in the question Richard could sense a mixture of anger and bafflement and, yes, of hurt feelings. Time to press harder.

'I chose her back in Soltau, and I have never regretted that.'

'I was there, too! Why her?'

'Yes, you were there, but you were too busy being untouchable and ruling the lives of everyone else. Helena is not like that.'

Margaret did not like that. 'Well, with her out of the way, you will see a different person.'

'No, I won't. You'll never stop trying to rule everyone. Sneer if you like, but Helena lets people get near her. You never do,' he challenged her.

She thought for a moment. 'Well, we will see.'

'No,' he said again. 'If you send Helena away, you'll have an enemy for life. You'll have to watch me every minute.'

She looked at him consideringly. 'And if I do not send her to Hong Kong?'

'Well, we'll see,' Richard said in his turn. 'But you have to decide now.'

The silence stretched out. Margaret's warring inclinations were visible in her face.

'Make up your mind,' he told her, and waited for her to strike him with the riding crop.

Margaret went slowly to the telephone in the hall. He heard her dialling, and then a one-sided conversation.

'Bruno?' she said. 'There has been a change of plans. Take my niece out of the crate and keep her there.' She paused, then, 'You heard me!' she snapped. The iron was back in her voice. 'Keep her there, I said. Yes, in chains. I do not want her running away. Naked, too,' she ordered. 'She will enjoy that.' The sneer was back.

He knew that Margaret was trying to make him worry about Helena, naked and in chains, in the hands of Bruno. She could not know that he and Helena had long ago decided that casual sex with others (including Bruno, whom Helena had known for years) did not matter. She always came home in the end. And so did he.

'All right. Just make sure she does not escape.' Margaret hung up and returned to the front room. 'There. Satisfied?'

'For now. I will need to speak to her in the morning.'

'Why?' she demanded.

'I think you know why,' he retorted. 'But what about tonight? Do you intend to spend all night whipping me?'

'No. I will spend the night in your bed.'

Richard smiled hopefully.

'Alone.' Margaret dashed his hope. 'You will stay here.'

'Your servant, madam,' he said with the faintest trace of mockery.

'My slave,' she replied. 'Get used to it.'

'Your slave,' he agreed, looking at the statuesque blonde in the skintight leather corselet. Her body, though proudly displayed, was untouchable. The only access was through the zipper down her back. But he was powerless to attempt even that. He tried another approach.

'What shall we do until madam chooses to retire?'

'We shall alternately lash our slave and tease her unbearably, but we shall not allow her to have another messy climax in her nice clothes. We shall teach her what self-control means,' Margaret announced unsmilingly.

She set the whip on the end-table and sat down next to him. 'Carrot time,' she said.

Richard was acutely conscious of her body pressing against his, of the hardness of her leather corselet exciting him even as it protected her, and of her subtle fragrance. He longed to touch her legs, to stroke the

67

smooth nylon of her tights, to rub her cunt (even if only through the leather), to . . .

Instead it was Margaret who did the rubbing. She settled herself snugly against him, her leather-covered breast pressing into his shoulder while she rubbed her thigh against his, the friction and the soft sibilance of nylon against nylon exciting him terribly. She tugged his skirt up to his waist. For a giddy moment he thought she was going to stroke his cock through the corselet, as Helena sometimes did when she wished him to come without undressing.

But this was not Helena. Margaret touched the damp patch on his tights and held the finger to her nose, sniffing delicately. 'A mess,' she announced. Then she brightened. 'Would you like to touch me?' she teased.

No reply was necessary. His stiff cock said it all.

'Oh, but I was forgetting,' she continued. 'The handcuffs. How awkward!'

'You could unlock them,' he suggested.

'No.'

He dropped the subject, for that evening at least. They might do better after she had taken some lessons in badinage from him, and he had taken more lessons in bondage from her. In the meantime, vamp till she was ready. Patience – and handcuffs – might see him through, although the insistent pressure of her thigh on his was hard to ignore.

Richard looked down, and then up at Margaret's face. Her hand rested on his thigh, near his crotch, rubbing the smooth glossy tights and, incidentally, his leg. Her expression was mocking, but he detected an uncertainty behind the façade. Is this what one did, she seemed to be asking silently.

The old Margaret would have simply done as she wished. This new Margaret presented problems he had never had to confront before. This hesitant Margaret forced him to consider his own actions. He wondered which Margaret he preferred. The old certainties, however painful, seemed more desirable now. But the handcuffs made all the decisions for him.

She moved her hand higher, into the damp patch on his corselet, smearing the half-dried semen into the corselet and tights, her hand growing more slippery – more exciting – as she stroked him.

His cock, never indecisive, responded with a jerk. Margaret grinned triumphantly. She knew how to handle him. His doubts receded. She took charge of his body as she had so many times in the past. He closed his eyes and imagined her naked (except for the essential stockings and suspenders) and helpless in his arms. The handcuffs and the straps that bound him vanished in his fantasy. He was Richard the lion-hearted, Richard the stiff-cocked, naked and rampant. Margaret the strong became Margaret the compliant, Margaret the eager, waiting for him, wanting him, helpless to disobey the imperatives of her flesh.

The handcuffs brought him back from dreamland. His wrists were still encircled by bands of steel, his ankles and knees still bound tightly together, and it was Margaret, not he, who was doing the arousing. And Margaret's hand was becoming insistent, squeezing his cock through the corselet, and her smooth thigh was pressed against his own, nylon-to-nylon, and he was groaning softly as the arousal continued, and then he was coming in sharp spasms as he lost control, the pleasure darting through him . . .

As usual, Margaret sensed when he was on the brink of orgasm. 'You were about to come,' she accused him. 'You weren't even trying to control yourself!'

'Guilty as charged,' he gasped, managing a smile as he declaimed, 'but your perfume and your leg and your hand made me dizzy with desire for your luscious body.'

'That is no excuse,' she said severely. Standing abruptly, she picked up the riding crop. 'Stick time,' she announced. 'I will teach you self-control yet.'

'Why?' he asked, before she could strike.

Margaret hesitated, the crop poised to strike. Slaves did not usually question her actions, and she had no ready answer for this one.

He pressed his advantage. 'Why hold back? Isn't sex supposed to be about letting go and having orgasms and feeling good?' A blunder, he saw at once.

Her confusion cleared and her face took on its usual haughty expression. 'Not with me,' she snapped. 'Sex is about pain and submission. The pleasure comes later, from the pain and submission. You came when I lashed your cock.

'But this time,' she continued, 'I will be more careful. I will arouse you with the whip but stop before you come. I will leave you begging for more, without knowing which you want more, the orgasm or the whip. You will learn to appreciate my methods, so that when I finally allow you to come, you will experience almost unbearable pleasure.'

The crop landed across his thighs with a crack, just far enough from his cock to make the point. 'Ahhhh!' he cried. The whip left another red weal in his flesh, followed by a stinging, burning sensation. Margaret had struck him much harder than before. Clearly she intended to drive home the lesson. 'Ahhh!' he cried again as the crop rose and fell, marking his thighs, his stomach and calves while carefully avoiding the bulging cock beneath the tight corselet.

When she tired of these targets, Margaret roughly seized his hands and pulled him forwards, tumbling him to the floor. There she turned him on to his stomach, crushing his hands beneath him as she lashed his back and bottom and the backs of his legs from ankles to thighs.

Richard cried out under the furious assault, to Margaret's evident satisfaction. 'That is much better,' she observed. Then, seeing him beginning to grind his

70

hips against the carpet, she ordered him to stop. 'You are not to come now!' she hissed, striking him again. 'You will only do so when I allow it.'

She sounded nearly hysterical, her voice high and shrill. He lay still at once. The pain did not daunt him so much as her rage.

Margaret planted one high-heeled shoe in the small of his back, pinning him to the floor as she continued to beat him. When she finally grew tired, Richard could hear her loud, harsh breathing. She removed her foot and sat down again. He risked a sideways glance. Her breasts were heaving and her face was red and sweaty from her labours. The pain and burning in his back and bottom bore witness to her vigour.

At length, with her foot, she rolled him on to his back, pressing him down once again as he tried to sit up. He subsided, and lay on the floor at her feet.

Margaret's breathing at length slowed to normal. She smiled lazily down at him. 'You may now kiss my shoes,' she said, as if granting him an enormous favour.

As indeed she was. Hadn't he fantasised about this very thing? He rolled on to his side, raising his head to kiss the shiny leather as she presented her foot to him.

'That is better,' she said as he kissed the shoe. 'Now the other one.'

When he had kissed both shoes, Margaret took them off. 'Now my feet,' she ordered, presenting one to him and then withdrawing it teasingly as he strained towards it. 'If you really want to do this, you will have to try harder.' Margaret continued to offer and then withdraw her foot.

When she finally held it still, he kissed her foot. The nylon of her tights was smooth beneath his lips. He caught the faint odour of her perfume mingled with those of sweat and shoe leather. His belly tightened with desire. Greatly daring, he licked her toes, taking them into his mouth when she did not withdraw. The odour of her feet filled his nose and mouth. This was heady stuff. As he continued to kiss and suckle Margaret's toes through her sheer grey tights, Richard knew he would never be free of his desire for this imperious woman.

At length Margaret withdrew her foot, the toe area of her tights damp with saliva. The taste of it lingered in his mouth as she planted it in his crotch and offered him the other one. Margaret seemed to be enjoying equally his submission and his attentions to her feet. He took her foot into his mouth as she casually moved the other one on to his cock and began to rub it backwards and forwards. The friction of nylon on elastic sent disturbing sensations to his southern regions. She smiled lazily as she felt his cock stiffen beneath her foot. 'Mmm,' she said. 'Keep licking.'

Richard's attention was sharply divided between the foot in his mouth and the one on his cock. He could not decide which was the most pleasurable. Straining even further, he managed to kiss her instep.

'Do not presume too far,' she warned. 'Keep to the toes.'

He did, while becoming seriously aroused by the casual way in which her other foot was massaging his cock. The foot was slippery from his saliva, and became more slippery as she moved it over the damp patch of semen in his crotch. The friction on his cock became less a matter of rasping and more a matter of sliding. Most disturbing, but he strove to hold back this time, not wanting to end the relative intimacy she had granted him. As he continued to lick and suck Margaret's toes, he began to wonder at what point she would consider that he had displayed the required self-control, and when she would strip off her leather armour and allow him a real go at pleasuring her.

Lost in a fantasy about getting Margaret into bed and himself into Margaret, he barely noticed when she stopped massaging his cock with her foot. Only when she withdrew the other foot from his mouth did he realise that the moment had passed. Margaret looked down at him. 'I like you at my feet, but that is enough for now. I could feel that you were on the verge of another nasty, smelly accident. We don't want another, do we?'

'Maybe you don't, but I wouldn't mind,' Richard croaked.

'Perhaps later. Next week. Some time after you have learned better self-control.'

He would have to be content with the half-promise. Clearly there was to be no more tonight.

'But, my goodness,' Margaret continued, 'just look at the time. I should have been in bed ages ago. Time flies when one's feet are being pleasured by one's slave.'

'I don't suppose you'd consider . . .'

'No. Do not ask again. However, I will allow you to sleep on the couch tonight. It will be more comfortable than the floor, though it is more than you deserve. You may climb on to it now if you wish,' she said as she rose to her feet.

She watched with interest as Richard strained to sit up and work his way over to the couch. 'I like to watch you struggle, Pamela,' she said as he finally got his chest and upper body on to the sofa.

While he struggled to lift himself further, she struck his bottom several swift, stinging blows with the riding crop. 'To help you along,' she said. 'The sight of your bottom stretched tight was too good to resist.' She came as close to a girlish giggle as a woman like her could.

Margaret went to fetch a blanket and pillow for him. Returning, she said cheerfully, 'See, I am not totally oblivious to your creature comforts, though I do not go so far as Helena would to satisfy them.'

Which was, roughly, why he preferred Helena to Margaret, though he did not say so.

'I think you will be more comfortable on your back, though you may sleep on your side if you prefer.'

73

'I'm spoiled for choice,' Richard said as he stretched out on his back.

Margaret looked down at him with a distant fondness. 'Poor Pamela,' she said as she reached down to pull his skirt up to his waist and to pat his cock before covering him with the blanket.

'Think of me naked in your bed as you go to sleep. That will keep you excited. But no wet dreams, whichever you choose.' She turned off the light. 'Sleep tight.'

She went upstairs, where Richard could hear her moving around and imagine her undressing. He groaned in frustration.

Things went quiet upstairs. Margaret, he guessed, was in bed. Maybe even asleep. Or just cat-napping. The leopardess in repose.

Richard found sleep impossible. Visions of Margaret naked (or, alternatively, still wearing her corselet and tights) kept him awake. There were other insomnia-inducing influences as well: the burning of his flesh where she had whipped him; the awkwardness of sleeping while bound; the other burning from his cock, which was suffering a prolonged period of frustrated priapism. He thought about turning on to his stomach and grinding himself against the cushions, but Margaret's warning about messy accidents deterred him. She was sure to check in the morning, and retribution was certain.

He thought about Margaret's emphasis on 'self-control'. It was something which *she* prized highly (though seemingly only in others), even if he did not. He merely wanted to please her, to get into her good graces, as it were, and if she had any. To work around, finally, to the point where he could regularly get into something more satisfying than merely her good graces, without losing the thrills of submission he was still learning from her.

It was dangerous to become *too* acquiescent, lest Margaret conclude that he was ready to renounce

Helena, which he would not do. He had clung to that idea in the face of Margaret's undeniable beauty and his own reactions to her dominance. It was difficult to decide on (and to follow) the right course. So he lay awake, thinking and imagining.

When Margaret came down in the morning, he was still awake, nothing resolved. She was carefully made up, her long blonde hair brushed and shining, arranged expertly in a French twist. As desirable – and as untouchable – as ever. She posed for him at the bottom of the stairs, smiled enigmatically and continued into the kitchen.

Ruefully, Pamela contemplated her own state: hairdo coming undone, make-up smudged, clothes wrinkled and smelly. She was looking frankly disreputable. A shower and a change of clothes would be welcome, but she was unlikely to get either.

He caught himself thinking as Pamela. A disturbing thought. Did he do it because Margaret saw him as Pamela most of the time – or because he was seeing himself that way? Did he, as Helena had once asked, really want to be female?

He had said no. He examined the question once more, and came to the same conclusion. Pamela was merely a role he played for the pleasure of it. Like an actor. He must always remember which role he was playing. Keep them separate.

Pamela rolled on to her side with some difficulty. The blanket slipped to the floor and her wrinkled dress rode high up her thighs, revealing the white patches of dried semen on her corselet and tights. There was nothing she could do about it. Either Margaret would understand her helplessness, or decide to punish her for untidiness and immodesty. She could do nothing about that either. The thought allowed her to relax, to enjoy the luxury of total dependence on someone else – no decisions; no responsibilities; no blame except that which her captor decided arbitrarily to assign to her, and for which she might be as arbitrarily punished.

Richard had become Pamela yesterday evening, at the exact moment of locking the handcuffs around her own wrists. It had been Pamela (and not Richard) who had revelled in the pain and the humiliation and the submission, the shoe-kissing and the toe-sucking, the arousal and the frustration, the sleepless tormented night and the renewed frustration as Margaret flaunted herself.

But it was Richard who had to rescue Helena from her aunt's clutches. No matter that the aunt in question had taken *him* prisoner as well and was showing every sign of keeping him helpless for the foreseeable future. The need to do *something* was accompanied by the knowledge of his powerlessness to do *anything*. He was back in the everyday world of decisions and frustrations and worries. He asked himself what else he could have done to discover where Helena was being held and what Margaret's plans were. Richard was forced to the uncomfortable conclusion that he had given away all freedom of action for nothing.

Unless one counted the undeniable pleasures of the previous evening (and the promise of more) as nothing. And so his thoughts went, round and round.

Margaret interrupted them by appearing with a cup of coffee in each hand. Richard looked at her with frank appraisal and admiration. It must be wonderful to always know that one is beautiful, desirable, and in control.

She sat beside him on the sofa, snuggling up as she had last night, her thigh pressed against his, the nylon-to-nylon friction as exciting as ever. Holding a cup of coffee to his lips, Margaret smiled gaily into his eyes. 'I believe this is where we left off last night. Drink some coffee. Then we can continue our discussion.'

He nodded his thanks, while thinking that the discussion had been largely carried on with the riding crop.

'Do not think that I am becoming your servant,' Margaret warned as she withdrew the cup. 'I am only doing this in deference to your ... indisposition.' Her gesture took in the handcuffs and straps. 'Really, you should be serving me, but for now we will go on like this.'

The delightful friction against his thigh was sending shivers of excitement through his belly and cock. It stirred and grew slowly erect.

Margaret noticed as well. 'I see you still fancy me, but you must not think of that now. Think of Helena. What are we to do with her? If I simply let her go, she will immediately set about getting you away from me. And if I let you both go, you two would simply settle down to fuck one another stupid, as you have been doing these past months. Surely you can see my dilemma.'

Margaret had obliquely admitted that she had been feeling like the outsider at the feast. Last night he had threatened her (however unconvincingly) with the stick of continued isolation. Now was perhaps the time for the carrot.

'Gretchen,' he began, ignoring her startled look at his use of her familiar name, 'don't you think it's time to make a deal?

'Gretchen' gave him a thunderous look.

'Listen to me!' he said intensely. 'You must know by now that simple force will not solve the problem of how to get what you want.'

'Oh, and you know what I want? Pray tell me what that is.' Margaret looked dangerous.

Richard remembered Margaret warm and naked in bed on her last visit. That had been a temporary thaw. He hoped for a more permanent softening. A compliment, he thought, might defuse the threatened explosion. 'Look . . . I mean . . . you must know I . . . want you. Want to fuck you, want to give you pleasure, want to know you enjoy being with me as much as I enjoy being with you.' When in danger or in doubt, tell the truth (sometimes).

'You . . . enjoy being with me?' A hint of surprise and gratification crept into her voice, but she was still in a dangerous mood.

He plunged on. 'I thought of you all last night. I couldn't sleep thinking of you naked in my – our – bed.' He deliberately let the ambiguity of the 'our' stand. If she chose to construe it as 'mine and Helena's', she might explode. If she thought he meant 'mine and yours', she might explode. She had said many times that her slaves were not to make presumptions about her accessibility or acquiescence. And if she took it to mean 'mine and yours and Helena's', as he had intended it, she might still explode. But he would risk it. Margaret could be dynamite in bed. Either the fuse was lit, or not.

'After your last visit, you must know I want you in bed, and that I – we – want you to be a frequent visitor in our house. We would like to be able to visit you as well, without the threat of becoming your slaves. Can't you declare a truce, get to know us as something besides possessions? Sharing might be more satisfactory than continual raiding and capturing. What is captured must be constantly guarded. What is given needn't be.'

Margaret finally spoke. 'And suppose I enjoy possessions more than shared gifts?'

Richard thought of leopards and their unchanging spots. 'Well, *do* you? You must decide. You don't have to answer now. But think about it. I'm not going anywhere.' He lifted his manacled wrists and let them drop again.

'Very well,' she said, rising and looking down at him. 'I will consider the matter. But at the same time I would like *you* to consider whether you prefer to be shared . . . or owned. Take your time, Pamela.' She smiled as she turned the tables neatly.

Touché, he thought ruefully. But he only said, 'I must see Helena today.'

Some of the satisfaction went out of Margaret's expression, but she shrugged her shoulders. 'Very well. But you must wait – unless Pamela relishes the idea of being driven in broad daylight wearing a gag and blindfold as well as her pretty dress and handcuffs.'

'Why do I have to wear anything unusual?

'Because I say so. I do not want you to know where Helena is being held. You might be tempted to mount a one-man – or woman – commando raid to recapture her. You offered to share your idyll with me, but how do I know what you might do once the handcuffs were off?'

'Margaret, you will just have to learn to trust others. Not everyone is as suspicious as you.'

She gave him a direct look. 'Yes. I will have to trust others, but they must first earn that trust from me. For now that means doing whatever I say. For now that means waiting until I am ready to take you to your paramour.'

He shrugged. Margaret kneeled to loosen the straps that bound his legs. 'Time for a clean-up,' she said. 'Get up.'

Richard struggled to his feet, tottering momentarily in the high heels.

'Upstairs,' she ordered tersely.

Obediently, he started up. She followed, carrying his leg straps and idly flicking his legs with them.

In the bathroom she lifted his skirt and ordered him to hold it up. Stooping, she unsnapped the crotch of his corselet and pulled his tights down. 'Sit,' she commanded. With a half-smile, she continued, 'You may shit when ready.' She pushed his cock, which was showing signs of interest, down inside the toilet bowl. 'Stay,' she said as she left the room.

Margaret came back a few moments later with his cock-ring and chain. She held a new brass padlock in her hand. 'I thought this looked familiar,' she said. 'All

79

finished?' After wiping him clean she locked the ring on to his scrotum. 'You look almost indecent without it,' she commented as she pulled his tights back into place and threaded the chain through the hole in the gusset. Performing the same task with the corselet, Margaret smiled to herself as she pulled his skirt back into place. 'Isn't that better?' she asked brightly.

Richard felt the familiar weight and constriction of the ring, remembering the first time she had locked it on to him, back at the beginning of his life as a slave and bondage devotee. The chain hung down between his legs, brushing against the insides of his thighs.

Margaret grasped the chain and tugged it sharply, leading him back towards the bedroom.

The bed, he noted, was carefully made up. Margaret was nothing if not neat and thorough.

'Sit there,' she ordered, pointing to one side of it. She pulled the chain from under the bed and joined it to his chain with a second padlock. She flourished the keys to remind him who was in control before stooping to bind his legs together again at knees and thighs.

The straps felt tighter than they had been. Yes, he decided as he worked his legs, they *were* much tighter. She had the advantages of more leverage and a severe disposition.

'I will be back for you some time later. You may amuse yourself until then, but I do not want any more mess. Do you understand?' Margaret cupped his chin, forcing him to meet her glance.

He understood.

Margaret went to Helena's wardrobe, selecting a pale gold skirt with black spots and a tawny gold blouse. She put these on over her leather corselet. Now she looked quite ordinary, although Richard was terribly excited by the knowledge of what lay beneath.

She stooped suddenly and planted a kiss on his lips. It lasted. If he was surprised, she seemed even more so.

Hurriedly she broke it off and stood erect, the dominatrix once more.

'*Au revoir*,' she said, making a quick exit.

He heard the tap-tapping of her high heels as she descended the stairs. The sound of the car driving away came to him as he sat on the bed, chained to it by his balls. He wondered how he would 'amuse himself' without breaking Margaret's injunction against 'messy accidents'. He weighed the arguments in favour of such an 'accident'. The lash, and her anger, outweighed them.

Silence, if not peace, returned gradually. He heard faint animal sounds and birdsong through the open window. The sun shone on the back garden, the river, the woods across the water. There was a quiet air of approaching winter in the scene. A cool breeze came in through the window, stirring against his legs. Outside the window people were shopping, driving children to school, working in the fields. He was enforcedly idle, a helpless prisoner of the erratic and unpredictable woman who had abducted his lover and was threatening them both with permanent separation and slavery.

He lay back on the bed, stretching himself out and admiring the play of light on the sheer glossy tights, enjoying the constriction of the straps and the tight corselet. Pamela emerged from her corner of his imagination – the helpless captive woman awaiting her captor. However much she might struggle to free herself, Pamela would always be the captive of her own imagination. Margaret was as necessary to Pamela as Helena was to Richard.

If Margaret shipped Helena to her friend in Hong Kong, he would become more like Pamela with every passing day, until she took control of his existence. He imagined wearing women's clothes for the rest of his life, Margaret's prisoner, perhaps her sometime lover, whenever the mistress of Soltau decided to allow such a liberty. Would that be enough without Helena? Pamela said an emphatic, 'Yes!'

The Richard part of him said a more sober, 'No.' He had to free Helena. Somehow free himself, too, of these mental shackles that bound him to Margaret and, more immediately, of the real ones that bound him to the bed. He saw no way to do either. But if he had learned anything from his bondage experience, it was patience. An enforced patience at first, but becoming more natural the longer he and Helena – and Margaret – played these games.

But were they really games, or an integral part of their lives? With a shiver of excitement he realised he would never be free of this dark desire to be held captive, to wear female clothing, to suffer under the lash and to experience those bursting, throbbing orgasms he had enjoyed with Helena – and Margaret. There had to be a way to ensure all that for the future.

Margaret returned in late afternoon. The low sun flooded the room, making colours seem more vivid. She burst in like a windstorm, bringing urgency and action to the peaceful house. Richard, startled from his hours-long reverie, sat up in bed and swung his feet to the floor. Lying down in Margaret's presence seemed somehow improper. He smiled inwardly at his eagerness to please her, difficult as that often was.

'Well, Pamela, did you enjoy your day?' She raised his skirt and felt in his crotch for telltale dampness. She rubbed his cock briefly, smiling as it stirred under her hand. 'Still glad to see me,' she said. 'But now we must prepare you for the journey to see little Helena. You *will* co-operate, won't you?

He nodded.

'Good. This will only take a little while, but I will try to make it enjoyable – Pamela. The first step is a gag and blindfold. Where does Helena keep the leather helmet she took from my house?'

He hesitated.

'Come now. I am not quibbling over a trifle. It has already been replaced with something more severe. But I need it now. Where is it?' She was looking annoyed.

He told her.

Margaret fetched it. 'Some leg-irons and a tyre pump,' she demanded.

He told her where to find them, too.

'Nearly ready,' Margaret said with a sardonic smile. Things were going her way, so she could afford to smile. 'First the helmet,' she announced. 'No ear plugs this time. I will need to direct you from time to time.'

He agreed to the conditions by keeping still and silent as she fitted the helmet over his head and stuffed the inflatable gag into his mouth. It may only have been thoroughness, but Margaret seemed to derive pleasure from making the straps as tight as possible. With the bicycle pump she inflated the gag, filling his mouth and forcing his jaws apart, making the helmet even tighter.

He sat in silence and darkness, waiting for the next move.

'Can you hear me?' she asked.

He nodded.

'Good. I am going to stand you up now.'

She helped him to his feet, steadied him when he swayed and nearly fell. With his ankles and knees strapped tightly together he was in constant danger of falling, but he managed equilibrium at last, with her help.

Margaret unlocked the handcuffs and loosened the belt, but his relative freedom did not last very long. She turned the belt around and tightened the buckles again in front. Guessing that she intended to handcuff his wrists behind him, he brought his arms behind him. Margaret grunted in satisfaction as she locked the cuffs on to him.

She loosened the leg straps then, and replaced them with the leg-irons. Only then did she unlock his chain from the bed. She snapped the dog-lead to his chain and tugged sharply: follow.

Down the hall she led him, the pull of the chain giving him direction. When they paused, his mental map of the house told him they had reached the staircase. Margaret's hand guided his foot on to the first step, then the pull of the chain compelled him to descend after her. He did so carefully, knowing that a fall was always possible. Margaret seemed oblivious of the danger, to judge by the relentless pull on his balls. At the bottom she pulled him towards the hallway and the front door.

There he balked. Being led out into the front garden at the end of a chain, dressed as he was, would be embarrassing. Suppose someone saw him. Margaret pulled harder, forcing him to follow. The procession of two crossed the driveway, gravel crunching under two pairs of high-heeled shoes. A pause, then Margaret's hand on the helmet guided him into the car. He went almost eagerly, anxious to be inside something and out of sight.

Margaret strapped him in and closed the door. The car sagged slightly as she got into the driver's seat. She started the engine and drove off with her helpless passenger.

Richard tried to keep track of the turns, which he could feel even though he could not see them. The knowledge might help him in case he got free and had to find Helena. But, tense with the fear of being seen, highly conscious of the handcuffs and the leg-irons and the female clothing, he only had the sense that they were headed west. He could not tell how far.

Eventually the car stopped. He felt Margaret get out, felt his own door being opened and the seat belt being unfastened, felt the sharp tug on his balls. He got out awkwardly, stood waiting for her directions. They came in the usual way. He followed the sharp, impatient tugs into a house of some sort. A strange house whose shape he did not know. Margaret led him quickly along a hall, as if wishing to get this over as soon as possible. A pause. Then he was thrust into a room.

'Richard!' Helena's voice was strained but there was no doubt that she was glad and relieved to see him.

'Pamela,' Margaret corrected her. 'You will have one hour together. The time will begin when I have removed the gag and blindfold.'

The gag was deflated, the straps loosened, the helmet lifted away. Light flooded in.

'One hour from now,' Margaret repeated. 'You have a great deal to discuss, so do not spend too much time feeling one another up,' she added ironically. She closed and locked the door.

'Oh, Richard, come here quickly.'

Helena was not entirely naked, as Margaret had suggested to Bruno, but she might as well have been. She wore only a troubled expression, a waist belt similar to his own, and a thick leather collar, by which she was chained to the bed. He guessed that her hands were handcuffed behind her back like his.

A chain was fastened to the front of her belt, disappearing between her legs. Knowing Margaret, he guessed that there were dildoes involved, the chain serving to hold them in place. Wires descended from her collar, also disappearing into her crotch. That was more disturbing, hinting at the presence of some electrical device. Again, knowing Margaret, he suspected some sort of torture was involved.

He was half right.

They met, Helena holding up her face to be kissed. The handless kiss grew longer, each striving to let the other know that, despite Margaret, nothing had changed between them. Prisoners both of the wicked duchess, they were still united against her.

'You *are* all right?' he asked anxiously

Helena nodded. 'You?'

'Yes. Did she threaten you with Hong Kong?'

'Yes. Aunt Margaret said I would be shipped there, to a friend of hers, who would teach me obedience. She showed me the crate I was to travel in. That frightened me, but I was more frightened that I would not see you again. I'm sure that she intended me to stay where I was sent.'

'That's what she said to me,' Richard replied. 'I told her that if she did, she would have to deal with me. She hesitated a bit, but in the end she called here and cancelled the plans.'

'So that's why Bruno kept me here.' She leaned against him, her face lifted again for a kiss. Afterwards, she sighed. 'I am so glad you stopped her. She frightened me badly this time. I believe *Mutti* is right. She wants to get rid of me so that she can have you to herself. You won't let her succeed, will you?'

'No,' he said, although he saw no immediate way to thwart Margaret. 'But, tell me, what else has she done to you?'

Helena, despite her worried expression, managed a small smile. 'Well, of course she beat me. With a thin cane. It hurt terribly, and in the end I came.' She shrugged her shoulders. 'You know me. Aunt Margaret was so furious she stopped beating me, but by then it was too late. I shook and shuddered and came for quite a long time. Her expression was priceless.'

'She did much the same thing to me. She was furious with me too,' he said.

'She beat you?'

'Of course. That's what Margaret always does.'

Helena smiled mischievously. 'And you *came*?'

'Yes.'

'Good. I am glad. But,' she went on, 'there is this too.' Helena indicated the wires that ran from her collar to her crotch. 'She has turned me on, I mean ... switched me on ... these dildoes inside me. They are

86

electrified. Aunt Margaret has a remote control. There is a receiver in the collar, with batteries. The wires lead to my cunt and arsehole. If I please her, she makes them vibrate inside me and they make me come and come until I think I will pass out. I can't stop.'

'I can think of worse things,' he said, trying to lighten the atmosphere.

'Yes, but there is the other side of the coin. If she is angry, she makes the dildoes give me low-voltage electric shocks. It's an expertly built machine. It feels as if there are red hot pokers inside me, and there is a terrible pulsating, stabbing sensation. I scream and scream when she does that to me. And I can't get them out.' She indicated the chain between her legs.

'Imagine she is beating you with the cane,' Richard suggested. He could think of no way to get them out either.

It was Helena's turn to look sheepish.

'You *have* been doing that,' Richard said delightedly. 'And you came.'

'Well, yes, but don't tell Aunt Margaret. She will only stop doing it.' She smiled tentatively. 'But it *does* hurt as well,' she said defensively. 'At first. She calls this thing her carrot and stick.'

'She used the same expression to me,' he admitted. 'The carrot was herself, though she only hinted at future delights.'

'Oh, Richard,' Helena said again. 'I can only hope the carrot was worth the stick. But what are we going to do? She won't just go away and leave us alone.'

'No. Of course she won't. We will have to make her change. She will have to begin treating us as people rather than possessions – without, however, stopping her mistreating us both sexually on occasion. Life without the whip just wouldn't be the same, would it?'

Helena nodded. 'I suppose not. But how do you plan to make her live with the new dispensation?'

'I could always threaten her with sexual deprivation. That should bring her to her knees. If that doesn't work, I might beat her, but only in places where it doesn't show. But Margaret herself keeps preaching about "self-control" like some medieval nun.'

'She is not a nun. Remember, I saw the two of you in bed on her last visit. She didn't behave like a nun then. Nor will she do so if we can get her into the mood and into bed again.'

'And me into her,' Richard added.

'That too,' Helena said with a smile. Suddenly she jerked away from him, bewilderment and surprise on her face. 'Aunt Margaret!' she gasped. 'She has . . . my dildoes.' She drew a great shuddering breath, and sank to the floor, where she lay thrashing in enforced pleasure as the electricity coursed through her body. She rolled from side to side, the cords in her neck tense and her muscles rippling in spasms. She fought her handcuffs, frantic to rip the plugs from her cunt and anus, her hands straining towards them, but quite unable to reach them.

Richard kneeled beside her, helpless as she was to do anything about her torment. Like her, he struggled futilely with his handcuffs. Helena continued to roll on the floor. Of Margaret there was no sign save the tortured body of her niece. Had Margaret been there, Richard would have taken her on despite the handcuffs. But there was nothing to be done. He watched her in helpless anger.

And as he watched, he wondered how Margaret had known the precise moment to 'switch Helena on'. Remembering the videos of Edwina and Lindsay and Walter Jennings in what they thought was the privacy of their own home, he suspected a video camera hidden in the room. No doubt Margaret was spying on her two captives. That was another thing they would have to cure her of.

But the immediate worry was Helena. He spoke to her, 'Think of the whip. Think of me lashing you between the legs, on your cunt and on your breasts. Turn the pain into pleasure as you always do.'

Helena opened her eyes, looking doubtfully at him through her tears. 'Oh, Richard, make her stop, please!'

'The whip,' he repeated. 'Think of the whip.'

His words seemed to calm her. She closed her eyes, imagining perhaps playing their favourite sex game: she was strung up by the wrists and writhing in ecstasy as he lashed her all over her body, but especially between her legs. Helena's cries subsided gradually, and changed, beginning to resemble her cries of pleasure as she was beaten.

Richard lay beside her, speaking intensely, reminding her of their past pleasures. And Helena worked her magic once more, the pain becoming sexual pleasure. She opened her eyes. They were much less troubled. 'Kiss my breasts, Richard. Tease me with your mouth and tongue and teeth. Help me to come.'

And so he did, kissing her full breasts, licking them, biting her nipples as they became engorged. 'Oh!' she moaned, her body tensing as she began to come. Then again, 'Oh! Oh, Richard, yes, yes, yes, oh, God, yes!' Great shudders went through her. Her cries of pleasure sounded like cries of pain.

Suddenly Helena's tense body relaxed and she opened her eyes. 'She has switched me off, Richard.'

He drew back. 'Are you sure?'

'Yes, but please don't stop.'

He resumed teasing and biting her breasts and nipples, and Helena closed her eyes once more, surrendering to the pleasure, her body tensing and relaxing as she climaxed and recovered, climaxed and recovered. Finally she rolled away.

'I must rest now,' she said. 'But thank you, Richard. I don't think I could have borne that without you. It was much more intense than before.'

'Are you all right?' he asked.

She gave him a wan smile. 'I'll live. Aunt Margaret doesn't want to hurt me. She must now know that the pain is not going to frighten me. She can't keep these things inside me forever. Nor can she keep me handcuffed every moment. One day she will make a mistake, and I will be ready.'

She struggled to a sitting position, grimacing as the dildo was forced deeper into her anus. Leaning against the side of the bed, she got to her knees and then to her feet. Richard struggled to stand also.

'Come sit beside me on the bed.' When he had done so, she leaned closer to whisper in his ear, 'Speak softly. I think Aunt Margaret has a microphone in the room. Can you think of any way to escape from her?'

'Not at the moment. But you said that Bruno is kindly disposed to you. Work on that. I will try to get into Margaret's good graces, if she has any. And one day she will make a mistake, as you said.'

'Very well. Then we must be alert for the chance when it comes. But now –' brightening '– I want to make you come. We will lie down, and you can lie against my back where I can reach your cock with my hands. Aunt Margaret will be furious, but we cannot allow her to stop us doing what we both like.'

'Margaret will indeed be furious. She has been telling me again and again not to come, but . . .' Grinning conspiratorially, he added, 'Let's do it! First you, then me.'

'Dear Richard,' she said with a tired smile. 'I have come many times, with your help. I must rest. But you have not. Come, lie on the bed.'

He did as she asked. Helena swung her legs up and lay down herself, worming her way across to him until he lay against her back, spoon fashion. They had often gone to sleep this way at home, though not when both were handcuffed. Helena gathered his skirt between her hands and raised it inchmeal until she could touch his cock beneath the tight elastic corselet.

'My, you are eager,' she said.

Richard heard the smile rather than saw it. His cock was erect. It had been so almost since the torture attempt had begun. He had been turned on by the idea of Helena undergoing sexual torture by remote control. But the agenda was quite different now. Helena's fingers rubbed and stroked and squeezed his cock and he surrendered wholly to her manipulations. Raising and lowering her hands to the limited extent allowed by the handcuffs and waist belt, she was able to touch him from the tops of his thighs to just above the tip of his cock as it rested against his belly. The slow pace of the stimulation imposed on them by their handcuffs was a pleasant change from the urgency that usually accompanied their sexual congress.

Richard was drifting towards orgasm, oblivious to their surroundings. Margaret was nearby. She might burst in at any moment to vent her fury on her helpless captives. But that did not deter him – or Helena.

Helena jerked suddenly against him. 'Oh!' she exclaimed.

Richard himself was jerked back to the present.

'Richard,' Helena said tensely, 'Richard . . . she has . . . turned me on again.' Seeing his alarm, she hurried on, 'No, not like before. This time it is the carrot. I am going to be made to come. I can't stop myself. Oh, what shall I do?' she wailed, her hips beginning to thrust backwards and forwards as she became excited – despite herself, as she might have said.

'Do the only thing you can do,' Richard advised. 'Come. Enjoy it. Don't be like Margaret.' Privately, he suspected that it was Bruno who had applied the carrot to his lover. Margaret was much more likely to use the stick. His own excitement was increased by the prospect of Helena coming 'despite herself'. The prospect of his own orgasm receded without any regret.

'If the dildoes make you come, that's hardly a fate worse than death. Enjoy it. Roll over so I can watch you.'

'Oh, no, please don't look at me when I can't help myself,' she begged. 'Not when Aunt Margaret makes me do it.'

'That excites me too. And anyway, where do you expect me to go? Go ahead.'

'I can't . . . avoid . . . going ahead,' Helena moaned, her voice rising as she had a small orgasm.

Richard saw her eyes lose focus momentarily as she came, accompanied by a small shudder. 'That's my horny little nymphomaniac,' he encouraged her. 'Come closer. I want to feel your body against me when you cross those peaks ahead.'

They wormed towards one another, until they were pressed together. Helena shuddered again as she came, another moan of pleasure forcing itself past her lips.

'Oh, Richard, kiss me, please. *You* make me come, not just this . . . thing . . . inside me.'

They lay face to face in a long kiss. Richard was excited by his lover's predicament, and Helena was being aroused by the vibration of the two dildoes inside her. She moaned as they kissed, the sound coming from her and going into his mouth, an intimacy they had often shared before. She twisted her upper body, rubbing her engorged breasts and nipples against him, arousing herself even further.

Richard broke off the kiss and slid down until he could kiss her breasts and tease the nipples with his teeth and tongue. As he kissed her, she moaned again. When he bit her nipples she came, shuddering and crying out, 'Oh, Richard, oh, God, yes, yes, yes! Oh, God, I'm coming! I can't stop!'

Had his mouth not been occupied, he would have told her not to try. Her mutually assisted orgasm was terribly exciting to him too. The idea of Helena being forced to come against her will was a delightful oxy-moron. He wished he could use his hands on her cunt and clitoris to give her even greater delight, but she was clearly going to come again without any further stimulation

Richard often fantasised about forcing Helena to come while she was helpless to resist and unable to stop until she was exhausted. He had never been able to realise it, because they had always ended up fucking.

Helena cried out again, 'Oh, God, oh, God, oh, God!'

Curious, Richard thought, how even the most militant of atheists, like Helena and Margaret, reverted to their early religious training in moments of stress. He had a vivid memory of Margaret screaming those same words as they drove one another to mutual orgasm on her last visit.

His cock was erect. He could feel it throbbing against the tight elastic of the corselet, rubbing against the sheer nylon of his tights.

Helena was by now thoroughly aroused, her orgasms almost continuous. But, even when she was almost delirious from the delicious sensations flooding through her helpless body, she thought of him. 'Richard,' she gasped, 'open your legs.' Her voice rose oddly as she came.

He did as she asked, and she bent her leg and thrust it between his, her thigh rubbing against his erect cock. She had discovered a way to make him come despite Margaret and despite their handcuffs.

Under the dual stimulus of Helena's ecstasy and the insistent pressure of her knee against his cock, Richard forgot all about self-control and Margaret's injunction against messy accidents. Messy this might be, but it would be no accident. Defiance made the pleasure more intense as he felt himself spurt inside the tight elastic, the warm flood soaking into the tights and the corselet. He groaned as he came.

Helena heard him through the overwhelming sensations of her own orgasm. 'Oh, yes!' she encouraged him. 'Come, Richard! Come with me! Come now!'

He did just that, and she moaned and shuddered with him.

Margaret out of sight, even Margaret out of mind, did not mean Margaret absent. The first indication that they were not alone was a furious shout from her: 'I leave you alone for a moment and you immediately start fucking one another!'

Hyperbole, of course. They had been together for nearly twenty minutes before discovering how to pleasure one another despite the handcuffs and her instructions. But Margaret was in no mood to debate the finer points of timing. She struck Richard with the seemingly ubiquitous riding crop, the blow landing across the side of his thigh. She struck at him repeatedly, the blows landing indiscriminately on both of them. Resistance was impossible. So was escape.

He cried out in pain and surprise as he was struck. Helena reacted quite differently. Only someone who was ignorant of her ability to derive sexual pleasure would have been surprised. But even Margaret, who knew her niece well, was betrayed perhaps by her fury. Helena, the dildoes still vibrating in her cunt and anus, almost immediately went into another climax as she was beaten, moaning and grinding her hips against Richard in her frenzy.

Margaret lost all control. She struck her niece in fury, the red weals appearing on her naked body at each blow. Had she been thinking clearly, she need only have stopped striking Helena and switched off the dildoes.

Richard risked a sideways glance at their tormentress. Margaret's face was red from anger and effort, but there were also tears of frustration and disappointment at the corners of her eyes. Angrily, she wiped them away with the back of her hand. Richard guessed that Margaret's jealousy was provoked by this latest demonstration of his and Helena's fondness for one another, and their ability to, as she had said, fuck one another stupid given the slightest chance. And, of course, one could not rule out a sense of standing on the sidelines while her slaves did to one another what the mistress wanted done to herself, but could not bring herself to ask for.

But he had to do what he could to protect Helena. 'Gretchen,' he said sharply, using the familiar name to get her attention.

It worked. She stopped lashing Helena and resumed beating him. Tears were now running down her cheeks.

When she paused to wipe them away, he spoke again. 'Gretchen, stop this right now!'

She gave him a furious look. 'Why should I? You have been screwing like animals. Look at you! No self-control. No discipline. I won't have that!'

Before she could launch into another sermon on abstinence and obedience, Richard asked her, 'Why not join us? Wouldn't you like to enjoy sex instead of trying to stop others from having any except on your own terms?'

'And ... and ... roll around like an animal? Like you?'

'Like us,' Richard agreed. 'Let go. Stop being the moral policewoman. Take your pants off.'

Margaret looked doubtfully at him for long moments, as if considering the proposition. Richard thought he saw desire in her eyes, but she turned away abruptly and left the room.

Helena, beside him on the bed, was still climaxing steadily, moaning as she came. She went on for long minutes. Then Margaret apparently got hold of the remote and switched her off, for she slowly subsided. She looked at him, smiling despite the red marks all over her naked body.

'That was marvellous. Thank you.'

'Well, your aunt helped,' he said modestly.

'I meant you handled her well too.'

'I thought you were too busy wallowing in lust to notice.'

'Into every sexual frenzy some moments of sanity must fall,' she said with another smile. Then she came to the main point. 'You want her, don't you, Richard? You know you can tell me. I will help you. Short of murdering her, I can't see any other way of getting her to give us some peace.'

'You're sure?'

'Of course I'm sure. And I'm not being wholly unselfish. Think how nice it would be for both of us if Aunt Margaret would visit us as *Mutti* did. We could be alternately her slaves – I am accustomed to the way she beats me – and her bedmates.'

'All right.'

'Good. New subject. Tell me what you two have been doing while I was a lonely captive in the wilds of Norfolk.'

So he did. When he ended, she asked only if he had enjoyed the interlude. 'All of it?'

'Yes.'

'Then we both need her to provide counterpoint. One can't always be having fun, can one?' she asked ironically.

'I don't see why not. It's Margaret we have to persuade.'

'We will both work on her. We will wear her down in time.'

A visiting leopardess would certainly banish dullness. Richard imagined several Pamela-days in succession: sucking Margaret's toes, receiving her beatings, being her slave, eventually (as a reward) sharing her bed and her body.

'I would have to find something to occupy myself while she visited, at least on those days when she wanted

96

you for herself. Then you could go see Lindsay and Edwina whenever she wanted to abuse me.' Helena sounded enthusiastic.

Once again Richard marvelled at her acceptance of what was not every woman's idea of a love-life.

'All right,' he agreed, 'we'll work on her. But how about working on one another right now? Unless you have something more urgent to discuss.'

'What could be more urgent than sex? It makes even the vilest of durance less onerous.'

'You've been at the thesaurus again,' he accused her as she settled against him.

Helena sighed with contentment. 'Do you think you could work on my nipples again?'

He bit her left nipple gently. 'Ah,' Helena moaned, once more squeezing her leg between his and massaging his cock with her thigh. They made slow, handless love to one another for far longer than the single hour Margaret had originally allotted them. She did not return, either out of forgetfulness, or from a disinclination to be too obviously the outsider at their banquet.

They were sleeping entwined when she came for him.

Margaret shook him awake roughly. 'It's time to go, Pamela.' She waited as he swung his legs to the floor and sat on the side of the bed. Wordlessly she reached under his skirt to snap the dog lead to his cock-ring, tugging sharply to get him moving. There was no time to bid Helena farewell. 'You've had enough of one another as it is,' she said, her anger barely contained.

Helena called out, 'Work on her, Richard!'

Margaret led him down the hallway and into the front room of what was evidently a two- or three-bedroom bungalow. From the windows he saw flat farmland stretching away. In the distance a typical Norfolk windmill stood in ruins.

'What did she mean, "work on her"? Work on who?' Margaret demanded.

'Why, work on you, of course. Have you made up your mind about us? Are we to be partners or possessions? I am working on earning your trust. You should work on learning to trust us. Any progress to report?'

'I am not obliged to report to you!' she snapped, her cheeks bright with anger again.

'No, you're not,' he agreed. 'But a continued lack of reporting, together with continued threats and incarceration, might fairly be construed as a negative answer. I – we – will have to plan accordingly.'

'Are you threatening me?'

'How could I do that when I am wearing your handcuffs?' he asked reasonably. 'But one day you will have to unlock us. And we won't be kindly disposed by then. That's a friendly warning, if you like.'

Margaret glared at him but did not reply. In silence she fitted the leather helmet, stuffing the gag into his mouth and buckling the straps tightly behind his head. She inflated the gag, forcing his jaws apart and cutting off all speech.

Richard offered no resistance, treating it as yet another trust-building exercise – as well as a terribly arousing experience.

Another sharp tug on the lead informed him that it was time to go. She led him to the car, strapped him in and drove away. Once again he tried to memorise the turns and estimate the distance between Bacton and Helena's prison. If Margaret did not relent, he might have to mount a raid to get her back.

As always, the return journey seemed to fly by. In minutes, seemingly, Margaret was drawing up at the house and bundling him inside. His confidence returned in the familiar surroundings. When she left him standing in the hallway, he was able to feel his way into the sitting room and sit on the sofa. There he awaited Margaret's next appearance.

She took a long time coming. But finally with another sharp tug on his lead she urged him to his feet and up the stairs. His hopes rose as she led him towards the bedroom.

He felt Margaret lock his lead to the bed, chaining him in place. His hopes rose still higher as she unlocked the handcuffs and removed the waist belt. The leg-irons were removed, followed by the soiled dress and the tights and corselet with their damp patches of semen. The only traces left of Pamela were the long wig and the carefully applied make-up, both out of reach under the tight helmet. Margaret showed no sign of removing that.

Naked except for the helmet and cock ring, he allowed Margaret to push him down on to the bed on his back and to bind his wrists and ankles to the bedposts. He hoped that this further acquiescence would be taken as a sign of trustworthiness. But his cock, ever alert, signalled that his motives were not all pure.

Was Margaret going to throw herself on to him, impaling herself on that rigid cock? Was she going to press her ripe, eager body against him and ride them both to a shattering climax? And then demand more, and still more, from him, until they were both exhausted and could do no more?

No. She was going to beat him, as he discovered with the first blow across his stomach. She was putting a lot of herself into it. But she avoided his cock, the most obvious feature of the landscape. Richard fought not to cry out. The gag helped, but before very long he was groaning loudly and fighting the ropes that bound him.

Margaret changed tactics and whips abruptly. A stinging blow to his cock informed him that she had switched to the pussy-whip she had used on him, first in her hotel room in Cromer and then later in this same room, during her earlier visit. And, as then, the stinging assault aroused him. His cock remained erect, jerking to the blows. As he became more excited he found it harder to practise the self-control Margaret was so desirous of instilling in him. He lay in darkness as she lashed him, all his attention focused on what was happening to his most sensitive parts.

When Margaret stopped at last, just short of making him come, he began to hope that *now* she would fling herself on him, stuffing his stinging cock into her warm, slippery cunt and . . .

But she didn't. As near as he could tell, she left the room.

Some indeterminate time later, she came back. Richard heard her approaching footsteps, so he was not totally unprepared for the touch of her hand. But he *was* surprised to feel it on his cock. His hope surged once again.

She grasped him firmly, which was her way, sliding her hand up and down while he grew erect. The soreness from the recent beating was forgotten in an instant as his thoughts turned fondly to sex with his blonde captor. The bed sagged as she sat down, still massaging him. Was she going to make him come, he wondered. His excitement grew. Her hand felt marvellous, now tight, now looser, squeezing and sliding along his shaft. She toyed with his cock-ring, turning it on his scrotum, teasing him with his helplessness. What about her previous insistence on self-control? He tried desperately to control himself, to hold back, resisting the hand that was so maddeningly urging him forward. His imagination showed Margaret sitting naked on the bed, the light of desire – for him – lighting her deep blue eyes.

Then, as he was waiting for her to straddle him and guide his throbbing cock into her eager cunt, she abruptly stopped, taking her hand away. He grunted, his cock afire. He tugged frantically at the ropes that held him. He felt the mattress rise as she stood up, heard her retreating footsteps. He was alone again, with an erection out to *here*, and no place to put it. Self-control, indeed. His helplessness increased his arousal. It felt as if he was going to come, spurting into the empty air, no one to share or help. No one to disapprove, or apply the whip. His cock leaped at the thought of the lash. But gradually the desire ebbed. The taut muscles relaxed, but his cock remained stiff. It was hard to have a limp prick with Margaret in the house.

More time passed. This time he did not hear Margaret when she returned. Perhaps she had taken off her shoes in order to approach him unheralded. The pussy-whip struck him, focusing his attention on his cock in a flash of stinging pain.

Like Helena, he felt himself becoming aroused by the lashing, his cock once more growing stiff and warm as it was struck from each side in turn. When the whip struck him between the legs, Richard cried out through the gag. He did not know himself whether the cries were pleas for her to stop, or to go on, to lash him until he came, or until she put him out of his misery by impaling herself on his erect member.

Margaret did neither, continuing to lash him within an inch of orgasm before leaving him once more struggling futilely against the ropes and with an aching erection. In his mind's eye he saw his tormentress striding imperiously away in her tight leather corselet and sheer grey tights, as he had last seen her, a haughty expression on her beautiful face as she enjoyed his helpless excitement. His excitement grew. This time he *was* going to come. He felt his cock quivering with the first tremors.

A cold wet cloth enveloped his prick before he could explode. He dropped from boiling point in an instant, though still aching with the desire to be inside something warm and wet and female. If Margaret had used a warm cloth instead of a cold one, he would have come there and then. Which was, of course, why she had not. He knew that she was going to stretch him out forever, never allowing him release. Perhaps an entire night of alternating pain and frustration lay ahead. It depended on how much Margaret wanted to sleep. His own desires and needs never came into it.

Beneath the cold cloth his erection subsided. When Margaret lay down beside him he groaned but could do nothing. She lay for a long time, her naked body pressing against him, while he lay in helpless frustration. Sleep was impossible.

The hours stretched out interminably. Richard tugged against the ropes while Margaret's body lay warmly against him. From time to time she woke and reached for his cock, stroking, squeezing, now tightly, throttlingly, now gently, sliding her closed fingers up and down his shaft. And always, unerringly, stopping just before he could come, her hand dropping away, her voice low in his ear, mocking him: 'Sleep now.' *She* did.

In the morning his head felt heavy and his eyes sore from the long vigil. He felt the mattress rise as she stood, the air cold against his side where her warm body had lain. Margaret untied him and removed the helmet. Pamela's smudged make-up and tangled hairdo emerged. Her eyes blinked in the growing light.

'Bath time,' she decreed. 'You smell of sex.' She wrinkled her nose in disgust. 'Give me the wig. I will take care of it this time, though you should not expect it every day.'

Did she expect to be there every day? Would she take him away with her in chains, pack him in a crate and ship him to Soltau? His cock stirred at the thought of Pamela waking to each new day of uncertainty and adventure. But what about Helena?

He could overpower Margaret now, of course, send her away, even beat her until she begged him to stop, promised to do whatever he wished. But would she tell him where to find Helena, knowing that her return would end their own time together? He would have to carry on. For Helena's sake, he told himself, while Pamela cried out for her own place in the blinding sun of Margaret's attentions, however painful that might be.

He and Pamela went to the bathroom, bathed, made their toilet. The ring locked tightly around his scrotum reminded him of who was in charge.

Back in the bedroom, Margaret made him sit down and paint his finger- and toenails. He was clumsy from lack of practice. Margaret was relentless, making him wipe off the badly done bits, forcing him to make a perfect job of it. When she was finally satisfied, she ordered him to take the maid's uniform from the closet. It would be the most appropriate for a day indoors, she declared.

She had brushed the brown wig until it shone, and arranged it expertly in a French twist. She adjusted it over his still-damp hair. The opaque tights came next, not the shiny, more dressy ones he had worn yesterday. A clean corselet and slip and false breasts followed. The false breasts were new, with prominent nipples that could be seen through the corselet and slip and, later, through the tight bodice of the silk uniform. He shivered with pleasure as he caught sight of them in the mirror.

The make-up came next, done with more flair and élan than he ever did it. But this was Margaret, not one of the other two women who had taught him the art of female impersonation. The wren was banished, the peacock to the fore. A more feminine, more striking Pamela looked out of the mirror at him. She was undeniably prettier. She gave him a troubled look before Margaret once more took charge. She dabbed perfume on the pulse points: behind and below the ears on either side of the neck; the insides of elbows; in the hollows behind the knees. The fragrance was dizzying.

Leg-irons, she said, would have to suffice for today. She would have liked to put handcuffs on him as well, but, she said, she expected him to clean and dust the house – only proper for the maid. You may, she added, work on your own things when the house is clean and the laundry taken care of.

'Shoes,' she commanded. The high heels were by now quite familiar. Margaret herself locked the leg-irons on to his ankles.

'You may begin with the laundry, Pamela,' she commanded.

It felt both natural and eerie to be the maid in his own house. He gathered the laundry, smelling his own semen and Margaret's perfume and body-odour as he carried the bundle to the laundry room downstairs. Pamela looked back at him from each mirror he passed.

In the kitchen he made fresh coffee and set about breakfast unasked: omelette and toasted bread, fresh marmalade and butter.

Margaret, attracted by the rising smell of cooking, came down.

'You may serve breakfast, Pamela,' Margaret said as she seated herself.

Pamela offered her an omelette, buttered her toast, poured coffee for her imperious mistress. She stood attentively as Margaret ate.

Margaret wiped her lips and rose. 'You may eat now, Pamela,' she said as she took a cup of coffee with her through into the front room.

When everything in the kitchen was tidy, Richard went through to receive his instructions for the rest of the day.

'I am going out soon. You will have the house to yourself. The garden, too, if you care to go outdoors.' Margaret smiled mockingly at him. 'I do not know when I will be back. I have several appointments today. I will tell Lindsay and Edwina hello for you when I call on Walter.'

'What about Helena?' he asked. 'I want to see her again today. It's the only way I can be sure she is being treated well.'

'Don't you trust me, Pamela? As you said – it was only yesterday – we will have to trust one another. In any case,' she said with some asperity, 'I would have thought that yesterday would have been enough to last for several days.'

'How do you know, Margaret? When was the last time you had a good, thorough fucking?'

She glared at him, angry. And ... eager? She mastered her feelings, became imperious once more. But she had no ready reply to the taunt. Instead, she left immediately.

As he dusted and hoovered and polished, Richard thought about Helena and Ingrid. He was not sure when he would see either of them again, and that thought was worrying. His thoughts turned to Margaret. They were worrying too. She had probably withheld her plans from him to increase his anxiety. Not knowing when she would be back, or in what mood she might return, would keep him on tenterhooks all day. When she finally did come back, he would be all the more grateful to see her. Good psychology if one were the mistress. Not so good if one were the slave.

There was no escape. The alternatives were the same: call the police or the fire brigade to cut away his leg-irons; walk down the road to Christine's house and ask her to lend him a hacksaw. Margaret, thorough as always, had ascertained that all his own metal-cutting tools were in the boathouse down by the river.

The hours flew for Pamela. She dusted and tidied up, clanking from room to room in her leg-irons. Knowing that Margaret might turn up at any moment with the riding crop spurred her on. What Margaret might do to a dilatory or slipshod maid excited her. She felt shivers of excitement at the thought of Margaret's disapproval.

For Richard the hours dragged. His work usually filled the hours, but now he was worried about Helena. At the same time Margaret occupied a large part of his thoughts. He listened for the sound of the returning leopardess with as much anxiety as Pamela.

When the leopardess returned at last, towards dark, she took them both by surprise. No car drew up to warn them of her presence. The sound of the front door closing echoed through the house, startling him. Margaret was evidently not in a good mood. Pamela looked at her mistress with the familiar mixture of dread and anticipation. Richard was looking for a crack in the stern façade.

'Damned car,' she fumed, looking harried. 'I do not see why I paid so much for something that always breaks down.'

Richard smiled, imagining an irate Margaret lashing her recalcitrant Mercedes with the riding crop, Basil Fawlty-fashion.

Pamela was anxiously searching for something to placate Margaret. A cup of coffee, she thought. That usually worked, if it were brought promptly and with the required servility and deference.

Richard-Pamela went to the kitchen to make it, considering meanwhile what to serve for supper. The coffee was received with the usual mixture of hauteur and minimal gratitude, but it had a calming effect on Margaret. Richard retired to the kitchen to prepare something for them to eat.

When the food was ready, he invited Margaret into the kitchen to partake of it. She had freshened up while he toiled. She came to the table looking more immaculate than before. Her hair was once more in place and her face cleaner. She also wore a loose wrap which, from time to time, opened to allow him to see that she was wearing the leather corselet once more, with shiny dark grey tights and black high-heeled shoes. Her legs looked, as always, stunning. Richard was suitably stunned.

Greatly daring, with Margaret in a bad temper anyway about her car, he sat down to eat also. Time for the help to assert themselves modestly. He asked her what had happened with the car.

'The damned thing', as she called it, had broken down between Norwich and Lowestoft, simply miles from anywhere. She seemed affronted by its leaving her stranded. Car and driver had required a recovery vehicle and a taxi, respectively. 'It will be repaired tomorrow,' she informed him 'You will go fetch it, Pamela.'

Going about his local haunts dressed as Pamela presented certain hazards, like recognition, he objected.

Margaret dismissed his worries. 'No one looks beyond the clothes. See tits and legs and high heels, expect a woman, not a drag queen. You can wear dark glasses if you're really worried,' she decreed airily.

Margaret seemed to have recovered her temper under the influence of food and Pamela's presence. 'That was a good effort, Pamela,' she announced. 'Not up to Egon Ronay standards, but quite passable. When you have finished the washing up, come into the front room with coffee,' she ordered as she exited.

Richard wondered if she ever gave unqualified praise. Her most characteristic appraisal was some form of 'could do better'.

In the sitting room Margaret had arranged herself on the sofa in a theatrical pose, the robe thrown back on her shoulders and one of her legs drawn up underneath her. The robe was open and revealed her breasts jutting proudly under the tight shiny leather. Her nylon-sheathed legs were a stirring sight to Richard, who was suitably stirred, the movement taking place mainly in his crotch.

She had also arranged other props ready to hand on the coffee table. The riding crop and the waist belt with its attached handcuffs were there, signalling another evening of pain and frustration rather than the hoped-for romp in bed.

He remembered his nights with Ingrid here on the sofa. Her half-sister was a completely different woman.

She pointed wordlessly to the belt. Richard picked it up and fitted it around his waist, handcuffs to the front.

'Hands behind you,' she ordered.

He loosened the buckles and turned the belt.

'Tighter,' Margaret ordered in her could-do-better voice.

'Help me, then,' Richard said, turning to face her.

With a resigned sigh she pulled the buckles tighter, nipping his waist in. She locked the handcuffs on his wrists and stowed the key away.

'Now sit down at my feet,' she commanded. 'My feet and toes may require some attention later. You will like that, won't you, Pamela?'

No reply was required. She ordered, he obeyed. He kneeled down before her and then settled down on the floor with a slight bump. Margaret spread her legs and motioned for him to sit between them with his back resting against the front of the sofa. She pressed her legs against his sides, the shiny nylon of her tights rasping against the silk of the maid's uniform. All cosy for an evening's telly, Richard thought.

Margaret appeared to lose herself in contemplation of the catalogue of disasters that made up the typical news programme. From time to time she shifted her position, her nylon-sheathed legs making exciting sibilant sounds and causing his cock to stir restlessly. But that was all it could do. The tight elastic imprisoned his shaft just as effectively as her leather corselet protected her cunt and breasts. Impasse, he thought.

This was his third consecutive relatively sleepless night. He drowsed from time to time, waking to find her legs pressed against him, holding him upright in both senses of the word.

Although Margaret was seemingly engrossed in the TV across the room to the exclusion of the other TV between her legs, Richard knew that sooner or later she would do something exciting and painful to Pamela. She was merely allowing the anxiety and anticipation to build and the imagination to suggest several possible scenarios. Pamela fantasised about sucking Margaret's toes once again. Perhaps to kiss her feet and legs. Maybe – the most dizzying possibility of all – Margaret might want her breasts and cunt kissed through the tight leather corselet.

Eventually she put an end to his fantasies by standing up. She stretched like a cat, arching her back and thrusting her breasts forward for him to admire. She picked up the riding crop.

Pamela watched her warily but expectantly.

'You didn't think I had forgotten your disgraceful behaviour with Helena yesterday, did you? Get up and kneel against the sofa,' she ordered, watching as he struggled to arrange himself.

When he was kneeling, lightning struck (as it usually does) the highest point. Margaret landed a stinging, burning blow across his bottom. She raised his skirt, exposing him from bottom to ankles, and then proceeded to lash him methodically over the whole area.

Richard thought the matter of Helena was merely a pretext. Margaret needed no excuse to lash anyone. It was part of her nature. And if this was in retaliation for his handless and cockless fuck with Helena, then it was a long time in coming. Margaret usually administered punishment immediately.

From waist to calves his body was afire as she landed blow after blow. He grunted as they landed, jerking spasmodically, fighting the handcuffs that held him helpless under her whip. Margaret seemed tireless tonight. The beating went on and on, almost devoid of any sexual content. Margaret avoided striking upwards between his legs, knowing that that would make him come. Of course, he was inflamed by the whip, but her avoidance of his crotch kept him from orgasm. When she finally tired, she simply stopped. She set the whip aside and resumed her seat on the sofa. She commanded him once more to sit between her legs.

But this time she took off her shoes, resting one foot between his legs and pressing the heel against his balls. The other foot massaged his cock through the tight elastic of the corselet. He became achingly erect but she stopped each time she sensed he was about to come. It was maddening. He could not say how long this went on, but it seemed an eternity of arousal and frustration – exactly the state he knew Margaret liked him to attain. He imagined their roles reversed, Margaret helplessly bound at his feet, begging for release, and he very nearly had the messy accident she deplored so strongly. She sensed his agitation, removing her feet and forcing him to subside before replacing them.

He looked at her feet and calves, longing to kiss them, lick them, adore them. He brought himself back with a mental jerk. Occasional slavery was exciting, but these thoughts led to utter subjugation. And what's so bad about that? Pamela asked. Subjection to Margaret meant renouncing Helena, Richard replied. And Ingrid as well. Don't forget her.

Remembering Ingrid's excitement as she fought her bonds and came repeatedly finally undid him. Despite the alacrity with which Margaret removed her feet, she was not swift enough to prevent him from coming, the hot spurts of semen soaking through the tights and corselet as his hours of frustration ended at last.

Even though he would have preferred to spend himself inside Margaret, this was relief of a sort. Margaret, of, course, did not agree. She bent her furious gaze on him. 'What brought that on?' she demanded. 'I was being most careful not to let you go that far.'

'I was thinking of Helena and yesterday,' Richard lied, partly to conceal Ingrid's visit from her half-sister, and partly to taunt her. Two spots of anger burned in her cheeks.

Richard thought Margaret would beat him again for his temerity. Surprisingly, she did not. Instead she stood abruptly and left the room, her face working. The leopardess was fighting back tears. Chagrin, he told himself. Not tears. In his scheme of things Margaret was not allowed to cry. She would be less than Margaret if she did.

He lay quietly, waiting for her next move, glad that it was not his decision. There was a sort of justice in this. She had taken the active part since her arrival, forcing the passive role on him. She had got herself into this state. She would have to get herself out of it again. Would she avenge her chagrin with more stern punishment, or accept his offer of a truce? Between anticipating more punishment and imagining Margaret naked and eager in his arms, he managed to maintain a respectable erection.

Margaret did not return for a long time. Two or three hours, as near as he could estimate. When she did, she was composed once more. She pulled him to his feet by the chain on his balls, none too gently. She led him up the stairs and into the bedroom. There Richard was surprised and excited to see that she had brought a straight-backed chair from the study. Memories of her last visit crowded his mind: Pamela tied to the chair while Margaret used the pussy-whip on her.

Margaret lifted the hem of the tight skirt above his waist and unfastened the crotch of his corselet. The tights were pulled down around his knees, freeing his cock and balls from their long imprisonment. His cock stood out stiffly as he imagined himself being fucked by Margaret.

'Sit,' she commanded.

He did.

Margaret removed his handcuffs and waist belt, then bound his wrists behind the back of the chair. She pushed the chain from his cock-ring through between his legs and fastened it to his wrists, holding him tightly against the chair-back. She tied his ankles together and pulled them back under the seat of the chair, tying them to his wrists as well. She fished his cock and balls from between his thighs. The effect was to make his prominent cock even more prominent, and extremely vulnerable to whatever she intended to do with – or to – it.

He shivered in anticipation as he waited for the next act in their ballet of pain and pleasure. He was forced to watch as Margaret undressed slowly, stripping her glorious body to his gaze, allowing him to look but not to touch. Ever the tease, he thought, when finally she stood naked before him. The ultimate reward but still untouchable. A slave's reach should exceed his grasp, or what is a mistress for?

But, of course, there was more. Margaret used the pussy-whip on him, lashing his exposed cock and balls while he squirmed and tried not to scream or to come too soon. Her face grew red and her breath short as the vigorous beating went on. Her nipples were erect, but that might only be due to the excitement of administering yet another beating.

Only when she dropped the whip and straddled him could he tell that she was wet and parted and eager. Margaret guided his cock inside her with one hand, her perfume filling his nostrils as he filled her body. The long slow glide into the warm sheath of her cunt ended when she sat on his thighs, impaled and excited.

He guessed that some of her arousal was due to the whipping she had given him, but then so was his own. If both giver and receiver got a sexual thrill from pain, it did not lessen the satisfaction or the excitement of being finally joined to his leopardess, inside her, as she rocked her hips and squirmed on his cock.

As she moved for them both, Margaret gave a small sigh of satisfaction, as if she too had reached a long-sought goal. She put her arms around his neck, pulling her breasts against the false breasts he wore, crushing them between their bodies. She moaned as her sensitive, engorged nipples rubbed against the satin of the maid's outfit and the firm false breasts beneath it.

Richard felt as if his cock had been plunged into a bath of fire. Why she had waited so long for this was a mystery. If the pleasure was so great, why not indulge more often? Perhaps Margaret was one of those people for whom the holding back made the final indulgence more pleasurable.

But even with Margaret sitting on his lap, naked and impaled and eager, he thought of another difference between his lover and her aunt. Helena needed frequent sex. She had never wanted to hold off so long that the waiting became an arousal. Better to plunge in whenever the urge struck.

But now there was the aunt to deal with. Or, rather, it was the aunt who dealt with him, sliding up and down on his cock by bending and straightening her knees. Her vaginal muscles clenched and relaxed around him as she moved towards her climax. She avoided his glance by laying her head on his shoulder, her breathing harsh in his ear, a sharp panting changing to a longer groan as she came.

Richard could feel her spasms of pleasure in his cock as he fought to hold back his own orgasm. At last he saw some value in the self-control Margaret so often advocated. The longer this went on, the better he liked it. And there was still the pleasure of coming at last with his now-not-so-distant mistress. He concentrated on giving Margaret pleasure.

And she evidently took great pleasure in the in-and-out movement, grinding her clitoris against his pubic bone at the bottom of her glide and becoming more

113

frantic with each contact. When Margaret came the next time, she pulled away from him and shook his upper body with her arms, her fingernails digging into him. Her eyes were wide open, staring at nothing.

That was what the Germans meant by *leer* – the empty stare of a person in ecstasy. Her eyes were a startling blue, so close that he could see tiny images of himself in their depths. Margaret's face and neck and breasts were flushed as she shook with one climax after another. She seemed insatiable, venting enormous emotional pressure at last in this fury. Margaret in ecstasy was a different person. Her beauty seemed intensified as she surrendered her body to pleasure at last.

With a deep groan Margaret climaxed once again, and Richard could hold back no longer. His own climax rippled through him as he spent himself inside this wild woman impaled on his cock. Margaret threw back her head and screamed, a full-throated cry of release and joy that raised the hairs on the back of his neck.

He held himself tense as Margaret spent herself in frenzy, and when she slumped against him he allowed his own muscles to relax. Still joined, they sat for a long time. Richard thought that Margaret might have drifted off into exhausted sleep. Her breathing became slow and regular, and small involuntary spasms shook her body. Her cunt tightened around him in tiny spasms. To his surprise and pleasure, he felt himself becoming erect again. Margaret too felt him stirring inside her body. She sat erect and opened her eyes, her own surprise showing as a hopeful question: again? So soon?

This time their coupling was slower, more studied, more intense. This time, Margaret did not jerk herself frenziedly about as she rode him. She moved slowly, regularly, up and down on his cock, moaning softly where earlier she had screamed, her cunt tightening around him in rippling contractions. And their release was longer, making up for the lessened intensity by increased duration. And afterwards Margaret did go to sleep, leaning against him, still coupled, as the long slow afternoon wore away and the shadows lengthened in the room.

When at last she arose from him, there was a relaxed, dreamy look on her face that reminded him strongly of Helena after sex. In Margaret the transformation from leopardess to sex kitten was startling. She kissed him on the mouth, long and lingeringly, their breaths mingling as her tongue darted into him. Then, wordlessly, she made her way to the bathroom, leaving him still bound to the chair.

In the quiet house he could hear her pissing. The sounds of running water came to him as she finished. There was a curious intimacy in the quiet, shared noises. Margaret had always been careful not to let him see her attending to her body's needs. For all he knew, she had been granted immunity from the toilet and the shower. But now she revealed her more human side. *Menschlich, allzu menschlich,* as she might have said, had she been given to admissions like that.

She returned, still flushed, her eyes puffy and her hair undone. Another unprecedented intimacy. She seldom allowed others to see her *en déshabillé* if she could prevent it. This relaxation made her more human, more approachable. Richard hoped she could somehow manage to maintain this mood – or at least to fall into it more often.

Margaret gave him another long kiss before lying down on the bed, naked, allowing him to look at her glorious body. To look but not to touch.

Richard would have liked to join her, to hold her naked body warm in his arms, to sleep with her in truth, and to wake to sleep again with her. On the other hand, by leaving him bound, she was holding out the promise of yet another wild coupling when she woke. Richard needed rest after the storm, but he could only drowse sitting up in the hard chair. His half-dreams kept him wakeful anyway, while the object of them lay naked but untouchable a few feet away.

Thoughts of Helena came to worry him as well. Margaret did not seem disposed to release her, or to let him see her again after the last visit. Rescue plans might soon have to be made, even at the risk of destroying this new-found intimacy with her aunt. Thoughts of quieter, more frequent sex with his lover were contrasted with Margaret's frenzied but sporadic and unpredictable lovemaking.

Margaret woke and rose from the bed. Without even stretching her body to tease him with her beauty, she came directly to him and kneeled in front of the chair. She took his cock into her mouth, breathing warmly on it as she caressed it with her tongue. His response was almost instantaneous. He groaned when she nipped his stiffening prick. Margaret continued to work on him until she was satisfied that he was fully erect. She stood and straddled him once more, guiding his cock into her as she sat on his lap.

Miraculously, she was wet and ready. Richard guessed she had been having erotic dreams, and had woken to realise them without delay. Not everyone was so lucky.

Wordlessly, staring into his eyes as if defying him to protest, she lifted herself off his cock and then slid back down until she was fully penetrated. She moved slowly, deliberately, at first, as if demonstrating that she could control herself in every way, but eventually her body's need betrayed her and she became more frenzied. The pace increased, his cock sliding in and out of her more rapidly, and she began to make small grunting sounds of effort as he slid home. She seemed unaware of the sounds, intent on the sensations from her cunt and belly. They must have been overwhelming. This time, she seemed not to care when, or whether, he came. Only the fact that he had spent himself twice into her willing body saved Richard from coming at once as Margaret virtually hurled herself at him. Her moans became growls of pleasure, torn from somewhere deep inside her. She sounded like an animal – his leopardess – as she began to climax.

She held herself proudly erect, staring into his eyes, as she ground her clitoris against his pubic bone. Her climaxes came so close upon one another that Richard could not tell when one ended and the next began. Devout Muslims at the end of Ramadan fell no more eagerly upon their first meal than Margaret fell upon him. Devout Christians (if there were any of them still about) at the end of Lent were no more ready for a good tuck-in.

In the end, there could be only one ending. When it came for him, Margaret squeezed her eyes tightly shut. The spasms as he emptied himself into her once again caused her to scream with her own release. The quiet house was filled with her cries. Richard imagined the entire village being startled out of its torpor, galvanised by this evidence of his visitor's ecstasy.

This time she sat still for a very long time, her breath slowing and her flush fading. When at last she rose, she looked bewildered and weary. Her progress to the bathroom this time was nearly a stagger. And when she came back to the bed she sat wearily on the edge. Richard had to remind her of his own desire for the loo. She untied him and watched him as he stood shakily in his turn. She seemed to be gauging the depth of his response to her by his weariness.

Evidently, she was satisfied. She smiled as he made his unsteady way to the toilet. He stripped off the dress and corselet and tights and wig. He showered, cleaning away all traces of Pamela. When he emerged from the bathroom the only trace of his submission was the obdurate ring locked around his scrotum.

'Richard,' she said when he entered the bedroom. She sat still on the edge of the bed as if too weary to move, but she had noticed his transformation at once.

He lay down on the bed, beckoning her to join him. After only the briefest of hesitations she lay down beside him, pulling the light covers over them.

Margaret looked at him questioningly. Her usual air of command and firm resolution was in abeyance. Richard wanted her to come to him on her own, take him into her arms as she had taken him into her body, but maybe it was too soon for that. Instead he put his arms around her, hugging her body to his own, feeling the initial stiffness and resistance gradually leave her. Margaret warm against his own flesh was a strong argument in favour of keeping her there. Or of ensuring that she returned often enough to keep them both satisfied.

She permitted herself a low sigh as she settled against him, her long blonde hair spread on the pillows and over his encircling arm. He bent to kiss her brow, her eyelids, her neck, and finally her lips. Margaret sighed again as she opened her mouth to him.

Margaret slept. Richard only dozed, waking each time to find the woman of his most recent dreams and fantasies naked in bed with him, and him not bound or restrained in any way. He could now touch her whenever he wished, and his cock stirred with the memory of his frustrated desires. But even though he was not bound physically, there was the equally strong mental bondage he had learned during these last three frustrating days. She had taught him that access would be only on her terms. That she had granted access only a few hours ago was no guarantee that she would welcome another penetration, especially as he was not tied to the chair and in her power.

But she *had* untied him. She had not put her clothes back on. She had not objected when he had lain down

118

and embraced her. But – how would she react to a stiff cock sliding into her without warning? Only one way to find out. He drew away slightly from her warm body and looked at her. In repose the leopardess looked like any other woman asleep. Margaret's face, relaxed from its customary sternness, seemed especially vulnerable. An illusion, he knew.

Nevertheless, he would have to test the depth of her acquiescence, and by great good fortune the tool he would use for the job was making itself ready without any effort on his part. It was evidently making itself felt, too, for Margaret stirred in her sleep when it pressed into her belly. She reached down and squeezed his prick familiarly.

What more invitation could a man want? He disengaged his arms, rolling Margaret over on to her back. Her thighs parted with the movement. Supporting himself on one hand over the sleeping leopardess, he used the other to guide himself into her.

Margaret came fully awake as she was penetrated. She stared wildly into his face, not recognising him at once. When she did, there was a momentary return of the fury he had half-expected. But it was gone in the next instant, when she remembered where she was.

Committed now, he slid all the way in. Margaret sighed as the slow glide ended with his pubic bone pressed against her clitoris. She stirred, adjusting her position slightly, and he felt himself slide in a fraction more. Margaret raised her arms and embraced him, pulling him down until her taut nipples were crushed against his chest. Even more surprisingly, she raised her legs, locking her ankles behind him with her heels pressing into the small of his back. She was as open as she could make herself, and in the pale morning sunlight, in the quiet house, she surrendered herself to him.

She admitted him at once into her body and into her rather narrow (as he knew) circle of intimates. That she might bar him from that circle at the next moment, demanding his submission and service, made the magic greater. Her heels pressed into his back, urging him onward. Her back arched as she offered herself to him.

And Richard, still wondering at the transformation, accepted the offer whole-heartedly. He raised his hips and felt himself slide from the tight sheath of her cunt. He sank back, gliding into her once more, and she sighed with pleasure. A normal morning's fuck, it might have been, with any other woman but her.

They moved languorously together in the dance of love. Mating would have better described the congress with the leopardess, he thought, as his cock slid in and out of Margaret while she rocked her hips in time with him and urged him on.

This time, slower, more deliberate, absorbed in pleasuring her, Richard was able to hold off his own orgasm more easily. The old Margaret would have been pleased. So, evidently, was the new. Her first orgasm took them both by surprise, even though she must have felt it coming on. She stayed relaxed until almost the last moment, until the sharp spike of her release caused her to tighten herself around him as she used her heels to drive him into her. She squeezed her eyes closed and moaned with pleasure as she came.

For long moments after her shudders ended Richard lay on top of Margaret, enjoying the warmth and wetness and tightness in which he was buried. She sighed as he wriggled to achieve better contact with her clitoris. He took the opportunity to kiss her eyes and ears, the side of her neck where the pulses beat close to the surface. He inhaled the mixed aroma of her musk and her perfume as his lips brushed her smooth skin.

Margaret opened her eyes. He gazed into deep pools of blue as she regarded him steadily. It wasn't a contest of wills this time. No one was trying to make the other look away.

'Richard,' she said, the single word signifying an entirely different relationship. 'Richard', not 'Pamela'. Not simply, 'you'.

'Richard,' she said again, her voice rising suddenly, his name becoming an exclamation, 'Richard, I'm coming again!' Surprise and delight in her face as the forces gathered within her body. He felt her muscles tighten around him, sensed her rippling spasms through his cock as her climax washed over her.

She kept her eyes open, gazing at him as the wave broke over her. Only at the last minute did she blink. Her discipline was amazing. He had never tried to hold Helena's gaze – or anyone else's – while he came. Margaret drove him into her with the pressure of her heels as she arched her back. The sudden warmth of her flesh around him signalled yet another climax as she held him to her, inside her. Then she was looking steadily at him once more.

He withdrew slightly and then slid home again. She sighed, a long sound of satisfaction. She relaxed her legs, signalling him to resume the pumping motion that pleased them both so much. He did so, seeing her face grow pink, the flush spreading to her neck and the tops of her breasts as she began the slow climb to another orgasm.

Margaret held his gaze once more, shuddering in the aftermath of her orgasm. This time, however, some of the old Margaret was apparent, challenging him to stay with her as she came. Richard, looking into her eyes, thought she might try to hold back this time, make him come while she watched in detached amusement. He watched her try. And fail. Her body betrayed her, plunged her into another series of climaxes. She began to pant and moan, shuddering with pleasure, the sounds forced from her as she exhaled. Her inarticulate cries became louder as she came. At the last she screamed again, her hips bucking under him, wild with pleasure, lost and vulnerable.

And he came too, spurting into her as she screamed and bucked beneath him. Margaret closed her eyes at the end to focus on her own ecstasy.

They lay coupled while the day grew about them, the dew of morning now made silver by the risen sun, and the first stirrings of the breeze bringing the scent of late-blooming flowers from the garden. At last, reluctantly, they parted, the signal given so subtly that he was almost unaware of it.

Margaret rose from the bed and stood looking down at him. The languor of their lovemaking was in her face, and an unaccustomed peace. Released momentarily from the role of dominatrix, she looked at him as a lover might before she turned away.

Richard was tired after the sleepless night and the morning's strenuous lovemaking. He was mentally tired as well with the balancing act: was it Margaret or Gretchen he was facing now?

When she returned from the bathroom, something of her old manner had returned to her. She looked more . . . purposeful. More like Margaret, less like Gretchen. The leopardess rather than the lover.

Richard looked at her with mixed relief and regret. The transformation had been magical. He was sorry to see it ending. Nevertheless, it was a relief to know that Margaret was still Margaret.

'Are you tired, Pamela?' Margaret asked. 'I hope not, for there is another busy day before you. You will have to travel to the garage to collect my car, and then you can tidy up around the house in the afternoon. And tonight I will find . . . something else to occupy your time.'

Richard showered and returned to find Margaret dressed. The Pamela-clothes he had worn the day before were wrinkled and soiled but she had selected another dress and some clean underwear and tights for the day's activity. He dressed under her critical eye. She applied the make-up and styled the wig, and Pamela was ready for another day of toil and servitude

'Call a taxi,' Margaret ordered. 'Here is the address of the garage which is repairing the car.' She handed Pamela a note with the address of a Norwich garage. 'Drive it straight back here. I wish to go out as soon as possible.'

But before he could summon the taxi the phone rang. Margaret went to answer it. Richard could hear her talking sharply to someone on the other end. One of her minions, from the tone of her voice. She did not sound pleased. When she hung up, she announced that the plans for the day had changed.

'Pamela, you will have to stay here today.' As usual, she offered no explanation for the abrupt change.

'What's happened?'

'Nothing that need concern you,' Margaret retorted sharply. 'But I think,' she said consideringly, 'that you would benefit from a day of darkness and immobility and sensory deprivation. You need time to contemplate the events of yesterday and last night. To put them in their proper perspective.' She smiled briefly. 'You should not expect such things to happen every day.

'But tell me,' she continued, 'what does Helena do with Pamela when she wishes to go out for the day?'

'Several things,' he said, with a thrill of anticipation. 'Sometimes she leaves Pamela in chains to do the housework, much as you originally intended. At other times she is taken to the boathouse down by the river and tied up.'

'And would Pamela like to do that today?' Margaret asked. 'Of course, she would have to get down to the boathouse first.'

Richard understood that she intended for him to walk down to the river in the Pamela-clothes. Not something he relished in the daytime. The silence grew as he wrestled with his warring inclinations and his native caution.

Margaret must have read his feelings in the silence. 'I think,' she said judiciously, 'that the boathouse would serve. If you really don't want to see the neighbours, I could put the hood on you before I take you there. Of course, I will then have to lead you across the garden. Yes?'

'No,' he croaked. 'I have to live here.'

'You could always leave. Come back to Soltau. Forget the neighbours. No one will say anything to you, no matter how bizarre your appearance. And I would be able to attend to your needs on a more regular basis. You would like that, I am sure,' Margaret said teasingly.

He shook his head. 'I won't leave Helena.'

Margaret looked annoyed at his continued loyalty to her niece, perhaps especially after the previous night's wild sex. But she only asked, 'What else does Pamela suggest, then?'

'The closet.' His heart lurched at the prospect of Margaret leaving Pamela bound and gagged in the closet.

'I suppose it will not hurt to humour you this once. Let's get started. I must leave soon.'

She ordered Pamela to don the waist belt with the handcuffs at the back. When she had put it on, Margaret locked the cuffs around her wrists.

'You look better already, Pamela,' Margaret remarked. 'Bondage becomes you.' She looked critically at her captive. 'Won't you reconsider coming back to Germany with me? Then you could do this every day – or something else even more exciting.'

He shook his head again. 'Not even if you took me to the top of an exceedingly high mountain and showed me all the dungeons of the world.'

'Not even if I drove you before me in bondage, lashing you all the way?' Margaret smiled ironically as she fitted the earplugs and gag and laced the leather helmet tightly on to his head.

He stood quietly as the gag was inflated, forcing his jaws apart and filling his mouth. She locked the leg-irons around his ankles. He felt Margaret snap the lead to the chain from his cock-ring. When she tugged, he followed, out of the room, down the hall, to the stairway, blindly, chained and helpless in the Pamela-clothes that were becoming so familiar. Even as he was led away Pamela's presence was becoming stronger in his imagination – a captive woman being led to an unknown fate. His cock stirred beneath the tight clothes.

At the stairway Pamela had a surprise. Instead of being led up to the second floor and the small closet that had so often been her prison, she was led *down* the stairs. Alarm flooded through her and she fought the leading chain and the handcuffs. Margaret paid no attention to Pamela's alarm, tugging sharply on the lead and forcing her captive down.

Resistance was impossible, but Pamela made her reluctance obvious with every step into the unknown. She grunted around the mouth-filling gag, shaking her head, hanging back until Margaret jerked the leading chain. The uncompromising pressure of the cock-ring decided the issue. On the ground floor she was led through the hall and into the kitchen, her own and Margaret's high heels clattering across the tile floor. A cool draught around her legs and up her skirt announced the opening of a door. Margaret, she realised in panic, was taking her outdoors in broad daylight. Under the tight clothes and hood Pamela went hot with embarrassment.

Her long note of protest made no impression on Margaret. The pull on the leading chain was unrelenting and irresistible. She was forced to follow through the door and out into the open air. Richard knew that the garden was private, shielded from the adjacent houses by a high hedge. Only one of them, he knew, had a view of the garden, and only from one window. Nevertheless Pamela felt as if the entire world was crowded into that window to witness her humiliation and embarrassment – a world that would brand her a pervert if it saw her in these clothes and in these chains.

Margaret set a brisk pace across the lawn, Pamela stumbling behind her as her high heels sank into the turf. Once she almost lost a shoe. Only the ankle strap kept it in place. She grunted once more.

Suddenly the leading chain went slack. Bereft of direction, Pamela stood still, metaphorically naked before the world in the sunlight and the cool breeze, though in actuality fully clothed. She cried out in protest, but there was no response. The chain dangled slackly between her legs. Pamela called again to her captor to lead her to shelter, get her out of sight. Margaret might as well have been in the next village.

Oh, God, Pamela thought. How did this happen? But she knew the answer. As always, her own acquiescence had led her to the brink of this precipice. And although she knew that the garden was smooth and level, she dared not move, as if an actual precipice yawned beneath the toes of her high-heeled shoes. Blind inside the tight leather helmet, Pamela felt that the slightest movement might cause her to tumble over the edge. She stood as still as one of the garden statues.

Turning her head from side to side, Pamela strove to detect any audible sign that Margaret was there to rescue her. The earplugs defeated her efforts. She sniffed the air. Perhaps she could catch the scent of Margaret's perfume. But the wily leopardess might well be standing downwind of her, within arm's length and perversely enjoying Pamela's evident agitation. Another desperate, muffled call brought no response.

Strive for calm, Pamela adjured herself. Think. But there was nothing to think of except her own exposure to discovery. Her thoughts tumbled over one another like ferrets. She took a tentative step forward. No precipice. Another step, hesitant, probing ahead with her foot before she set it down. As far as she could tell, she was moving towards the river – assuming that Margaret had been leading her towards the boat-house.

The river was not a good place to be when one was blind and helpless. Pamela turned around until she was facing back towards the house: shelter and safety. She set out hesitantly in that direction. In her agitation, her fear of being seen, any shelter, even only a wall at her back, seemed most desirable. And if she could get back to the house, she would be out of sight from the one crowded window that overlooked the garden. She would be safe from discovery and humiliation.

Margaret had thought of that. Before Pamela had taken even two blind steps, the chain came up taut between her legs. She was tethered to something, something immovable, something that would keep her in full view in the centre of the garden. Renewed panic swept over her. What was she fastened to? Pamela desperately scrabbled to reach the chain with her hands, but the waist belt did not allow sufficient freedom of movement to grasp the chain and tug at it.

Unable to use her hands, Pamela kneeled carefully in the grass, feeling the cool damp through her tights. She shuffled forward on her knees until the chain once more came up taut between anchor point and cock-ring. This time the angle was not so great. She was able to grasp the chain and pull at it. It was unyielding. The Richard-part of her came up with the answer: there had been a concrete block with a ringbolt set into it, sunk into the earth and used to tether his uncle's dogs when visitors came.

Now Pamela was chained to it like a dog. But no dog had to endure the constant panic at being seen. Dogs were routinely chained up. People, not. Pamela was often in chains. Does that make me more of an animal, less of a person, she mused. Animals didn't enjoy this perverse delight in their helplessness. As she kneeled in the grass, her tights becoming damp, Pamela thought of how she courted her own helplessness, savouring it as no animal would. Margaret aided her, but the desire to be bound was hers.

As usual when blindfolded, Pamela lost track of the time. She kneeled in the grass as if in worship, through what seemed at once an eternity and an instant. Margaret had offered her up as a victim to whomever might find her, the ultimate sacrifice of her dignity to her mistress's whim.

Margaret eventually came back. With a tug on the chain she indicated that Pamela was to follow her. Pamela struggled to her feet and followed the tug of the chain once again, glad and relieved that she was once more under control, back in the familiar world she knew and liked. Her destination was not important. It was only revealed when Margaret urged her to climb a nearly vertical ladder. Then Pamela knew that she was in the disused mill by the river.

Blindfolded, in leg-irons and unable to use her hands, Pamela struggled upwards. Margaret, she reflected ruefully, was good at setting hard-to-impossible tasks for others. The tight skirt of her dress also hampered her efforts, hobbling her at the knees. It was a nice dress, but not the sort of thing for this kind of work.

Perceiving the difficulty, Margaret stopped her to pull the skirt up around her waist, freeing her legs sufficiently to allow Pamela to climb. Margaret climbed behind, steadying her captive and urging her upwards. In this fashion they climbed four flights. Margaret urged her through the trap-door that closed off the small room at the top while Pamela mused on captive princesses in high and inaccessible towers.

Arrived in the aerie, Pamela waited for Margaret to join her. Margaret pulled down the hiked-up skirt and led her to the couch which was the main furnishing of this seldom-used retreat.

Richard's uncle had converted the small room to a study when the mill became redundant. As a boy growing up here, Richard had often climbed the ladders to look out at the world from the small windows that pierced the thick walls. He remembered that there was also a desk, which he and Helena had disassembled in order to get it in. A chair and some bookshelves completed the outfitting. The trap-door, he remembered, bolted from below. Once it was bolted, Pamela would be unable to escape even without the added handicaps of the handcuff-belt, the leg-irons and the hood.

Margaret pushed her down on to the couch and proceeded to make things even more difficult by removing the leg-irons and strapping her ankles and knees tightly with the leather straps. Pamela would not even be able to stand up, let alone try to open the trap-door. When Margaret left, no one would know where to find her.

Margaret's exit was more felt than heard, a vibration in the wooden floor as she allowed the trap-door to fall closed. Pamela could not hear the bolt being shot, but she knew that Margaret would not overlook such an elementary precaution, even though her captive was immobilised.

Pamela remembered that the wooden steps below this topmost room could be removed quite easily. Richard had been nearly marooned there once when his uncle had taken them away. Margaret had shown a surprising knowledge of the small details of the house and grounds. She had known of the concrete block in the garden. She had known about this room. She must have devoted considerable time to a survey of the area. So it would not be too surprising if she had discovered the secret of the steps.

Pamela shivered with the familiar combination of excitement and dread as she contemplated her helplessness and isolation. Beneath the tight elastic corselet and the smooth black opaque tights her cock stirred in response.

So, helpless and isolated and excited and frustrated, Pamela passed an unmeasured time awaiting further developments. Mindful of Margaret's preferences (and of her zeal in punishing any transgressions), she resisted for a long time the urge to induce an orgasm by struggling against her chains. But in the end the combination of isolation and helplessness overcame her resolve to be 'good', as Margaret defined that term. She began to imagine herself the female captive of a brutal captor who would do awful things to her against her will, who would force her to obey every command. And she came, the warm fluid soaking through the corselet and tights and making a sticky patch between her thighs.

When the excitement and pleasure began to fade, the thought of what Margaret would do to her upon her return made the cycle begin all over again. Pamela jerked and struggled in her chains, her body aflame with desire and dread. She came again, this time longer and more intensely, leaving her weak and drained. And still Margaret did not return. As the hours passed, Pamela found herself prey to the old fear that her captor had had an accident, and that no one would come to release her – ever.

Pamela's dark dream of abandonment ended when her leg-straps were removed and replaced by the cold steel embrace of the leg-irons. She guessed that her captor would lead her back down the ladders, but after that, what? Would she be taken into the house, or left once more in the garden? When they finally reached the ground floor, the temperature suggested that it was dark outside. The air was cold on her legs. The tights offered almost no protection.

They moved across the garden, Pamela guided once more by the sharp tugs on her leading chain, her high heels sinking into the grass. The feel of a hard surface under her feet told her she was being taken across the patio and into the house. The cold air on her nylon-sheathed legs was replaced by a warmer flow as the door closed behind her and the outside. She felt both relieved and apprehensive – and excited once again. A move of any sort usually heralded some sort of erotic play – the whip, perhaps, as Margaret punished her for her lack of self-control. Perhaps another evening of toe-sucking humiliation and frustration lay ahead. Perhaps (though less likely than the other scenarios) another night of sex with Margaret. That possibility caused renewed interest in a predictable place.

She was led up the stairs. Counting the steps, Pamela knew that she was being taken to the second floor. She guessed that the closet was her destination. The lead went slack and she stood still, directionless. She was pushed suddenly from behind, stumbling, the taut chain joining her ankles causing her to trip and fall heavily on to a mattress. Winded, Pamela felt her captor remove her leg-irons and replace them with the leather straps, pulling them savagely tight, biting into her flesh through the sheer nylon of her tights.

Gagged and blindfolded, Pamela lay for a long time, waiting for something else to happen. When it didn't, she struggled into a more comfortable position and probed her surroundings with her bound legs. The door was closed. Locked, too, she knew – not that it mattered. Helena had made Richard remove the handle on the inside so that a captive, such as Pamela, would not be able to escape even if not bound. But Pamela was always bound before being confined.

She resumed her solitary vigil, and soon was working herself into a state of trembling anticipation and excitement as she imagined what Margaret would do to her when she returned.

Pamela was on the verge of an orgasm when the straps were loosened and hands urged her to her feet. The removal of the hood and gag revealed, not Margaret, but Helena.

She held up the key to the handcuffs. 'Is it to be Pamela or Richard who welcomes me back?' she asked with a smile. 'I'd prefer Richard,' she said. 'I've been pining for the whip and the cock (in that order) for days. So, Pamela, go get undressed and have a shower. Send Richard to me when you see him.'

'Margaret?' Pamela began.

Helena held a finger to her lips. 'Shh. Later there will be time to tell our tales. Sex first. Sex second and third too. Then, maybe, talk. If I'm not worn out.' She grinned lewdly as she urged Pamela towards the bathroom.

Wondering how Helena had come to be here, and what had happened to Margaret, Pamela undressed and showered. Richard got out of the shower and dried himself. His cock, even though still encircled by the ring, was growing stiff as he anticipated lashing and fucking Helena. He followed his cock into the bedroom.

There, he lashed Helena all over her naked body, paying special attention to her breasts and cunt, while she screamed in the mixture of pain and ecstasy that was her body's gift to them both. And she screamed again later, in unmingled pleasure, as he mounted her and guided his cock into the warm wet sheath of her sex.

'What happened to Margaret?' Richard finally asked.

'I happened to her,' Helena replied, 'even though she doesn't know that yet.' She told him that she had escaped from the bungalow by seducing Bruno – not a difficult feat, she said with some pride. Freed of her chains, but still naked, she had escaped into the dusk and raided an outdoor clothesline at a nearby farm. 'There were dogs barking as I took the clothes, and I had visions of being chased across the fields in the altogether. But they were indoors, apparently.'

Hitchhiking had proved easy enough, she said. 'I just waggled my hips and looked distressed.'

'And did you have to pay the usual price?' he asked.

'One day I'll answer that question. But would you care if I did?'

'Not really. But be careful. Bruno and your aunt are not the only crazies about.'

'And we're sane?'

'Most of the time, though I have my doubts about you. But how did you find ... Pamela? And where is Margaret?'

'Margaret is now where ... Pamela ... was. I would guess she isn't very happy about it either. Finding Pamela was pretty easy. The key under the flowerpot got me into the house. When it became obvious that Pamela was not in the closet or the bedroom, the only other places to look were the boathouse or the mill. As soon as I found the ladder leaning against the wall in the mill, I knew where to look. So I left everything as I had found it and brought her back here and left her in the closet while I dealt with Aunt Margaret.'

And how did you deal with her, he asked.

Margaret, Helena said, had strolled across the garden as if she owned the place and had gone directly up to Pamela's prison chamber. She, Helena, had followed softly behind. When Margaret had replaced the ladder and unbolted the trap-door, Helena had allowed her aunt to enter the upper room. She reasoned that Pamela's absence would not be immediately apparent in the darkness. It was merely a matter of closing the trap-door before Margaret could discover her captive's absence.

'It was a near thing, though,' Helena said. 'Aunt Margaret can move fast when she has to. She must have heard the door closing. I got it bolted just in time. She pounded and stamped on it and screamed at me to let her out. She may have cooled down a bit by now, but she will be very angry when we do finally let her out.'

Richard asked if she thought it wise to keep her aunt captive all night. 'It will be cold in that room,' he said.

'There are blankets there,' Helena retorted. 'She can wrap up and keep warm. That's more than Pamela could have done. She might have left Pamela up there all night with no way to wrap herself up against the cold.' Besides, she asked, did he really feel like getting out of a warm bed, getting dressed and crossing the garden in the dark to fetch Margaret?

'We'd only have to deal with an angry leopardess all night,' Helena continued. 'Anyway, would you prefer to go get her or fuck me again?'

Thoughts of Margaret receded. Richard reached for Helena and pulled her on top of him.

'We shall overcome,' she said with a grin as she guided his cock into her body.

They rose late and had a leisurely breakfast. Richard's conscience had been considerably pacified by Helena's repeated demands for sex during the night. But after breakfast there was no further reason to delay what they knew could be a hard job. Richard fetched handcuffs in case her night of solitary confinement had not subdued Margaret. Helena took a dog lead and collar. 'For the good of her soul,' she said.

It was a foggy day. They made their way down to the river. Richard reflected that Pamela would have welcomed this fog the day before. But then as likely as not Margaret would not have left her exposed in the garden.

The brick tower loomed suddenly before them out of the mist, its top lost in the white blanket. Margaret would not have had much of a view from the tiny window of her cell.

Richard climbed the ladder and unbolted the trap-door. He pushed it open and then waited cautiously in case Margaret chose to vent her anger by stamping on his hands with her stiletto heels. When there was no immediate attack he poked his head into the room.

Margaret, wrapped in blankets and dishevelled from her night in jail, glared at him from the couch. When Helena followed him up, the glare was widened to include her. Margaret was obviously not well disposed toward her jailors.

'Did you expect me to submit quietly to handcuffs and a dog chain?' Margaret asked.

'No,' Helena told her. 'But I knew we could force you if it became necessary – just as we did last time we sent you home.'

Margaret did not like this reminder of her ignomini-ous retreat with dildoes stuffed up her cunt and anus and held there by an improvised chastity belt of chain and padlocks.

'I will come quietly,' she said. 'This time.'

And she was as good as her word, following them back to the house. There, she made straight for the bathroom.

Richard and Helena were enjoying a second cup of coffee in the kitchen when Margaret came down again, looking more refreshed and less angry. Wordlessly, she poured a cup for herself before joining them.

Richard caught Helena's eye and nodded impercep-tibly at Margaret. In the recent past she would have demanded that someone serve her. An angry leopardess at the breakfast table would have been awkward. Just now she looked pensive. They all knew the issue before them. Margaret knew that they were prepared to defend themselves against her attempts to enslave or separate them.

They both waited for her to speak.

'A truce, then,' she said finally. The words came reluctantly, but they had been said. A promise. She was too proud to renege on it, but the future would have to be negotiated on a day-by-day basis.

Richard and Helena both nodded their acceptance. They knew that there would be no other acknowledgement of the altered relationship.

'Breakfast, Aunt Margaret?' Helena asked, steering away from the touchy subject.

'Yes,' she said. 'Thank you.'

'Is the car all right now?' Richard asked, likewise treading on neutral ground.

Margaret nodded.

Richard could not resist one more question. 'Why didn't you tell me yesterday that Helena had escaped?'

'Would Pamela have submitted tamely to being exposed if she had known that fact?' Margaret replied. 'And I thought there might be some chance of recapturing her. That would have restored the status quo. More satisfying than the present situation, but I am a pragmatist. We cannot change the past.'

'Where will you go today, Aunt Margaret?' Helena asked.

'I will have to see to Bruno,' she said heavily. 'I will be back around what you so quaintly call teatime.'

Just as well not to be Bruno today, Richard reflected.

When Margaret had gone Richard went back to his neglected plans and drawings. He visited the building site, where he felt a stranger after the crowded events of the last few days. Margaret's whirlwind visit had driven out all thought of the workaday world.

The house was quiet when he got home in the early evening dark. There was a note from Helena: Margaret had called to say that she wanted to speak to Richard on her return. 'I know what she means,' Helena had written. 'I will make myself scarce this evening. Enjoy her. Build bridges for the future.'

Richard cooked spaghetti bolognese for tea and left it in the oven to keep warm. Food and a welcome for Margaret might ease the strain of what would be the first evening of the rest of their relationship.

Margaret did not ask about Helena when she arrived. Perhaps she had even asked her niece to stay away. She made no comment when Richard (not Pamela) greeted her. She hung up her coat, smiling nervously when he tentatively embraced her. Like teenagers on a first date, he reflected.

He took charge of the evening. He lit the fire in the sitting room and set the table in the kitchen while it warmed up. Food and wine – an unambitious Australian Chablis from the village shop – got them through the first awkwardness. He took coffee and brandy through into the sitting room and they watched the evening news in awkward silence.

Richard broke it abruptly, taking the direct approach.

'Margaret. What are you wearing under your dress?'

'Unzip me and see for yourself.' A faint echo of challenge to remind him of the leopardess.

There was nothing except Margaret and a pair of tights under the dress. Richard thought he should have noticed her bra-less state, but he had been too preoccupied with plans to cope with a recently reformed leopardess. The magnificent breasts, standing firm and pink-tipped, emerged from the dress as he eased it down her body. He stopped long enough to kiss each nipple, causing Margaret to take a sharp breath.

The tights were a momentary disappointment. He would have preferred stockings and suspenders, as being more suitable for seduction/sex. Then he noticed that these tights, smooth and sheer and glossy, had no crotch. Margaret's crisp blonde pubic hair stuck out boldly through the opening. His disappointment evaporated.

137

She sat erect on the sofa, her breasts proudly on display, the pink of her labia just visible between her parted thighs. Richard knew that she must have chosen to dress as she had, must have bought the tights recently, since he had never known her to wear them before. Yet she looked indecisively at him.

'I have never been particularly interested in vanilla sex,' she said. 'Sex without bondage or pain or humiliation as prelude or background has always seemed boring.'

'That's because the idea of surrendering to someone else is so foreign to you. But you could try to think of the surrender itself as a bizarre act – as it will be for you. Don't just lie back and dream of beating someone else. Think of yourself as a trembling virgin about to have sex for the first time – with the enormous advantage of long experience.'

Margaret stood up abruptly. 'Take me then,' she said. She strode to an armchair and bent over behind it, grasping the arms and presenting her cunt and arsehole to Richard's cock.

His stiff cock led him across the short space that separated them and found its way between her thighs. The warmth of her cunt was an unmistakable target. He buried himself in it while Margaret sighed with pleasure and clamped down on the shaft inside her.

He bent forward so that he could cup Margaret's breasts. The taut nipples invited his fingers. Margaret sighed, fully penetrated, her breasts cupped in his hands, her nipples teased by his fingers. She met his thrust with her own, moving with him, moaning softly at each in-stroke. If she had any remaining inhibitions, Richard could not detect them. Margaret may well have been thinking of chains and slavery – for others, of course. Richard was thinking only of having sex with the leopardess.

Margaret, afterwards, seemed satisfied. Richard could almost believe that she had turned over a new leaf. She consented to share the bed with him. But just before drifting off to sleep, she said, 'That was nice, but don't expect things to be this way forever.'

3

The English Visitors

It was more than two months later before they heard from Margaret again. In that time, both Richard and Helena began to think that she had forgotten her promise to mend her ways towards them. But they agreed that there was nothing to be done about the matter. So they also agreed that they could not live in daily fear of another raid from the fastnesses of Soltau, and gradually resumed their daily routines.

When Margaret's note finally did come, it was almost as if she had been calculating how long to leave them alone before springing her next surprise.

In token of her new resolution to allow certain others to enjoy their lives without constant interference, Margaret wrote, she was inviting them to visit her. She promised not to enslave them, not to dominate them each minute (while reserving the right to do so sporadically), not to hold one or both of them hostage. For the leopardess of Soltau it was a big concession.

So big, in fact, that both Richard and Helena decided to arrive early, knowing that Margaret would be away for at least another day on business before she was due to entertain them and a select few others. Reconnaissance was their only defence against a surprise attack.

Helena called her foster-mother from Margaret's house to let her know that they were in town. There was no reply. She asked Richard to stop by the shop when he went into town later.

It was early afternoon when Richard arrived to find Ingrid's shop closed. Odd, he thought. She normally opened during business hours. Her assistant at least should have been there, but was not. He went around to the back entrance, where deliveries were made in the enclosed yard. The gate was closed, and the door was locked.

He let himself into the rear hallway with the key she had given him. Since the shutters in the shop windows were closed, there was little light in the hallway. He looked around in the dimness at the place where he had taken the first steps towards becoming Pamela Rogers. He had practised walking up and down these stairs in his high-heeled shoes. Ingrid had helped him choose the first dresses and underwear in the darkened shop, and upstairs she had helped him with the details of his transformation.

He recalled his transformation with a thrill of excitement as he climbed the familiar stairs to her flat. The door at the top led to the well-remembered sitting room overlooking the street. It too was dark. There he found Ingrid, but someone else had found her first. Margaret, he guessed.

Ingrid was shackled into a rigid frame that resembled a cross with two short cross bars, one near the top and the other at the bottom. The device forced her to stand upright with her hands held out to each side of her at shoulder height. Her elbows were bent and her wrists were shackled in irons welded to the upper cross bar. Her ankles were shackled to the ends of the lower cross bar. A steel collar encircled her neck. Another went around her waist. Both were welded to the frame, keeping her neck and head and waist back against the steel bar that formed a kind of backbone.

Naked, she stood near the window. She would have been visible to anyone passing by in daylight. The drapes were wide open, left so deliberately, he guessed, by Margaret, the more to humiliate and embarrass Ingrid, who could not move from her strained position. Richard wondered how she had been able to maintain her balance. Then he saw the chain attached to the steel backbone of Ingrid's frame. It led to a stout hook in the ceiling that had not been there on his last visit. She could not fall no matter how strained or tired she might become.

The strain of standing for long hours showed in her face. The possibility of being seen was also part of the ordeal. Ingrid's relief when he called her name showed plainly.

'Oh, Richard, I am so glad it is you who found me. Anyone could have come upon me – and done whatever they wished to me.' She was shaking with relief and strain.

Richard went to her, intending to free her from her restraints, but she stopped him.

'Kiss me,' she said. 'I have been thinking of you all afternoon. I was hoping you would come. Margaret said that you were coming to her weekend party. I knew you'd come to see me too.'

They kissed lingeringly. Richard embraced Ingrid, his arms around the steel bar that held her rigid from neck to heels. Unable to touch him, Ingrid nevertheless made him welcome with her lips and tongue. She sighed when the kiss ended. When he drew back she almost lost her balance, and would have fallen but for his arm and the chain that held her frame upright.

A close examination of her restraints revealed that they were locked on to her. When he asked about keys, she replied that Margaret had taken them away with her.

'How long have you been here?' he asked.

'Hours and hours,' she replied.

'And has anyone . . .?

'If you mean, has anyone come to check on me, the answer is no. If you mean, did anyone see me, I would imagine that several people did. I could not move from this place.'

'And you mean that no one came to investigate – or called the police or the fire brigade?'

'Do you think anyone in England would interfere in such a situation?'

'Probably not. At least not for a long time, anyway. Too embarrassing. And suppose it – you – turned out to be a cardboard cut-out, or merely a photograph stuck to the inside of the window?'

'Exactly,' Ingrid replied, 'although there was one man who looked at me for a long time. I don't think he believed I was a photograph. I was afraid he'd break in.'

'But he didn't, probably because that's not the sort of thing one does either – at least not in broad daylight.'

'Still, I am glad that you are here now,' Ingrid said.

'Do you need to go to the toilet?' he asked, looking for a bucket to hold under while she peed.

'Margaret took care of that,' Ingrid replied. 'Look.'

Richard noticed then that a catheter had been inserted into her urethra and led to plastic bag now nearly full of her urine. 'What would happen if the bag filled up?' he asked.

'Then I would have had a very uncomfortable time,' Ingrid replied matter-of-factly. 'Nothing can be done until Margaret returns with the keys.'

'She's gone too far this time.'

'Margaret has indeed gone too far this time. She is in Dresden on business, and won't be back until tomorrow morning. But I am sure that there is someone at the house who has been told to look after me, because . . .' She stopped speaking abruptly, and a curious look of distress crossed her face. 'Oh!' she said suddenly.

'What is it?' he asked sharply.

Ingrid did not reply. Her attention was focused on internal matters. Richard looked at her closely, and noticed again something he had not seen before. Along with the tube of the catheter which disappeared between Ingrid's thighs, there were wires leading to her cunt and anus. More of Margaret's subtle torture, he guessed at once. There had to be dildoes inside her, and they were connected to the telephone socket via a black box which had to be the control device. Clever, he thought, simply dial your victim's number and the control box dispensed judgement for you.

'Does she shock you with electricity?' he asked, thinking of Margaret's fondness for hooking her victims' genitals up to batteries.

'What?' Ingrid asked vaguely. 'Oh . . . yes. Sometimes. But there are . . . other things . . . she does as well. She makes me want to . . . come. That is the worst. She always stops me before I can reach a climax. I don't know how she does it, but that has been happening all afternoon. I sometimes think I will make it this time, and I shudder and cry out – and she stops me again. Now – oh, God – she is doing it again!' Her voice rose and her body tensed as if she were on the verge of orgasm. 'I can't stand it any longer. I have to come! Please!' she cried desperately to her absent torturess.

She shuddered in her restraints as the signals came down the telephone line and into her body via her two orifices. Richard could see her arousal. Ingrid arched her back; her nipples grew taut and her breath became ragged. She moaned with desire and frustration, twisting as far as she could in her heavy irons. She swayed on her feet, the chain alone holding her up as her knees went weak. Ingrid was trying hard to reach orgasm, her need plain on her face.

Richard could see her taut belly as she clenched her vaginal muscles in anticipation. The cords in her neck stood out with the intensity of her effort. And suddenly the terrible tension left her, and she groaned. 'Oh, God! I can't come. She won't let me! Please help me, Richard. Touch me. Make me come! Please make me come!'

He kneeled in front of the tortured woman and buried his face between her thighs. He kissed her labia as she writhed in her need. Ingrid was warm and wet. He could smell the musk of her arousal. The clean salty taste of her was in his mouth as he teased her clitoris with his tongue and teeth. And he could feel something hard buried inside her – the dildo which had brought her to the brink of orgasm and then stopped her. But there was no stopping Richard. As he kissed Ingrid's labia and bit her clitoris, she moaned loudly, shuddering as she came once more to the brink of orgasm. He took her over the edge while she cried out with pleasure, jerking in her irons. She had forgotten her exposed position by the window, her restraints, her long afternoon's sexual frustration.

'Oh, yes!' Ingrid cried as the waves of her orgasm swept through her, tautening her belly and making her knees buckle. 'Oh, yes! Oh, God, yes!'

When he broke off momentarily to ensure that Ingrid would not fall, she became frantic.

'Oh, God, Richard, please don't stop now!'

'Just a moment.'

He looked around for a safer place for Ingrid. He finally decided that the floor would have to do. He unhooked the chain that held her upright from the ceiling and caught her beneath the arms from behind. She cried out in alarm as she felt herself tilting backwards.

'Shh! I've got you. Don't worry.' He kissed the back of her neck, just above the steel collar. She stopped fighting as he laid her on the floor on her back. 'Is that all right?'

Ingrid nodded. Spread open like a starfish in the heavy irons, she looked incredibly desirable. And desirous. 'Oh, Richard, make me come again! It has been so long.'

He kneeled between her thighs and once again used his lips and tongue and teeth to arouse her. Unable to move in her restraints, Ingrid nevertheless managed to signal her pleasure by a tautening of her muscles and a continuous low moan as she came, the sound rising and falling in time with her orgasms. The muscles in her thighs and stomach stood out in relief as she came. Her hands opened and closed convulsively in the heavy iron bracelets, and her toes curled.

Richard, looking up momentarily from his position between her thighs, saw a sudden flood of urine pass down the tube and into the bag as she came. Ingrid, until then only moaning, screamed in ecstasy at the double release. The bag filled rapidly as she screamed in pleasure.

When she went limp, Richard realised that she had passed out. He checked her over anyway. She seemed all right. He unclipped the bag and took it into the bathroom, where he emptied it into the toilet. Back in the front room, he reattached the bag to Ingrid's catheter and paused to examine the arrangement. He had never seen a woman with a catheter.

He spread her labia and saw the tube disappearing inside her, but he soon lost sight of it as it passed up the urethra. He tugged on it, feeling resistance. He let go of it. So long as Ingrid was locked into her restraints, it was best to leave the tube in place.

In any case, Margaret would know all about it. That idea excited him too. How would a catheter feel? Margaret would no doubt enlighten Pamela if she only asked. There would no doubt be a practical demonstration as well. Pamela knew she was going to ask.

In the meantime there was Ingrid He sat beside her, studying the contrast between her smooth skin and the unyielding irons that held her prisoner. This was what bondage was all about. And why he liked it so much.

Ingrid opened her eyes and looked contentedly at him. That's what sex is all about, he thought – making a woman look at you like that. Helena did it too. Could Margaret be taught the trick? Would she want to learn?

'I feel like a stranded turtle, Richard. I must look like one too. But a satisfied stranded turtle. It was wonderful, what you did to me. I thought I would go crazy from frustration. You know, before we met I could go for weeks without thinking about sex. Now I think about it – and you – all the time. Not bad for an older woman, is it?'

'All right, I know when I'm being provoked. I promise to spank you as soon as I can get you out of these irons.' He spoke lightly, but he was glad to know how Ingrid felt. Knowing that he was loved and appreciated by Helena and her foster-mother made him proud and happy. He bent to kiss Ingrid. She opened her mouth to him again as she had opened her body.

They sat quietly for a time, Richard leaning back against the front of the sofa, Ingrid in her stranded-turtle position on the floor. It was Ingrid who spoke first.

'You know, I was right about Margaret. She is definitely after you. And she is quite jealous of anyone who seems like a rival.'

'Do you mean yourself?'

'Yes. She knew about my visit to you and Helena. And she knew – or guessed – that we did not spend a great deal of time going around the village or the local attractions. She thinks that we spent most of the time in bed – or at least in some form of sexual play. Which is what we did.' Ingrid smiled fondly in recollection.

Richard smiled too. 'When did Margaret do all this?' he asked, gesturing at her irons.

'Early this morning,' Ingrid said. 'I have been here all day.'

'Until I came, and then you came.'

'And then I came. Thank you again.'

'Ingrid . . . do you think you could come again?'

148

'Yes, if you will help me. Gladly.' Her nipples were growing erect at the prospect.

'I meant . . . the two of us,' he said. 'I want to come inside you.' His voice was tense with excitement.

'I cannot stop you,' Ingrid said with a smile. 'As you see, I am helpless. But, of course, I want you to enter me. There is only the small matter of the plug . . . and the catheter.'

'I can get the plug out. I'm afraid the catheter will have to stay, but I'll be careful not to hurt you.' Richard grasped the base of Ingrid's dildo and pulled the long, thick plug from her cunt. He laid it on the floor beside her supine body.

'I cannot open my legs any further,' Ingrid said apologetically. 'The irons . . .' With a small motion of her head, she indicated the rigid bar between her ankles.'

Richard stood to remove his clothes. His cock sprang free of his shorts, and Ingrid gasped in anticipation.

'I do that to you?' she asked wonderingly.

'Of course you do. You know that. As Margaret says, it's the sincerest compliment a man can pay a woman. She always says that just before she refuses to accept it in the place where a woman is meant to.'

He lay down on top of her pinioned body, guiding himself into her with one hand and supporting his upper body with the other. Ingrid, unable to move, nevertheless managed to welcome the penetration with a small squeeze of her vaginal muscles. When he was fully inside her, she sighed happily. The catheter was an unfamiliar pressure on his cock. He clamped down hard to keep himself from coming too soon.

Ingrid sensed his excitement. 'Dear Richard, come now if you want to.'

'Not yet,' he said through gritted teeth. 'I want you to come too.' He lay still on top of her as her vaginal muscles clamped his cock. He could feel her growing warmer and wetter as he lay on her. When she moaned he felt the first rippling spasm of her cunt as she had a small climax.

'Oh!' she sighed. 'That feels so good.'

Richard risked a small withdrawal and return, testing his control and her arousal. He was excited by Ingrid's restraints. Making love to a beautiful woman who could not move was one of his favourite fantasies.

Ingrid clenched her fists in the shackles as she came again. He felt the spasms as her body tensed and relaxed, tensed and relaxed. As Ingrid fought the unyielding restraints, he fought the desire to lose himself in a wild climax of his own. Her body was totally motionless below him, but her internal muscles, unrestrained, responded to his movements.

Ingrid moaned again with her climax. She was panting and her cheeks were flushed – like Margaret's when she was aroused, or angry. 'Oh, Richard! Oh, yes!' she moaned.

He knew that if she were not locked into the rigid steel frame that her body would be moving against his own. As he imagined all that energy being restrained he lost control. Her helplessness and immobility were too much for him. He came in sharp spasms, spending himself in her while her muscles clamped his cock, milking him as she groaned with her own climax.

He lay on top of her only briefly, even though he would have liked to remain longer. It must be terribly uncomfortable to be locked into those unyielding restraints. Lying beside her on the carpet, he listened as her breathing slowed. He reached to clasp one of her manacled hands, feeling her fingers close over his own and squeeze hard.

'I would like to lie in your arms, if I could,' Ingrid said.

'Take the wish for the deed. We'll do it soon enough. In the meantime, what shall we talk about?' They exchanged news of everything that had happened since her visit, the banal conversation seeming bizarre in the circumstances.

It was Ingrid who got them back to the main subject. 'Richard, I am getting excited again,' she admitted. 'I have never worn such severe restraints as these. Do you think you could manage another . . . fuck?'

He nodded. 'Even if it kills me but, this time, you get on top.'

'Oh, Richard, do not laugh at me. You know I cannot move.'

'You can if I do the work.' He bent over her rigidly confined body, raising her with his hands beneath her shoulders until she was nearly vertical. Then he rotated her and laid her down on the floor on her stomach. 'Stranded turtle, back view,' he commented.

'Would you like to enter the stranded turtle by the back passage?' Ingrid asked.

'I know lady turtles prefer it that way, but they don't usually wear chastity belts like yours. I'm afraid we'll have to use the front entrance again. Try not to be bored, will you?' He chuckled.

Richard kneeled beside Ingrid to kiss the back of her neck. She tried to turn her face, her mouth, to him, but she could not. He kissed her hair and the lobe of her ear, inhaling her fragrance as he moved over her. His lips moved over her shoulders and down her back. He kissed the backs of her thighs and the hollows behind her knees, moving down to brush her ankle bones and the soles of her feet with kisses. She sighed with happiness.

He lay beside her and reached across to pull Ingrid and her crucifix on top of his body. She could not assist in any way, so the operation took time. Eventually she lay on top of him in her iron frame. He guided his cock into her, and found her ready.

Ingrid lay looking down at him, her head held rigidly back against the steel bar by the collar around her neck, her hands raised to her shoulders as if in surrender, held by the steel bands around her wrists.

Once again he felt the unaccustomed pressure of the catheter against his cock as he moved for both of them. It was more difficult this time with her weight and that of her restraints bearing down, but the look on Ingrid's face was reward enough as he rocked his hips, moving his cock inside her in slow slidings and pressures. He raised his head and their lips met in a long kiss, Ingrid breathing out into his mouth in contented sighs as he moved within the tight sheath of her cunt.

Her breasts were flattened against his chest, and since she could not move or lift her body he had to forgo the pleasure of teasing her nipples. Ingrid did not seem to mind.

He felt her climax as a tightening of vaginal muscles around his cock. It was a ripple compared with the storms that had shaken her earlier, but her face showed pleasure as it passed through her.

And so they rocked gently together, giving and taking pleasure in one another's bodies despite Margaret's attempt to make it impossible. Richard was still excited by the novelty of the catheter and of making love to a woman who was unable to move any part of her body except those supremely important internal muscles. Ingrid relished her helpless immobility as she was thoroughly fucked.

She reached several smaller climaxes, gradually building in intensity to the point where her whole body stiffened and she cried out in release. He felt the catheter swell against his cock as Ingrid urinated at the moment of climax. He felt he could relax his own control after that, and so when he came a few moments later Ingrid was able to match him with a more sighing gentle climax.

This time, with Richard taking her weight, they were able to lie joined for some considerable time. From time to time he raised his head to kiss her lips and eyes and cheeks while he stroked her back and bottom, from time to time touching the steel that imprisoned her. When he slid out from under her at last, he admired the back view of the woman he had just pleasured lying imprisoned in her steel frame.

Finally he turned her over on to her back once more. More to admire that way, he thought as Ingrid smiled up at him. Her face was relaxed and more beautiful after the long pleasure of their multiple couplings. He remembered thinking the same thing about Margaret after she had finally stopped trying to dominate *their* coupling. He kneeled to kiss Ingrid once more.

'Richard, would you please clamp the catheter and empty the bag once more? And thank you for the fucking. It was wonderful.'

Pleased that she was pleased, he did as she asked, returned with the empty bag and reattached it to the tube that disappeared inside her.

'OK, now what?' he asked with a grin. 'Shall we speak of science and art and the possibility of life on Mars? Make the beast with two backs again?'

'Truthfully, I don't think I can come again after what you did to me. So let's talk now. You will have to leave me here, but I would like company for a while.'

'I don't mind talking to you, but I am not going to leave you here like this.'

'What else can you do?' she asked.

'Either bring the keys here, or take you to the keys. I'll have to call Helena to decide which course to take.'

When he finally reached her at Margaret's country estate, he described Ingrid's predicament and told her about the loose stone in the fireplace where Margaret had once hidden her keys. 'Go look,' he suggested.

She returned with the news that the hiding place was empty. Helena thought that her aunt would have taken

153

the keys away with her. 'What now?' she asked. 'We can't leave her there like that.'

He suggested that she choose the vehicle with the most luggage space and drive into the back entrance of Ingrid's shop. There they would load Ingrid aboard and transport her to Margaret's estate.

Helena agreed that that was the best solution. She would leave immediately. 'Expect me in about thirty minutes,' she said.

She hung up and Richard went to sit beside Ingrid once more. 'We are going to transport you to Margaret's estate, where we can look after you until Margaret gets back with the keys. Helena will be here shortly.'

'But ... but,' spluttered Ingrid, 'what if someone from the village sees me? It will be all over town in minutes. Please just leave me here.'

He shook his head. 'It's nearly dark outside. By the time Helena gets here there will be no one about. Helena is going to back the car up through the gates at the back and it's only a short distance from the door to the car. We will load you into the back, and away we'll drive over hill and dale. You just relax and enjoy the ride.'

Ingrid still objected, afraid of being seen.

'Shut up. You're coming with us. Leave everything to Helena and me. We'll cover your face so no one will recognise you,' he said, thinking of ostriches in sandy country. He smiled at her.

Ingrid failed to see the joke. 'And who will they think is being taken from my shop in irons if not me?'

'Shut up,' he said again. 'Let's talk about something else. Tell me what you would do if we left you here and some intruder did manage to get in and find you.'

'I would lie back,' Ingrid retorted, 'and think of ... Germany. Or I would pretend it was you.'

'Flattery will only get you another fucking,' he told her.

When Helena arrived, they had both run out of things to say and were sitting in companionable silence. They both heard the back door open, and the sound of her feet on the stairs. She came into the room and went straight to her foster-mother.

'Did Richard make you come, *Mutti*?'

After a startled silence Ingrid smiled. 'Yes, he did. Many times.'

'Then you are luckier than me. I have been waiting for him to come back and fuck me for hours and hours,' she said. 'And all that time he has been here fucking you.'

Turning to Richard, she demanded, 'Aren't you ashamed of yourself?'

'No,' he replied.

'Good. I would have been ashamed of you if you had been ashamed of giving *Mutti* pleasure, shameless woman that she is.' Practicality returned. 'How are we going to move her, Richard?'

Ingrid started to protest again.

'You don't get a vote in this. And you can't stop us. So be quiet,' Richard said again.

To Helena he said, 'You take her feet and I'll take her shoulders. The stairs will be the tricky bit, but if we're careful we'll manage.'

Helena laid the urinal bag on her foster-mother's stomach and coiled the catheter so that it would not snag on anything. 'Is it uncomfortable, *Mutti*?' she asked.

'Ask Richard,' Ingrid replied. 'It makes fucking more exciting on this end.'

'On this end also,' he said. 'But let's get you under way.'

Helena grasped the spreader bar between Ingrid's ankles while Richard lifted her by the spreader bar that held her wrists apart. On his signal they lifted the helpless woman in her iron frame and carried her towards the door.

'Was there anyone about when you drove up?' Richard asked Helena. 'Ingrid is afraid of being seen by the neighbours. I told her we would cover her face so that she would not be recognised.'

Helena too failed to see the joke. She replied seriously, 'We will need to cover her with something when we get her into the car. It has grown cold outside. We may get snow later.'

Together they carried the immobilised woman down the stairs. The big Land Rover was backed up to the rear door of the shop, its own rear doors propped open to receive their cargo. Ingrid in her iron frame just fitted into the rear space. Helena spread a car rug over her naked body and indicated that Richard should ride in the back.

'I know the way best,' she said. 'You sit with *Mutti* while I drive. And if you choose to keep her happy on the way, I won't mind very much. You might try feeling her up. We all know how much she likes that. But whatever you do keep her quiet.'

Ingrid gave a scandalised gasp which Helena ignored as she got into the driving seat.

They drove through the silent streets of the town and out into the country, Ingrid fearful the whole time of being stopped by the police. 'How will you explain me?' she asked.

Helena told her they would say she was a statue they had stolen from a church.

'Be careful,' Ingrid warned. 'I don't know what we would say if there were an accident.'

'I do,' Helena replied. 'We will tell the police that you always travel this way. Your version of seat belts.' To Richard she went on, 'Can't you do something to make her shut up? Try biting her clitoris or something.'

'Helena!' Ingrid protested.

'Go on, you know you love that. I would bet you've never been had while driving through the countryside.

Do you think you could do her now, Richard? I'll drive slowly if you'd like to try.'

Ingrid made more dissenting noises.

The car turned into the gates of Margaret's estate. Now that they were on a private road, Ingrid was less anxious, but still worried about 'people' seeing her.

As they drew up outside the front entrance Helena hopped out and said she was going to fetch some of the slaves to help carry Ingrid.

Ingrid was not in favour of that either.

'Well, at least Heidi and Bruno,' she said with a grin as she and Richard lifted Ingrid from the back of the car. 'And we could use some more light out here.'

'Stop teasing her, Helena,' Richard finally said. 'It's cold out here. Let's get her inside.'

Helena used one hand to ring the door bell. Ingrid scolded and protested as they waited to be admitted, but they had to wait.

The woman who opened the front door to the bizarre trio did not seem surprised. She looked over the burden they bore before stepping aside to admit them. 'Hello, Frau Wagner,' Heidi said. 'Will you be staying with us tonight as well?'

'I thought we could put her in the barn, Heidi,' Helena said to the beautiful blonde servant. 'She has been making too much noise. She needs to be where she won't be heard.'

Heidi smiled. 'You know your mother would not like the barn. Come. We will take her up to the bedroom I have prepared for you.'

To Ingrid she said, 'You will be comfortable there. I will look after you.'

Ingrid went scarlet with embarrassment and protested that she would be all right on her own, that she did not want to be a nuisance. As she spoke the bag of urine slid to the floor. Ingrid flushed more brightly as Heidi picked it up and laid it on her stomach once more.

'Someone will need to help you until we can get you free of your shackles,' she observed.

'Don't worry, Heidi. We'll stay with her,' Richard said. 'But maybe you can help us get her up to the room. We'll use the lift.'

Heidi led them to the lift and opened the doors for them. There was room for only three people inside. When they had manoeuvred Ingrid into the lift and leaned her against the back wall, there was only room for two. Heidi stepped inside.

'We will meet you on the second floor,' Helena said.

The doors closed and Ingrid began her journey upwards.

Upstairs they reversed the process, carrying Ingrid to the bedroom and laying her on the bed. She was still scarlet with embarrassment. Heidi bent to kiss her cheek. 'Do not be embarrassed. Everyone here is accustomed to bondage of one type or another. Look.' She lifted her skirt to show Ingrid her chastity belt. 'I wear it all the time, but,' she said with a smile, 'Richard managed to get around it on one memorable occasion.'

Ingrid looked less uncomfortable. 'He manages to get around most things in time.'

'He even got around *Mutti*'s iron frame and catheter today,' Helena remarked.

Ingrid's blush returned full strength. 'Helena!' she scolded.

'And they spent the whole afternoon fucking,' Helena went on as if she hadn't heard. 'Just look at her. She should be worn out by the non-stop sex, but she was trying to seduce him again on the way over here. Once she is free of the rack, she'll give him no rest. All I get is what she's left.'

'Speaking of racks, do you know if Margaret took the keys for this one?' Richard asked Heidi.

'I do not know.'

'We'll go have a look.' Richard beckoned for Helena to follow him. To Ingrid he said, 'We're going to look

for the keys. Heidi will entertain you until we get back.'
To Heidi he said, 'She likes to have her clitoris licked
and bitten, but be gentle. She's had a long day.'

Ingrid flushed with renewed embarrassment. 'Don't
you dare!' she said to Heidi.

'Pay no attention,' Richard said. 'Once she feels your
tongue she'll change her mind.'

Heidi climbed on to the bed and settled herself
between Ingrid's parted thighs. She wet her lips and
bent down to Ingrid's cunt.

Ingrid thrashed futilely in her irons, unable to move
away from the descending mouth. Her protests followed
them down the hallway.

As he had suspected, the search for the keys turned up
nothing. They went into the kitchen to prepare some
food and coffee. As they ate, Richard and Helena
discussed how they would face Margaret. With determination, they decided. They took some food upstairs in
case Ingrid was hungry.

Upstairs there was silence. Opening the door, Richard
saw Ingrid lying on the bed in her irons, asleep. The
tube from her urethra led to a nearly full bag on the
floor beside the bed. Heidi was not in evidence, but it
looked as if Ingrid had enjoyed herself despite her
earlier protests. Helena went to the bed and looked
down at her sleeping foster-mother anxiously, but
Ingrid was merely sleeping. Helena unclipped the bag
and went to empty it in the toilet. She reattached it to
the plastic tube without waking Ingrid.

Together they undressed and got into bed beside
Ingrid, one on each side. Richard took one of her hands
in his and Helena the other, and together they slept
peacefully.

In the morning Richard woke up first. Ingrid slept
uneasily beside him in her iron frame, moaning occasionally and twisting as far as her rigid irons allowed –

which wasn't much. He wondered what had woken him. There was no change in the room or in the house. Helena still slept. The dawn was barely grey. The late March day had barely begun for civilised folk. Then he remembered: Margaret was due to return that day. He did not know if she had done so already, but the promise of her presence was enough to make the atmosphere electric.

By taking Ingrid back to Margaret's house, he and Helena had no doubt incurred the wrath of the leopardess. She had clearly intended to leave her half-sister imprisoned in her own flat, to teach her the dire consequences of disobedience. Even Ingrid, helpless to resist, would be in her bad books. Richard felt his cock stir with excitement as he contemplated Margaret's wrath. Would she decide to whip them all? Perhaps. She might order him to find Pamela, and he would do it. The idea of becoming Margaret's personal slave, and of suffering under her strict discipline, excited him further.

He could not lie in bed with Margaret due to return.

As he rose, Ingrid opened her eyes. 'Good morning, Richard,' she said softly, intimately. Yesterday she had been his lover, and they both knew she would be again. Whether Margaret would join them, especially after she discovered that Ingrid was already a member of their circle, was uncertain. Her pride and jealousy might rule her still, as they had for so many years. Something like an epiphany was needed to change her.

Richard leaned to kiss Ingrid a lingering good morning. She returned the kiss eagerly, promising pleasure later, whether or not she were freed. Her nipples grew erect, and he caressed them softly. She moaned, the sound covered by his mouth. Nevertheless, it was loud enough to wake Helena.

'Don't I get a good-morning kiss – or are you too busy with *Mutti*?' She smiled at them both, waiting her turn before rising to embrace Richard.

'Poor Richard,' she murmured as she drew back, 'having to choose between two women so early in the morning.'

'Both of whom want him,' Ingrid added.

'But he has only one cock,' Helena replied. 'He has to decide who gets it first.'

'Have you forgotten who is coming today?' he asked. 'Very soon none of us may be able to decide about cocks and who is going to get one. Your aunt is not likely to appreciate our interference in her plans. We need to decide how to face her wrath.'

'There are only two ways,' Helena said practically. 'Either we submit to her, or we defy her. The three of us can overpower her if we must.'

'Ah, but do we have the moral force to resist? All of us will be tempted to submit – and take the mostly pleasurable consequences of that submission. All she has to do is show you the whip,' he said to Helena.

'And you the Pamela-clothes,' she retorted

'Touché. But that hardly solves the problem.'

'We don't need to change anything we have already decided,' Helena reminded him. 'We said we would take her into our circle if she wishes. If she does not, we will have to leave her alone to get on with her own life, even if that means we must be on guard forever. But no matter what we do, we first have to make her free *Mutti*. She cannot wear that frame forever.'

'But there is nothing to keep Margaret from locking her up again once we have gone.'

'*Mutti* can come live with us if necessary,' Helena said decisively. With a mischievous grin she added, 'Then you will have to choose between us every day.'

The woman in the middle looked from one to the other. 'Are you serious? That means I would have to give up my business, and my home, and settle in a foreign country. And I do not know if I would . . . fit in in England.'

Richard replied, 'If you stay here, and Margaret does not relent, you can expect to be locked into that frame regularly – or into whatever other device Margaret decides to use on you. She is hardly likely to be overjoyed once she knows that you've been helping us to defy her. And that you've been enjoying the kind of sex that she craves but can't bring herself to submit to. But don't worry about "fitting in" in England. Or in our house, which is probably what you also meant but didn't like to say. Helena managed the change, and we would both be glad to have you with us.'

'Especially Richard,' Helena said. 'Not many men have two willing sex partners.'

'Only Walter, that we know of,' he said.

'*He* gets along well enough,' Helena reminded him. 'And so do you – with Lindsay and Edwina. If he can cope, so can you.'

'Who are Walter and Edwina and ... Lindsay?' Ingrid asked.

'We'll tell you later,' Helena said. 'We have to deal with Aunt Margaret first. Anyone have a specific plan for that? A deadfall trap at the front door, or a pitfall in the lift-shaft, for instance?'

Richard smiled. 'No. As you said, we must make her decide here and now about the offer – give her no more time to dither, or for our resolve to dissolve.'

'And then what?' Helena asked.

'We'll have to see what she decides.'

'All right,' Helena agreed. 'But what do we do now, while waiting for the confrontation?'

They both looked at Ingrid, lying helplessly on the bed.

'Shall we do her?' Richard asked with mock gravity.

'Only if you think she would enjoy it,' Helena replied, matching his tone. 'Perhaps we could ask her.'

'Let's not,' Richard said. 'Protest is better than supine acquiescence. Ask any red-blooded male.'

The potential victim said encouragingly, 'I could do nothing to stop you.'

'Wouldn't do anything, you mean,' Helena said affectionately. 'You are not a good role model for shy young women, *Mutti*.'

'You are not a shy young woman. Neither is Richard a retiring young man. Nor am I young.'

'That's twice in the last twenty-four hours she's asked for a beating,' Richard remarked. 'Shall we give her one?'

'Or two?' Helena asked. 'I know where Aunt Margaret keeps the whips.' She left the room naked, a normal condition in Margaret's house. Returning, she displayed the pussy-whip. 'Look what I found,' she said brightly. 'Does anyone know what it's used for?'

Ingrid, apparently, did. 'Not that! Please!'

'Anyone would think she was a shy young virgin facing sex for the first time,' Richard joked.

'Instead of a seasoned B&D freak like us,' Helena added. 'You'll like this, *Mutti*. Trust me. Even Richard is turned on by it – especially when *Tante* Margaret is on the other end of it.'

On the bed Ingrid wriggled in her rigid irons, whether from fear or anticipation they could not tell. Her eyes were wide with apprehension as she followed Helena's every movement. Unlike Helena, she had taken some time to exhibit a proclivity for sexually oriented pain.

Helena swung the pussy-whip experimentally. Ingrid's eyes followed it.

'She is looking forward to this, Richard. Do you want to beat her, or shall I?'

'You do it. I'll watch.'

Ingrid went white. She shook her head as far as the iron collar allowed. Her body stiffened with anticipation when Richard nodded to Helena to begin.

The first blow landed with a crack across the fronts of her thighs, just above the knees. Helena raised her

163

arm to strike again, working gradually up her thighs to the apex, where she teasingly allowed the whip to trail between Ingrid's legs and over her labia – a promise of future delight. Ingrid writhed in her irons, panting from the pain and from the anticipation of the greater pain to follow. She was watching Helena closely, no longer objecting.

Helena struck her foster-mother a stinging blow across her full breasts. The force of it flattened Ingrid's nipples, but they sprang erect immediately. She cried out at the unexpected assault on her tender flesh, but she writhed gently in her restraints with the pleasure of it. Richard, watching closely, saw her hips rise and fall slightly. If she had not been locked into the rigid frame, he guessed, she would have been pumping them up and down with excitement. He too was aroused by the spectacle of a beautiful woman being whipped to arousal while unable to move or escape.

Helena lashed Ingrid's breasts, making them glow redly with the broad stripes of the pussy-whip. Because it was so short and broad, even a full-strength blow would not break the skin or leave permanent marks. But it would certainly let the victim know she was being lashed. Helena left Ingrid in no doubt. Her heavy breasts bounced and shuddered as they were lashed. Her nipples grew taut and crinkly with her excitement, springing erect again after each blow.

The lash travelled slowly down Ingrid's helpless body, leaving her stomach and belly glowing like her breasts. Helena changed her stance and swung the short whip between Ingrid's legs, landing squarely on her labia and cunt. This time Ingrid cried out, her scream filling the room and seeming to hang quivering in the air. Her next scream, of mingled pleasure and agony, must have been heard down the hall, but no one came to investigate. In Margaret's house such screams of torment were common. No one in that house would dare interfere when the mistress was administering discipline to one of her erring slaves.

Helena was now concentrating on Ingrid's crotch, lashing her repeatedly between the legs and drawing a scream with each blow. Ingrid was fighting her irons, her body bucking and jerking. Richard was once more struck by the eroticism of her helplessness and arousal. His own cock was erect. Helena's nipples were taut with her excitement.

Helena looked up and saw his erection. Playfully, she struck his cock, making it bob comically and drawing a grunt of surprise from him. She laughed delightedly. He grinned ruefully.

'Do you want to get into her now?' Helena asked.

He shook his head. 'Carry on.' He kneeled beside the bed to fondle Ingrid's abused breasts and nipples while Helena continued to lash her belly and legs and cunt.

Ingrid went wild with excitement from the mingled pain and pleasure. Her stomach muscles tightened in rippling spasms as she came. Her leg muscles grew tight, and Richard saw the sudden flow of urine through the catheter in the excitement of her release. Ingrid's hands were clenched tightly and her body vibrated as she fought against the heavy shackles that held her immobile. She screamed again and again as Helena drove her into repeated climaxes, giving her no respite.

When the lashing ended, Helena was panting slightly from her exertions, while Ingrid was gasping and shuddering, on the verge of another orgasm. Helena stood aside and motioned for Richard to mount Ingrid. 'She's nicely warmed through.'

His cock was so hard it hurt, a fact that Helena noted with a grin. She grasped it and squeezed. Richard almost came in her hand. He had to clamp down hard in order not to – which Helena also noted with glee.

'Don't you dare come yet,' she ordered, guiding him into Ingrid's cunt as he lowered himself.

He slid into Ingrid's helpless body with a sigh. She gasped as she felt him penetrate her, tightening the muscles inside her vagina around the invading cock. Unable to move, she stared into his eyes as he slid home.

'Fuck me, Richard! Fuck me hard!' she gasped.

He felt her body tense as she fought the restraints, attempting to move beneath him as she had done on other occasions, when she was not immobilised. 'Don't struggle,' he told her. 'Let me do the work.'

Her taut body relaxed somewhat, though she kept her vaginal muscles tight around his cock as he raised and lowered himself on top of her, sliding rhythmically in and then out again.

Ingrid's mouth opened in a gasp of delight as she felt the maddening friction of his cock against her clitoris. She gasped again when Helena reached between their joined bodies to fondle her breasts.

'Relax and enjoy it, *Mutti*,' she said affectionately, voicing the ancient wisdom of the Orient. She pinched her foster-mother's nipples between thumbs and forefingers.

'Oh, God!' Ingrid cried. 'Oh, God!'

Richard felt her clamp down on his cock as she came. Once again her body tightened beneath him as the orgasm swept through her. He rode with her, letting Ingrid feel him inside her but not distracting her by extraneous movement. He kept himself pressed fully inside, grinding his pubic bone against her clitoris.

Ingrid moaned repeatedly as the climaxes shook her helpless body. Her eyes were wide open, but it was doubtful if she were aware of anything but the fiery pleasure that coursed through her.

Richard only began to move again when he felt her orgasm subside. Ingrid's eyes focused suddenly, smiling at him, telling him wordlessly how much pleasure he was giving her.

He had to clamp down hard to stop himself from coming, wanting to prolong the ecstasy for them both

Sometimes he lasted longer than others. Sometimes he pushed his partner to orgasm, and sometimes she pushed him over the edge.

This time it was Margaret who decided things. The door flew open, crashing back against the wall as she stormed into the room. She must have been listening outside the door, Richard thought later. Or perhaps she had heard Ingrid's screams of ecstasy from a greater distance. In any case, she was furious as she burst in on the trio.

'How dare you!' she screeched.

To Richard, even then, it sounded melodramatic. That was what outraged women always cried. Nonetheless, she *was* outraged. Seizing the whip that Helena had let fall earlier, she began to lash them all indiscriminately, the blows landing on every bit of exposed flesh.

Helena, to her credit, ignored the blows and continued to tease Ingrid's breasts. Ingrid was past noticing anything short of an earthquake as she shuddered in ecstasy.

Margaret was doubtless thinking in terms of throwing a bucket of cold water over coupling dogs, but her actions were more like throwing petrol on a fire. Under the rain of blows Richard felt his self-control slip away. With Ingrid clamped tightly around his cock and moaning with pleasure he felt himself coming in hot spasms as Margaret set about them with the whip.

Margaret saw what was happening, but instead of stopping (although it was doubtful whether anything would have held him back by then), she lashed him even harder – a sure sign that she was losing control. 'Stop that! Stop this instant!' she screamed at them all. She sounded hysterical.

But Richard didn't. The whipping receded into the background as he and Ingrid experienced a shattering orgasm. Margaret's cries of fury sounded in his ears like the distant cries of birds. Ingrid's moans of pleasure were far more real to him.

When it became evident to Margaret that the main event had already occurred despite her efforts to prevent it, she threw the whip down angrily.

Richard, lying on top of Ingrid, turned to look at Margaret for the first time. He was surprised to see her weeping. That was the second time the leopardess had shown her feelings so obviously. He hoped that Margaret's tears stemmed from a feeling of being excluded from the magic circle, and not because she was genuinely angry. If the former, there was hope for her yet – and for them all. If the latter, it was back to guarding themselves against her.

Helena was smothering her laughter. Don't laugh, he urged her silently, but he too saw the funny side. He managed to keep a straight face. 'We ... er, didn't expect you back so soon.'

'Evidently,' Margaret ground out.

It was not exactly a propitious moment to open negotiations for a change of policy. Margaret was still furious, but she was still the one who would have to change. He was still lying on top of the woman he had just fucked – was still joined to her in fact. Not the best position from which to negotiate. That gave Margaret an advantage, but getting up too abruptly and allowing her to think she had rushed him would likewise give her an edge.

Still the matter had to be addressed without delay, without letting Margaret regain her composure or strengthen her resolve to resist.

Helena came to the rescue. 'Aunt Margaret, you must set *Mutti* free now. Give me the keys to her irons.'

Margaret immediately turned the full force of her anger on to her niece, allowing Richard to withdraw gracefully from Ingrid while the two women faced one another.

'Why should I?' she blazed at her niece. 'So that he can fuck her more easily? How long have they been fucking!' Margaret rarely swore, preferring irony and contempt when dealing with her slaves.

'Since you sent me to her to learn how to dress and act like a woman,' Richard answered her. Standing up was definitely a better position from which to argue. He mentally thanked Helena for intervening when she did.

'But that's not the point,' he continued. 'She has been locked up for more than a day. Her muscles will cramp, and the catheter has got to come out. We don't know how to get it out without hurting her. You'll have to do it.'

Margaret switched her attention, and her anger, from Helena to Richard. 'You have been giving her plenty of exercise, haven't you?'

Despite her hostility, he pressed on. 'The keys, Margaret.'

She glared at him for a long moment. She might yet retreat into the familiar old role. Taking orders was not her strong point.

Time for a small olive branch, something to save her face. 'You know she can't stay locked up any longer.'

Margaret continued to glare at him, but she slowly removed a long gold chain from around her neck. The keys emerged from inside her dress. Richard imagined them lying between her breasts. The keys were warm in his hand as she passed them over.

Richard set about the lengthy process of freeing Ingrid from her heavy frame. Even when she was free she could barely move. He had to help her swing her legs to the floor, and support her while she recovered the use of her body. He remembered fondly his own recent use of it.

Margaret turned once more on Helena. 'You knew about . . . him and . . . and her all this time? That he was fucking your mother? And you did nothing to stop them? What kind of a daughter are you?'

Helena responded coolly, 'Don't be so Victorian, Aunt Margaret. You're hardly in a position to moralise about us. Pots and kettles, remember?'

169

Margaret, taken aback by her niece's defiance, gave her an *et tu, Brute?* glare.

Helena plunged on, ignoring her aunt's mood. 'You will have to stop treating us as errant children needing correction and chastisement. We are adults. Richard and me – and *Mutti* – have asked you to stop playing the slave-driver and join us in an adult relationship. You must decide now. What are you going to do?'

'I do not have to listen to your demands,' Margaret retorted, the old hauteur returning.

'You don't have to accede to them, but you must give us an answer. Today. Now,' Helena insisted.

Margaret did not reply at once, the warring desires plain to them all: the drive to control everyone striving against the yearning for sexual gratification and acceptance.

Helena used one more argument. 'You need not let your other slaves know that you are treating us differently. We will save your face whenever we are here. Only we need to know.'

Bad policy, Richard thought, making a separate peace, but the only one likely to achieve the desired end. So much for solidarity among the downtrodden.

After a silence Margaret spoke softly, tentatively: 'I will . . . try.'

Helena smiled. Richard and Ingrid (still carrying the bag of urine attached to her catheter) joined her and they embraced one another, opening the circle to admit Margaret.

Margaret seemed fascinated by the vistas opening before her. Her life was bound to change – for the better, they all hoped. Characteristically, she signalled the change by actions rather than words. She took the bag of urine from Ingrid's hand and moved towards the bed. Ingrid followed at the end of the plastic tube. Margaret signalled her to lie down, stooping to remove the catheter.

Richard, watching closely – he might want to try this on Helena at some time – could not see clearly what she did. Ingrid winced, but the tube came out with no obvious discomfort.

Helena was more direct. 'Show me how to do that, Aunt Margaret. I might try it with Richard one day. Is the process similar for a man?'

Margaret looked at him, the dominatrix measuring up her slave for some future urethral humiliation.

Richard shivered with anticipation as he imagined Helena or Margaret inserting the tube into his cock and leaving him bound and gagged in the Pamela-clothes before going out for the day.

Only Ingrid, rubbing herself reflexively where the catheter had entered her, showed no direct interest in the process of inserting tubes into tiny orifices.

'Later,' Margaret said. 'I will show you how to use the catheter later.'

When she looked at him, he imagined she was weighing him up all over again, no longer certain of their relationship. Margaret looked as desirable as ever. He allowed himself to speculate when he might get her alone for long enough to see how deep these changes ran. She might well be waiting for the same opportunity, in order to isolate the three conspirators and deal with them separately. Divide and rule was usually an effective strategy. Richard had fewer doubts about Helena and Ingrid than he had about himself. Alone with the dominatrix, he might once more be tempted to prostrate himself before her as he had done at Bacton.

As if reading his thoughts, Margaret spoke to Helena and Ingrid. 'I would like to speak to Richard now. Alone. Please.' The please was an afterthought. She seldom used the polite forms she urged upon everyone else who passed through her hands or under her lash.

Helena looked at Richard, who nodded imperceptibly. 'Don't let her talk you around to the old arrangement,' she said. 'She has two powerful arguments at her disposal. The whip is only one of them. And remember how malleable Pamela can be.'

She and Ingrid, both naked, left the room. They could wander through Margaret's house all day without clothes and no one would remark on it. At most, anyone who saw them would assume that they were being disciplined by their capricious mistress for some real or imaginary infraction of the rules by which the house was run.

Richard and Margaret faced one another in the bedroom. Not the best place for a confrontation, he thought. The bed was too near. He was naked, and she was fully clothed. And Margaret was still Margaret – still able to bend him to her will, as Helena had pointed out. Worse still, his cock was growing erect as he looked at her. Even fully clothed, she was able to affect him that way.

'I see I have your attention,' she said with a mocking smile.

Richard thought her opening remark unpromising, but she did not follow it up. She became serious instead.

'Sit down,' she commanded, taking one of the armchairs.

Richard took the other, his cock and his attention at full stretch.

'We need to talk about the future,' she said. 'Tell me again about what I have promised to try. I like to have things as specific as possible. And please stop waving that thing in my face. It's . . . distracting.'

It was Richard's turn to smile. 'Tell it to go away. Most things obey you.'

'That is one of the things that does not obey,' she said. 'Fortunately. But we must postpone further explorations for now. Unfortunately. Talk.'

'Helena told you what we want. I can only add that you should stop harassing us in our business lives. Stop putting pressure on our clients and financial sources. And treat us as adults. Consenting adults, usually.'

'And . . .?' she prompted.

'Continue to play the dominatrix when we visit one another, subject to the no-harassment rule. You know we all like what you do. That's not too much to ask, is it?' Olive branches to lady leopards, he thought.

'No,' she agreed. 'Go on. Tell me how far I am allowed to go with you when I am the . . . dominatrix.'

'That's for you to decide when you are the . . . dominatrix. We don't want to limit you, nor preclude the possibility of further experiments – which we are sure you will come up with. But, in general: no grievous bodily harm or permanent scars. Pretty much as you have been doing. We trust your experience and common sense.'

'I am so pleased,' she said dryly.

'And don't lose your sense of humour,' he said.

'Anything else?'

'What more do you want?'

'Well,' she said, waving at his cock, 'is that part of the bargain too?'

'If you want it. Do you?'

Margaret flushed but did not reply. He did not press her. It would be a long time before Margaret begged for sex. If she ever did.

'Is there a . . . pecking order?' Margaret smiled ironically.

'First come, first served,' he replied. 'No favourites. Democracy in action.'

'Not even Helena?'

'Helena waited while I was fucking Ingrid. And she is not shy about what she wants. Do you think you could emulate her – or Ingrid – if it came to that?' Margaret could seldom resist a challenge.

'And will I be expected to join in with other women? With Helena and Ingrid? Lesbian stuff?'

173

'Not unless you want to. Consenting adults, remember?' Prompted by the imp of impudence, he asked, 'Have you ever done it with another woman?'

After a long silence Margaret said, 'No.'

'Afraid?' he asked. Another challenge.

Margaret was silent once more, debating perhaps whether, as dominatrix, she should offer him a reason. Finally she said, 'It's . . . disgusting. Unnatural.'

'And what you do – what we all enjoy – that's natural?'

'Of course! As you said, you all like it.'

Richard decided to stop needling her. 'Any other questions?'

She shook her head.

'So what now?' he asked. 'Ready to turn over a new leaf?'

'I said I would try. I cannot be any more definite than that, now.'

'Then that will have to do – for now. But I – we – want you to know that you are wanted. We want you to be at ease with us and to share our relationship whenever you can come to Bacton, and whenever we visit you here. Or at the Seaside Hotel in Cromer,' he added with a smile.

Her answering smile was brighter. 'Yes. You liked that, didn't you?'

'And the rest of it. But don't worry. Things haven't changed that much. Would you feel better if I asked Pamela to come and see you?' His heart lurched in the old familiar way as he thought of what that might entail.

'Perhaps . . . later. At the hotel in Cromer. Or in Bacton.' She changed the subject abruptly. 'What do you think of Ingrid's frame?'

'It was exciting to fuck a woman who couldn't move, but leaving her in it for too long might produce muscle cramps.'

'Even with you and Helena around to loosen her up?'

'We probably helped. Was the frame your idea?' he asked.

'Yes. I had it made locally to my design. There will be another one soon – for a man.'

'It was a good idea,' he told her. Another olive branch for the leopardess, he thought, while imagining himself being locked into the other frame, with Margaret officiating.

'Well, think of it for the future – when you come to visit next time, perhaps,' Margaret said with a knowing smile. 'But for now, we must make do with the one we have. What I will do is take off my clothes. What you will do is lock me into the frame. After that, what we both do will be determined wholly by you. Do you have any ideas about how to proceed?'

'Several,' he said, his excitement rising at the idea of Margaret immobilised, his prisoner. The reversal of roles was breathtaking. And sudden, leaving no time for demur or revision. Typical Margaret, even though she was going to be the passive partner.

She stood up abruptly, giving herself no time to change her mind, and performed the woman-undoing-a-back-zipper contortion which Pamela had found so difficult to learn. The top of the dress loosened, and Margaret shrugged out of it. It fell to the floor and she stood before him in her underwear. Through the translucent pale yellow bra her nipples and areolae were clearly visible. So was the blonde mass of her pubic hair, flattened against the lower curve of her abdomen by the tight sheer pants. A few tendrils peeped out at the leg openings.

She wore a matching suspender-belt under her pants, the better, Richard imagined, to strip them off while leaving her shiny dark grey stockings in place. For him?

'I was expecting you to be here,' Margaret said. 'Even if things hadn't changed, I thought you would like to know that I had dressed as you like a woman to dress. It would have been fun to tease you with glimpses of forbidden delights.'

'And now?' he asked.

'As I said, you will have to decide. Unless you are too tired after the workout with my sister.'

Richard smiled at his own vanity as he approached her. As if he would ever admit to being too tired, especially to this woman. He put his hand on the back of her neck, beneath the thick mane of her hair. 'Kiss me, Margaret,' he commanded. A test.

Which she passed by tilting up her face and opening her lips to receive him. She melted against him as he embraced her, her skin soft and warm against his. The kiss went on, Margaret showing no inclination to draw back.

It was Richard who broke off, pulling back to look at her once more. Her cheeks were flushed and her breathing rapid. He unsnapped her bra, allowing her full breasts to spring free of their confinement. They bore the imprint of the bra's seams. He traced the lines with his fingers while Margaret stood as if carved from stone.

When he touched her nipple lightly she shuddered and then steadied beneath his hand. He stooped to take the nipple into his mouth.

Margaret gasped with pleasure and brought her hands up behind his head to hold him against her.

When he bit her nipple, Margaret cried out with surprise and delight: 'Oh! Oh!' Her hands tightened, holding him fiercely against her breast. She arched her back, pushing her hips against him, shivering as his stiff cock brushed the silk of her pants and slid between her thighs. She closed her legs around him, and he felt the heat of her flesh.

They stood together for long minutes, Margaret beginning to breathe heavily as he teased and fondled her breasts and nipples. When he slid his hand under the waistband of her pants she did not protest. The pants joined the rest of her clothing on the floor.

'Lie down now, Margaret,' he commanded.

Only then did she hesitate, on the verge of objecting to his assumption of control.

'Lie down,' he repeated.

She lay down with her back against the rigid steel frame and raised her hands to shoulder level for him to lock the irons around her wrists. Her eyes were wide, fixed on his, betraying her uneasiness at giving control to someone else. She seemed to be seeking reassurance at the moment of truth.

Richard fastened the steel bands around her wrists, turning the keys in the locks.

Committed now, unable to escape, Margaret relaxed slightly. She lay still as he parted her legs and locked her ankles into the spreader bar. The steel collar around her neck and the steel band around her waist were not nearly as disturbing to her as surrendering her hands to the manacles had been.

Richard paused to look at his prisoner, formerly his mistress. She was every bit as alluring as Ingrid had been. She lay helplessly on her back with her legs spread invitingly, waiting for him to decide what to do to her. The sheer stockings and suspenders were in marked contrast to the unyielding frame that held her prisoner. *Le mot juste*, he thought, was breathtaking.

Margaret looked up at him apprehensively. This was unknown territory to her. The woman who had always made all the decisions for herself and others now waited uncertainly for his decision. Margaret as prisoner looked somehow smaller, less threatening. An illusion, he reminded himself.

Her eyes followed his hand as he laid the keys to her irons on the bedside table. They might as well have been at the bottom of the North Sea for all the good they

177

would do her. Even if she held the keys in her hand, she would still be unable to reach the locks.

The moment passed. She looked up at him with some of the old challenge in her glance. 'Well, what now?'

'I thought I'd enjoy the view. It's not often I get to see such a sight.'

'Well, do you like what you see?'

'I'm not sure,' he said teasingly, watching the familiar anger flare in her eyes.

Margaret struggled briefly against her restraints, though she must have known that she could not escape. After all, she had designed them. She shifted her gaze to his cock, now only half-erect. 'Lost your courage?' she taunted him.

Richard sat on the bed beside his captive. He looked at her for a long time, so long in fact that her eyes wavered and turned aside. Margaret stirred irritably in the rigid irons, but said nothing further. There was nothing but moral force that could prevent him from doing whatever he wished to her, and he knew that she would never beg him to stop, to let her go.

He stroked her legs through the sheer stockings. Margaret relaxed slightly, the tense muscles loosening. Moving higher, he ruffled her pubic hair with his fingers before tracing her labia down to her cunt.

Margaret stiffened momentarily as she felt his finger slide inside her, but when it brushed her swollen clitoris she moaned softly with pleasure. She grew warmer and wetter as he pushed his finger further inside.

Just like any other woman, he thought, when she lets herself go. But the letting go – that was the problem. Richard guessed that Margaret was only able to respond now because she could not do anything to prevent her arousal. He remembered his own feeling of release from responsibility when Margaret or Helena had bound him. Even dominatrixes, seemingly, needed to be set free from responsibility for their bodies' responses every once in a while.

Margaret groaned suddenly, her belly muscles rippling in a sudden spasm. Richard suspected that she had had a small orgasm – her first under the new regime. She wriggled in her restraints, moving her body as much as she could while he continued to probe her with his finger.

He looked at her nipples, as taut and swollen as he imagined her clitoris to be under his finger. Her breasts were engorged, heavier, firmer than usual. He pinched one of her nipples, hard and suddenly. The effect on Margaret was explosive, as if she had needed just that one small push to drive her to full orgasm. Gasping and groaning, fighting her irons, she came. One moment she was merely enjoying a pleasant sensation. The next she was wild, out of control, her body in full charge.

This was the first time he had been able both to initiate and observe a climax in Margaret. The sight was breathtaking as she surrendered to pleasure. His own cock was stiff merely from looking at her, but at that moment he wanted to watch her more than he wanted to bury himself inside her body and share her release.

Margaret was lost in ecstasy, moaning from her repeated orgasms. She did not notice the door opening to admit Helena. Like Richard, she was captivated by the sight of her aunt moaning and writhing in her irons. She looked down at the woman on the bed with something like awe.

Then she kneeled on the opposite side of the bed, taking her aunt's other breast with both hands, cupping and fondling it, taking it into her mouth, sucking and kissing and biting it.

Margaret's first reaction was another series of explosive orgasms, but as they subsided she seemed suddenly to be aware that they were no longer alone. Her eyes focused on her niece. She flushed a deep red. 'No! Don't touch me! Go away at once! Richard, make her go away!'

179

But Helena did not go. Nor did Richard try to eject her. Instead they drove Margaret out over the edge of self-control once more. She tried to fight them, to ignore what they were doing to her, but her body had its own agenda. Despite herself, Margaret came again, trying to choke back her wild cries, embarrassed to be seen in this state but unable to prevent them from manipulating her rebellious body. She closed her eyes and averted her face but she could not stop coming.

When she felt Richard mount her, however, she opened her eyes and looked wildly at him. His cock parted her labia and slid into her wet cunt as he supported himself on stiff arms above her helpless body. 'Ah!' she sighed as he slid home.

Helena continued to caress and tease her breasts and nipples as Richard lifted his hips, thrusting himself in and out. Margaret closed her eyes again briefly as if to blot out her surrender, but a rippling spasm in her belly made her look at him again. She glanced once, quickly, sideways at Helena but thereafter kept her gaze fixed on Richard as he drove her slowly, thoroughly, to orgasm. Shivers of pleasure passed through her belly and breasts and legs as her fucking went on.

Involuntarily, unconsciously, Margaret clenched her hands into fists as the waves of ecstasy washed through her. The muscles in her stomach were taut with her pleasure, her leg muscles standing out beneath the sheer nylon of her stockings. Her toes curled tightly.

Helena sucked her aunt's nipple, circling it with her tongue, kissing it.

'Ah! Ah! Ah!' Margaret moaned.

When Helena suddenly bit the nipple Margaret came, her moans changing to screams, her head twisting helplessly from side to side.

Richard rode with her, feeling the play of her internal muscles around his cock as they clenched and relaxed in time with her eruptions of pleasure. He thrust faster, sliding part-way out and then back in again, Margaret's screams and moans rising and falling as wave after wave of sensation swept through her body. And suddenly he came, emptying himself into the tight warm sheath of her cunt. Margaret screamed again, the sound filling his head, the room, announcing to the world (if it was listening) that here was a woman driven beyond control, deep into ecstasy, no reservations left.

They lay joined for a long time, breathing slowing and bodies cooling and relaxing.

Margaret was exhausted. She barely felt the hands and cock withdraw from her body before she fell into sleep.

She woke in the dark. As far as she could tell she was alone. Memory flooded back, and she twisted in her irons. Someone had covered her with a blanket, for which she was grateful. Naked, unable to move, and unwilling to call for help, she would have grown cold without a covering of some sort. She had no choice but to lie back and wait for someone to come to her.

The next time she woke she felt an urgent need to pee. She did not, positively did not, want to wet herself and the bed. She had berated countless others for doing the same thing, even though she herself had made it impossible to do anything else. It would be unthinkable for her to be forced to wet herself. But unless someone came soon to free her, she would do just that.

It was Helena who finally came. Margaret was vaguely irritated that it was not Richard, but the urgency of her need was paramount.

'Let me go at once,' she commanded, 'before I . . .'

'Before you wet yourself,' Helena finished for her.

'Let me go!' Margaret repeated. She sounded more shrill than commanding. She strove to control her voice and her bladder. 'Let me go.' That was better, she thought. Calmer. More her old self.

'Say please,' Helena teased.

Margaret flushed with anger. 'How dare you?' she shouted, almost losing control once more. She felt herself leak, the urine running down her crotch. She clamped down harder on her bladder and strove for control. With a visible effort she said, 'Please. Please let me go.' She was both angry and desperate – a bad combination.

Helena saw it. She smiled. 'Hold on, Aunt Margaret. I'll go get the catheter and bag. You'll have to tell me how to fit it to you.'

Margaret lost control entirely at the ignominious suggestion, struggling furiously against her restraints and demanding to be set free at once. When Helena calmly told her that Richard had taken the keys, she screamed in frustration and simultaneously lost control of her bladder. The urine spurted down her legs, soaking both her stockings and the bed.

Helena still smiled.

An infuriated and embarrassed Margaret glared at her niece, determined not to let her know what had happened, or how relieved she felt.

'You've wet yourself, haven't you, Aunt Margaret? I can smell it. And the blanket has a big wet spot,' Helena said with a certain satisfaction.

Margaret glared silently, still struggling. Helena lifted the blanket, to her aunt's helpless chagrin, to look at her soiled body. Margaret grew red in the face as she struggled against the irons.

'Why are you doing this to me?' she asked finally.

'It's not revenge, Aunt Margaret. Think of it as an education. You are learning what we all learned from you: helplessness, domination, humiliation and, yes, the extraordinary sexual release that comes from all these.'

'And that is not revenge?'

'No. We enjoy it. But you needed to know at first hand what it's like. Even when you do the same things

182

to us – and you will – you will have a better understanding of what you're doing. That does not mean that we want you to change your ways. Just understand what you are asking us to do.'

Margaret was uncharacteristically silent. Finally: 'All right. Are you going to let me go now?'

'The lesson isn't over yet,' Helena replied.

Margaret looked worried. 'What else is there to do?'

'Oh, lots of things,' Helena said cheerfully. 'For one thing, we would all like to give you a good old fossicking – as they used to say in England – to offer you a real welcome to our circle.'

Margaret looked alarmed at the 'all'. She had apparently not considered all the implications of their joint offer. 'What will you do?' she asked with some apprehension. She was not familiar with 'fossicking', but the context made its meaning clear.

'Well,' Helena said consideringly, 'we might introduce you to the pleasures of three in a bed. Or four. More bodies, more fun. Up to a point, of course,' she said judiciously. 'One should avoid excess in all things.'

'And just what do you consider excessive?' Margaret asked with a tremor in her voice.

Helena detected it at once. And, like many people detecting weakness in another, she could not resist the urge to tease her aunt a bit more.

'Well, probably no more than six,' she said, 'though I know that others set a different limit. But anyway, let's get you cleaned up. I'll just give the servants a call. They might like to join in, don't you think?'

Margaret shouted, 'No!' at once, her distress evident. 'They are not to see me! You promised that they wouldn't know about any of this! Don't do this to me!'

Helena summoned a disappointed look. 'All right, if that's what you really want. I'll just get Richard and Ingrid. And then, after you're cleaned up, we'll let you enjoy being fondled by three pairs of hands. How's that?'

The parts of Margaret that could be seen outside the wet blanket turned a bright red. She struggled again, shaking her head wildly.

'Oh, don't be such a stick-in-the-mud, Aunt Margaret.' Helena sounded exasperated. 'I can see we'll have to drag you kicking and screaming into the twentieth century. But now I'll just get the others to help me drag you into the bathroom.' She left before Margaret could protest.

Helena returned after nearly an hour with the others. Margaret, it appeared, had been expecting them back instantly, and had not appreciated the delay. She looked crossly at them and demanded to be set free once again.

They looked with interest at the damp, angry leopardess. Helena was amused, Richard disinclined to set her free, Ingrid merely worried.

'I've forgotten the keys,' he explained.

'Then go get them!' she blazed at him, wriggling in her restraints to emphasise her wish to be freed immediately, if not sooner.

Helena moved to the bed and lifted the blanket from her aunt's imprisoned body, looking down at her assessingly. The dark patch on the bedspread and the damp patches on her stockings revealed the more vulnerable side of the woman – which did not please Margaret in the least.

'Go get the keys!' she snapped again. 'Let me go at once!'

Instead, Richard and Helena lifted the frame from the bed and bore her, wriggling and protesting, into the attached bathroom. Ingrid, looking worried and doubtful, followed.

They propped her against the wall near the shower head. There was ample room for the four of them in the area.

'Don't struggle,' Richard ordered her.

Margaret understood the danger of falling as well as anyone else. She stopped wriggling and looked silently at them all.

'Richard,' Helena said, 'you begin soaping Aunt Margaret down. I will go strap on that huge double dildo you got for me in Norwich. *Mutti*, you can use another dildo for yourself, and leave both hands free to stuff Aunt Margaret's arsehole with one of the spare dildoes in the bedroom. We might even find one for your own arsehole if you'd like.'

Helena spoke lightly, as if discussing nothing more outre than seating arrangements at the dinner table. She winked broadly at Richard.

'You'll enjoy this, Margaret. Really you will. Just relax,' he told her.

Margaret, however, was far from relaxed. She looked from one to the other with a trapped expression, appearing to cringe in her irons. 'No,' she said in a small voice, shaking her head. Then, more strongly, 'No! Let me go at once! Let me go, do you hear?' She struggled once more.

Helena looked at her aunt and said helpfully, 'Don't worry, Aunt Margaret. I know you'll like this. You won't know how you ever survived without it. I'll be back in just a minute.'

'No!' Margaret screamed once again as the stream of water sluiced down her body. She shook her head wildly, fighting the restraints. She was scarlet with embarrassment and outrage. 'No! No! Stop!'

Richard stood behind Margaret, supporting her with an arm around her waist. With his free hand he soaped her full breasts. That did not mollify her. He felt the tension in her body. Even when he began to tease one of her slippery nipples, she continued to shake her head, whimpering, 'No! No. Please don't. Stop.'

Ingrid, until then reluctant to cross her half-sister, appeared to undergo a change of heart. She picked up a bar of soap and began to lather Margaret's helpless body. She stood in the stream of water as she worked on Margaret's thighs, the suds running down her legs in the wet stockings. Moving higher, she worked the soap into Margaret's cunt and labia and clitoris.

Margaret whimpered helplessly as she looked down on her half-sister. She was becoming aroused against her will, even as she begged them to stop.

The pleas, coming from someone who never begged, had a marked effect on Richard. His cock stiffened, poking her from behind. Margaret gasped as she felt the pressure against her bottom. Her buttocks tightened as if to repel an invasion even as she moaned in despair and rising excitement under their hands.

By the time Helena returned, Margaret's protests had almost ceased. 'Oh, please. Please don't,' she moaned, her muscles rippling as they stroked her under the stream of warm water. Her long blonde mane, soaked, dishevelled, lay over her breasts, imparting to her a wild, Naiad beauty. She still struggled weakly against her obdurate restraints, her fists clenching and relaxing, but the hands on her body, stroking and teasing her relentlessly, had driven her beyond real resistance.

Ingrid had begun to masturbate herself. She too was lost in her own pleasure. When she came, Richard noticed, she stopped abruptly to give her whole attention to what was happening between her legs and in her belly. She resumed when the spasm subsided.

The sight of Helena strapping on a double dildo almost undid all the careful work on Margaret. Her muscles stiffened once again. 'No!' she shouted, without any discernible effect on her three captors. Margaret must have known by now that she was going to cross this final frontier willy-nilly. Her protests came from somewhere as far beyond her control as what was happening to her. She watched with a mixture of wide-eyed fear and anticipation as Helena stuffed one of the dildoes into her cunt and adjusted the straps around her waist and thighs.

'Look, everybody,' Helena said brightly, 'dildoes for every opening!' She had indeed brought a handful of variously sized and shaped instruments. Some were clearly intended for the anus. Ingrid looked at them all with interest as Helena laid down her burdens and approached her aunt.

Margaret's gaze was drawn irresistibly to the dildo intended for her. Her eyes stretched wide as she watched her niece approach with the long heavy shaft bobbing between her thighs. She mouthed a last silent 'no' as Helena stood before her and guided the shaft into her cunt, the hard serrated rubber sliding on her soap-slippery flesh, parting her and gliding inside, the serrations bumping her clitoris as Helena slid home. 'No. Oh!' Margaret cried as she was impaled. And, as Helena moved the shaft inside her and against her clitoris, 'Ah!'

The conquest was nearly complete, Margaret surrendering herself to the relentless hands that touched and stroked and caressed, that pinched and teased her helpless body beyond the control of her iron will. Only one bit of her remained unconquered.

It fell to Ingrid. Rising to her knees under the shower that ran down their bodies, she chose one of the slenderer dildoes from Helena's assortment. She lubricated it with soap and thrust it slowly into Margaret's anus.

The mistress of Soltau clamped her anal sphincter tightly shut to resist this last invasion of her territory, but Ingrid was patient and relentless. She simply kept the head of the dildo against the locked door until Margaret could not resist the pressure any longer. When Helena rubbed the serrated dildo against her aunt's clitoris, her resistance crumbled at last. As Margaret cried out with her first lesbian orgasm, her muscles relaxed and the shaft slid fully into her anus.

Ingrid worked the dildo in time with Helena's thrusts. One-handed, she chose another dildo for Helena, pushing it into her anus slowly as she had with Margaret.

Helena moaned softly and closed her eyes as she was stuffed full.

Ingrid chose two more dildoes, pushing one into her cunt and the other, more awkwardly, into her anus. She sat down, pushing the anal invader firmly into herself, using one hand to work the dildo in Margaret's anus, and the other to move the shaft inside her own cunt.

To a detached observer it might have looked like a complex machine, its several parts moving in regular patterns. But, unlike most machines, whose functions were often enigmatic, this one produced a clearly identifiable result.

Richard continued to support Margaret with one arm around her waist while he used his free hand to cup her swollen breasts and to tease her taut nipples. At the same time he kissed the back of her neck, her earlobes, the pulses beating wildly in the side of her neck.

Assaulted simultaneously in all her erogenous zones, unable to escape the embrace of her rigid irons or the touch of her three tormentors, Margaret bucked and shuddered and twisted her head helplessly from side to side. And she came. Her screams must have been audible outside in the hallway, and perhaps down the stairs as well. The other occupants of the house must have known that someone was being driven to ecstasy behind the closed bedroom door. But such things were common in Margaret's house.

Afterwards, when she had recovered her composure, Margaret worried aloud that surely the slaves knew by now what had happened to their mistress. 'How will I be able to face them after this?' she wailed.

Richard told her not to worry. 'One scream of ecstasy sounds very much like any other from outside.' Even if one of the slaves had stayed around to see who came out of the room (which would have been a very foolish thing to do), he or she would have no way of knowing who had been screaming, Richard said. 'Unless,' he added teasingly, 'we pushed you out into the hall naked.' Margaret's horrified look was his reward.

But that was later. This was now, and a very intense now it was. Margaret appeared to have abandoned even the pretence of resistance. Her moans and screams were continuous as her captors showed her new horizons of sexual release.

But this was not solely for Margaret's pleasure. Helena, naked, slippery with soap suds, penetrated by the other end of the dildo on which her aunt was impaled, was thrusting frantically as her own orgasms racked her. Ingrid paused in her manipulation of the shaft in Margaret's anus to reach up between their joined bodies to rub Helena's slick pubic mound and the under-slope of her belly. Helena moaned with pleasure, gasping for breath as her foster-mother's efforts augmented her own. Her own body, as unrestrained as Margaret's was rigidly held, thrust and stabbed with the twin shafts and brought ecstasy to them both. Helena's screams joined with her aunt's at the end as they both had a shattering orgasm that left both women exhausted.

Only then did Ingrid rise, leaving Helena and Margaret still joined, to rinse the soap from their bodies. Helena withdrew from her aunt and sat weakly on the wet tiles, the Margaret-end of the double dildo jutting up aggressively between her legs and the Helena-end still buried deeply inside her. She leaned wearily against the wall, watching as Ingrid and Richard lifted the exhausted Margaret from the shower and carried her, dripping, into the bedroom.

Ingrid came back for towels. She paused briefly to kiss the top of Helena's head and to caress her cheek gently. 'Rest, *liebchen*.' Helena smiled and closed her eyes, not quite asleep and not fully awake either.

Richard and Ingrid laid Margaret on her back on the floor. She too was drowsy, exhausted by the recent ordeal-by-ecstasy. They dried her carefully, so that only her hair and her stockings and suspenders were still damp. Ingrid stripped the soiled bedclothes and replaced them, and they both laid Margaret in the clean bed. Margaret drifted off to sleep as they covered her with a blanket.

Between them they helped Helena to her feet and led her unprotestingly into the bedroom. They dried her too. When Ingrid made as if to unstrap the double dildo, Richard silently stopped her. 'Later,' he mouthed. Helena neither questioned nor protested, standing quietly as they towelled her dry.

Richard led her to the bed and had her sit on the side. He asked Ingrid to fetch some rope. Sitting on the floor at Helena's feet, he stroked her legs and tugged at the dildo jutting upwards in her lap.

Helena smiled with pleasure as he toyed with her weary body. She kissed the top of his head and ruffled his hair.

When Ingrid returned, he told Helena to get into the bed with Margaret. He and Ingrid helped her to lie on top of the sleeping leopardess. Ingrid, smiling impishly, guided the dildo into her half-sister's cunt.

Margaret made sleepy protests but didn't wake up. When Helena was lying between her aunt's legs and Margaret was fully penetrated, Richard and Ingrid used the rope to tie her in place. She smiled at them both as they tied her wrists behind her back and her legs at ankles and knees. In order to keep her from slipping off they used more rope to tie her body on top of Margaret. Helena wriggled experimentally, causing the dildoes to move inside each of them.

Margaret moaned in her sleep. Ingrid covered their joined and helpless bodies with the blanket, and then they both kissed Helena goodnight.

'If Margaret says anything, say the devil made you do it,' he told Helena.

She turned her face to him and opened her lips. 'Mm,' she sighed as they kissed, wriggling and causing the dildoes to stir.

'Sleep well,' Ingrid said, 'if you can.'

They turned out all the other lights in the room, leaving only a night-light. Making up the pull-out bed in the settee for themselves, Richard and Ingrid could just make out the shape of the two women in the other bed. Helena was not lying quite as still as she might have been, nor was Margaret as silent as a sleeper should be.

'Animal noises,' Richard said to Ingrid.

'Will we make animal noises too? Or will you tie me up?'

'Which would you prefer?'

Ingrid thought for a moment. 'Animal noises first,' she said. 'Tie me up later.'

'Passed by acclamation.'

'Stockings and suspenders for me?' Ingrid asked.

Richard nodded, and she went to rummage in the bureau drawer. She returned with a pair of the crotchless tights Margaret had worn in Bacton. These were black and glossy in the dim light. Richard watched with pleasure as she put them on, pulling the sheer nylon up her legs then settling the waistband in place. Her belly and bush stuck impudently from the front opening.

'I am open in the back, too,' she said encouragingly as she slid under the covers.

They made animal noises. Other, similar noises came to them from across the room in the intervals. Richard, waking later, heard the same noises again. He wondered where Helena got the strength, but he was glad she had it. Ingrid, her wrists bound behind her back and the ropes biting into the sheer nylon of her tights at ankles, knees and thighs, slept contentedly beside him. He stroked her belly through the opening in the front of her tights as he drifted off to sleep.

4

Pamela and Margaret

By the following Tuesday Margaret seemed to have recovered her former poise and air of authority. She appeared at breakfast that morning wearing a business-like but stylish pinstripe skirt and jacket combination with black tights and high-heeled shoes. Her working clothes, she called them. Her business-as-usual suit, Richard thought with a frisson of excitement. He remembered wearing a similar outfit on the trip to Zurich, when Margaret had 'given' Pamela to Hannelore Bern in order to separate him and Helena.

Margaret announced that she had business in Zurich, and that Pamela was to accompany her as her assistant. They would be leaving within three hours, she added. It was a typical Margaret-tactic: spring a surprise decision on the unsuspecting so that there was no time for debate or demur.

Helena gave him a long look: Can we trust her – and you?

Richard shrugged: Do we have any choice?

Margaret informed them that she and Pamela would be away for some three days. On her return, she said, there would be a fancy-dress house-party to celebrate what she called half-ironically her new-leaf policy. There would be contests and both indoor and outdoor sports (weather permitting, she said, sounding as if she were

193

daring the elements to defy her), and prizes for the most original costumes and presentations. 'I will judge all the events,' Margaret declared.

Well, Richard thought, we didn't want her to become too shy or retiring. He asked her if Hannelore Bern might attend. In that event, he said, she might consent to do some of the judging, allowing Margaret more time to enjoy the festivities.

With a dark look Margaret informed Richard that she would enjoy the day even more if she were sole judge. 'Setting standards, and holding others to them, is one of the things I enjoy most, However, I may invite Frau Bern to attend with some of her entourage.'

Handing the guest-list to Helena, Margaret announced that her niece and Ingrid would be in charge of arrangements in her absence. 'But for now, go tell Pamela to get ready to travel, chop-chop.' She made shooing motions at them as she turned to make her own exit. She paused at the door to add, 'And, Helena, make sure Pamela wears her cock-ring.'

So it was going to be one of those trips, Richard thought sardonically as he rose from the table. But on the whole he was glad to see Margaret reassuming control. He would revert gladly to letting her make all the decisions. The last few days had been a pleasant interlude, but they had all missed her abrupt manner and capricious behaviour. They had missed being beaten and disciplined and dominated by her. Given the choice, they would have preferred to have no choice except to obey her – if only she bore in mind the new conditions.

Upstairs, Richard showered and carefully shaved his legs and face while Helena chose and packed the clothes that Pamela would need on the journey.

'Pay attention to all this,' she admonished him. 'I won't be in Zurich to help you pack and select your clothes.'

Pamela's travelling outfit lay ready on the bed: the corselet and tights, the false breasts, the slip, the wig, and the navy pinstripe skirt and jacket she had worn on her first trip to Zurich. A pair of black high-heeled shoes stood on the floor beside the bed.

Helena locked the cock-ring around his scrotum. 'Her orders,' she reminded him. It felt familiar and somehow comforting to be wearing once again the badge of his submission.

Helena helped him to dress and do the make-up. She brushed and styled the wig, and when Richard finally looked into the mirror, Pamela looked back at him.

Margaret came to collect him. Helena handed her the key to the cock-ring and she fastened it to the long gold neck chain. She settled the key ostentatiously inside her blouse, between her breasts. She inspected Pamela from several angles before nodding curtly. 'That will do,' she said in her customary could-do-better tone.

Pamela carried her case down stairs, Helena following. Margaret led the mini-cavalcade to the store room where she kept the bondage equipment. From it, she chose the fashion accessories Pamela would wear: hand- and thumbcuffs, leg-irons, leather hood and gag, ear-plugs, a dog lead, and the leather waist belt she had worn while Margaret's captive in Bacton.

More promisingly, she selected the leather collar which Pamela recognised as the one Helena had worn – the one that supplied mild electric shocks or pleasant vibrations to the relevant bits of the anatomy. An anal dildo, a control box and the necessary electric leads completed the selection.

'For later,' Margaret promised, catching Pamela's look of anticipation. 'Put down your case and come here.'

Margaret compelled her to buckle the belt around her waist. 'Hands in front, please,' she ordered. She herself checked the belt for tightness. 'Inhale,' she commanded, tightening the twin buckles behind Pamela's back and nipping in her waist.

Pamela grimaced. Margaret looked pleased.

After threading the handcuffs through the elongated steel ring rivetted to the belt, Margaret cuffed Pamela's wrists together, then added the thumbcuffs for good measure. The leg-irons were applied to her ankles. The earplugs and the leather hood and gag completed the arrangements. Pamela stood quietly, helpless in her chains and unable to see, speak or hear.

after lifting her captive's skirt, Margaret snapped the dog lead to the chain from the cock-ring. With the usual sharp tug she led Pamela out to the waiting car.

Bruno took the case and stowed it in the boot along with Margaret's rather more extensive travelling wardrobe. From the porch Helena watched her aunt install Pamela in the rear seat, strapping her in then climbing in beside her. She watched in silent trepidation as Bruno drove them away. When the car was out of sight she turned away to begin the preparations for the party.

Helena and Ingrid spent the next days, and quite a lot of Margaret's money, on the arrangements. They arranged for a marquee to be erected, and for the caterers to deliver the food and drink, leaving the actual serving of the guests to Margaret's household staff. 'Best keep our frolic secret. If the rest of the world knew what we were doing, they would probably try to stop us,' Helena remarked.

On the evening of Margaret's return she and her foster-mother were sitting on the patio with drinks admiring the large marquee and going over last-minute details.

'I hope the weather will be fine,' Ingrid said. 'I am looking forward to the party.' Diffidently, she added, 'I know most of the things have been settled, but do you think we might put the iron frame in some prominent place with a woman locked into it as a sort of "this way to the party" sign?'

Helena smiled at her foster-mother. 'And were you thinking of being the woman selected to point the way?'

Ingrid blushed. Answer enough, Helena thought. 'Where do you want to be?'

'Inside the front door? In the hallway?' Ingrid suggested, still blushing.

'Think big, *Mutti*,' Helena advised her. 'Why not out by the gates, in case a guest needs to be shown where to go?'

'Helena!' she exclaimed. 'Stop teasing!'

'Who's teasing? I'll have a word with Bruno when he gets back. He can get one of the gardeners to help carry you down the drive and set you up at the gate. Unless you'd care to walk there yourself and have them lock you in after everything is ready.'

Ingrid was horrified.

'But what would you wear?' Helena asked, as if she had not noticed the effect her proposal was having on her foster-mother. 'Stockings and suspenders? High heels? The men would like that. You don't want to be too dressy. I suppose we could allow you that nice rubber hood and gag you're so fond of – if you really don't want to be recognised. But I would suggest just the gag,' she said. 'If you've got the looks, let the world know, I say.'

In her agitation Ingrid spilled her drink.

'I suppose,' Helena went on regretfully, 'we'll have to chain you – or the frame – to the gate to prevent casual passers-by from carting you off to a fate worse than death. You used to tell me about the days when you could leave your things lying about and the doors unlocked without fear of burglars. Those times are over, I'm afraid.' She paused thoughtfully while Ingrid made a strangled noise of protest. 'We *could* leave someone with you to ensure that you don't get stolen, or collect too many grubby hand prints on your bod, or get too many . . . things poked into your, er, orifices. Alas, we live in evil times.' Helena spoke as if she had gathered the sad wisdom of a lifetime.

Ingrid struggled to her feet, as if by fleeing she could escape her foster-daughter's outrageous suggestions. But her flight was aborted by the arrival of Margaret, with Pamela in tow.

Pamela wore the little black dress that Ingrid had made for her, with glossy white tights and black high-heeled shoes. The leather waist belt held her cuffed wrists before her at her waist. She wore the thumbcuffs and leg-irons and the tight leather helmet she found so exciting. Helena, seeing the familiar control box in Margaret's hand and the training collar around Pamela's neck, inferred the presence of the anal dildo and the branch circuit to the cock-ring. The homeward journey must have been interesting for Pamela.

'Did you have a nice journey, Aunt Margaret?' Helena asked innocently. '*Mutti* and I were just discussing what she should wear to the party.' To Ingrid she said, 'Would you like to tell Aunt Margaret about your idea, *Mutti*? I'm sure she will approve.'

Ingrid remained scarlet and silent, clutching the empty glass nervously.

'Cat got your tongue, Ingrid?' Margaret asked.

Ingrid remaining silent, Helena took up the explanation. At the end she asked Margaret with a straight face what she thought about *Mutti's* idea. It sounds good to me,' she said supportively. 'Simple and elegant.'

Ingrid spluttered incoherently, 'She . . . she . . . I never said . . . anything like that!'

'But you did, *Mutti*.' Helena spoke earnestly and innocently. 'Don't you remember saying you'd like to wear that nice rubber helmet and gag that you enjoyed so much when you visited us? Go on, tell Aunt Margaret,' she urged.

Margaret looked quizzically at her half-sister. 'What made you into an overnight bondage fanatic and exhibitionist, Ingrid?'

'Bad influences,' Helena said at once. 'She was like a wild woman at our house. And after you left her locked into the frame in her flat – you remember, you left her by the window so that everyone could see her – well, she's been talking about that for hours.'

At last Ingrid spoke. 'Margaret, I swear that Helena is making it all up! Tell her, Helena. Tell her it was all your idea. I could never do anything like that.' When Helena remained silent, she burst out, 'You know I couldn't! Tell her!' Ingrid said desperately, casting about for an escape from her tormentors.

'But you suggested the iron frame, *Mutti*. You know you did.'

'Yes,' she admitted grudgingly, 'but I never said anything about being left naked by the gate! That was your own invention!'

'We weren't going to leave you *naked*, *Mutti*,' Helena said reprovingly. 'We had decided on stockings and suspenders. And the rubber hood if you want it.'

'No!' Ingrid shouted. 'It's all your invention!'

'Perhaps I misunderstood, then,' Helena conceded, looking disappointed. 'But maybe Aunt Margaret should decide. After all, it's her party.'

Margaret looked steadily at her half-sister, as if weighing up the merits of the suggestions. With a faint smile she said, 'That might work. It's certainly an original idea.'

Ingrid looked desperate once more.

Margaret smiled at last, letting her off the hook. 'Stop teasing your mother, Helena. I think instead that it should be you at the gate. I have not forgotten the liberties you took with me a few days ago.'

If the idea dismayed Helena, she gave no sign. Clearly the gate was not the place for her or anyone, but she wouldn't mind being on display somewhere, preferably near a whip. To Margaret she said mock-deferentially, 'I'm sure that you will find something suitable for us all. But how was the trip for you and . . . Pamela?' she asked again.

'Good enough on the business side. Hannelore Bern and I concluded several deals. Some of the profits will pay for the party, in fact. But Pamela disgraced herself. Didn't you, Pamela?' She stabbed the control button sharply.

Pamela grunted, staggering.

Margaret continued, 'I shall have to devote some more time to instilling self-control – toilet training in particular. Won't I, Pamela?' She pushed the control button once again.

Pamela grunted again, her knees buckling.

'Oh? Do tell us about it, Aunt Margaret,' Helena said eagerly.

Pamela, on her knees, unable to rise, might or might not have been blushing beneath the leather hood. She shifted her weight minutely, the chain between her leg-irons clinking softly. A dark stain spread down the glossy white tights that sheathed her legs.

'You see?' Margaret gestured disgustedly. Handing the control box and lead to Helena, she said, 'Take Pamela upstairs and get her cleaned up. I will need her tonight. You can ask her yourself about her experiences.' She turned away and ascended the stairs.

Ingrid, now calmer, and Helena, still grinning after the exchange, helped Pamela to her feet and led her up the stairs to the bedroom they had been using. There they removed her hood and gag.

Helena indicated she was to sit in the armchair. 'The truth now, Pamela,' she said in a fair imitation of Margaret's sergeant-major voice. 'You will tell us all about the trip . . . or else.' Helena brandished the control box.

Pamela looked at her two warders with a queer expression. 'I don't mind telling you about it, but just who is telling the story – Richard or Pamela?

'I believe Pamela knows the story best. Let her tell it,' Helena said.

Pamela nodded. 'You saw how I left here,' she said. 'That was interesting, but the real adventure only began the next day.'

'So tell us about that,' Helena commanded.

Pamela began. Margaret, she said, announced the next morning that Pamela needed some exercise. 'You have been spending entirely too much time indoors.'

Pamela forbore to ask whose fault that was, waiting for Margaret to remove her handcuffs and leg-irons. Finally freed of her restraints, she took a shower and put her soiled clothes in the hotel laundry bag. Back in the bedroom, naked save for the cock-ring and chain, she laid out a fresh outfit and was about to dress herself when Margaret interrupted her.

With a minor flourish Margaret produced the leather dog collar with its battery box and trailing electrical leads. Pamela suspected (correctly, it turned out) that it had been modified since Helena had worn it. It was now *her* turn to learn of its effects at first hand.

Margaret buckled the collar around Pamela's neck and locked the buckle behind her head with a small padlock. A short length of chain dangled from the collar, reaching down to the region where it could be joined to the cock-ring. Margaret threaded the chain through the ring on the anal dildo and motioned for Pamela to bend over. Margaret lubricated the dildo with jelly. 'Electrical conducting jelly,' she explained encouragingly.

The dildo went into Pamela's back passage, leaving her feeling very full indeed, and Margaret pulled the chain tight between her legs and arse-cheeks. She joined the chain to the cock-ring with another padlock. The dildo was now held in place until Margaret decided to remove it. Being unable to rid herself of the means of torture and subjugation excited Pamela.

The wires were connected to the dildo and the cock-ring. Pamela shivered as she imagined the effect of the electric current on the affected areas. She felt her stomach tighten as she contemplated this newest form of sexual coercion to which she would soon be subjected.

Signs of interest became apparent shortly, to Margaret's amusement and to Pamela's chagrin and frustration. This ceremony was not going to end in bed, she knew.

Margaret guessed what she was thinking. 'Think of it merely as a special dog lead,' Margaret advised, apropos of the obvious signs of interest. 'A means of controlling people in public where a normal lead might arouse unwanted interest. Nothing to get all excited and erect and expectant about – unless you have a deep fondness for being walked.'

The box containing the battery and the stinging circuits pressed against the back of Pamela's neck. Margaret said that the wig and a high-necked blouse would conceal it from public view. 'And you could always wear a scarf.'

The tug of the chain and the full feeling from her arsehole reminded her of what could be done to her at any time. The opaque black tights came first, then the tight black panty-corselet. Margaret helped Pamela pull it into place, making sure that the leading chain from the cock-ring emerged through the hole in the gusset and dangled between Pamela's thighs. Next she ensured that the wires led clear from Pamela's crotch up to her neck. False breasts, slip and dark blue pinstripe dress came next. Pamela was beginning to look like any of thousands of career-women going to the office. No one could guess what her clothes concealed.

Margaret helped with the make-up and the wig. Finally it was time to slip into the black high-heeled shoes. The transformation was complete, and Pamela was ready to be walked by her mistress.

She laid down the ground rules. 'A light touch means to return to me. Heel, in other words. Two means you should hurry, lest I become impatient.' She showed Pamela the control box. 'I will have this at all times. Be sure you are always available and alert for my signals.'

'Where are we going?' Pamela wanted to know.

'That doesn't concern you,' Margaret replied. 'But since you've asked, I can tell you that we will be going wherever I wish to go, and staying as long as I wish. Happy now?'

She wasn't, but knew that further questions would elicit no more information, and would likely anger Margaret. She was in no position to provoke her mistress. It was a familiar situation. If she had harboured any doubts about Margaret losing her dominatrix's touch as a result of the agreement with Richard and Helena and Ingrid, she could forget them now. It was at once a relief and a thrill.

'In case you are wondering what it feels like,' Margaret broke in, 'I will now conduct a test. Please report the results to me.' Margaret pressed the button sharply.

Pamela felt a surge of electricity inside her anus and through the cock-ring. She gasped in pained surprise.

Margaret said, 'I will take that as message received, but do try to be less demonstrative in public. You will attract attention to yourself.' Margaret pressed the button twice more, causing Pamela to jerk spasmodically and to clutch at the affected areas.

'I told you not to be so obvious,' Margaret scolded her. 'What will the man in the street think if the woman across the street suddenly clutches herself intimately?'

'It's not every woman who has such good cause to clutch herself,' Pamela gasped.

'It's not every woman who is so lucky,' Margaret countered. 'Not every woman has such a watchful guardian.' This time she held the button down for what seemed to Pamela to be an eternity.

She emptied her lungs in a single explosive gasp of pain and surprise. Her knees buckled as the electricity surged through her body. Pamela sank to the floor, jerking spasmodically and rolling from side to side.

Just before Pamela lost consciousness, Margaret released the button. She watched in a detached manner as Pamela drew deep shuddery breaths, her muscles relaxing slowly.

Pamela groaned and reached reflexively for her crotch and anus. A quick stab of electricity stilled her hands.

'That's better,' Margaret said approvingly. 'With a bit of practice you'll be able to mask your reactions perfectly. You are aiming for a ladylike wince while your face betrays no sign of distress to your interlocutor.' She continued to watch as Pamela struggled to her knees.

'Some weaker persons have been known to soil themselves. Even the strong can be taken unaware. You would not like to be seen with urine – or something even nastier – running down your tights, would you? I can do that to you,' Margaret said threateningly.

'I have already let you do all this to me.' Pamela's gesture took in her clothes, the collar, the room that was her prison, the recently-removed shackles. 'What more do you want from me?' Even as she spoke she felt a thrill at the idea of such public humiliation as Margaret had described.

'An interesting question. I will leave the answer for you to work out. Tell me when you do. In the meantime you can take all this –' and her gesture encompassed everything that Pamela's had done '– as my way of reminding you that the liberties you took with me have not been forgotten. You said that you wanted me to continue as your tame dominatrix. Well, that is what I am doing. How do you like it?'

Pamela got unsteadily to her feet without answering. She put a scarf around her neck to conceal the collar. Margaret took that as a token of her continued obedience. Stowing the control box in her handbag, she led the way to the lifts. Pamela followed silently.

No one paid them any attention in the lift, or in the lobby, or out in the street. Pamela felt naked. Everyone, she felt, knew her secrets. She felt like cowering from the gaze of the passers-by. Margaret betrayed no sign of disquiet, and the rest of the world followed her example. The sun shone alike on the slave and her mistress and the general public.

Their first stop was a small bookshop which bore the discreet title, *Erotische Buchandlung*. There Margaret selected several books dealing with bondage and transvestism, dominance and humiliation, sadism and masochism.

'One should always be on the lookout for ways to further one's education,' she murmured to Pamela as she gave her the books to take to the till.

Pamela endured the knowing glance of the cashier as he added up the total. He placed the books in a plain black carrier bag, which Pamela was made to carry. It, too, made her feel naked under the gaze of the people in the street.

The next stop was several streets away, a dress-maker's establishment not unlike Ingrid's. The proprie-tress spoke deferentially to Margaret – who was obviously a regular customer – in rapid German. Pamela had trouble following the conversation. Exactly what Margaret was buying was not clear to her. Her vocabulary did not include the familiar words for female undergarments and lingerie. She caught only *die Strum-pfbände* – stockings. She did, however, understand when Margaret told the lady behind the counter that she was buying all this for her assistant, nodding at Pamela – who blushed fiery red.

She never saw what had been ordered. Margaret had evidently given the order some time ago, and was now merely confirming the details as she accepted and paid for the contents of the gaily coloured boxes that went into the carrier bags emblazoned with the boutique's name and logo. Pamela attempted to slip the black bag from the bookshop into one of the carrier bags, but Margaret, who understood the minutest details of her humiliation and embarrassment, shook her head minutely.

Margaret next decreed a coffee break, as if exhausted by the effort of shopping. She chose the sidewalk terrace of a small restaurant and ordered coffee and croissants for both of them without consulting Pamela. She lingered over the repast, and Pamela wondered why. Normally Margaret adhered to the not-a-minute-wasted principle.

A chauffeured Mercedes drew silently up to the kerb.

Ah, thought Pamela, mystery solved. Obviously Margaret had ordered Bruno to collect them. She was relieved that they would be driven back to the hotel in privacy. She had a long way to go before she would be as nonchalant as Margaret about public bizarrerie, however well concealed.

Margaret stood up and led the way to the car, leaving Bruno to settle the bill at the restaurant. He returned and they drove off. But not back to the hotel. They passed through the financial district, past Hannelore Bern's bank, and then out of the city along a familiar route.

Pamela's stomach plummeted as the metaphorical penny dropped. She was being taken back to the woman she had escaped from. Margaret, it appeared, had reneged on her promise to stop interfering in their lives, and was about to 'give' Pamela to Hannelore Bern once again.

Margaret reached into her handbag and withdrew the control box, her finger poised warningly over the button. Pamela's protest died in her throat. She watched Margaret as a bird watches a snake, her heart thudding in mingled fear and anticipation of the *rencontre* with the banker/dominatrix. All of her own ambivalence rose up to choke off coherent thought.

Satisfied that Pamela would try nothing rash for the moment, Margaret laid the control box in her lap and rummaged once more in her handbag. This time she produced a pair of handcuffs, which she tossed into Pamela's lap.

'If you please,' she said with a smile.

Pamela hesitated. Margaret reached for the control box.

'Do it,' she said warningly. When Pamela still hesitated, Margaret gave her a short shock that caused her to gasp and jerk erect, spilling the handcuffs to the floor.

'Pick them up and put them on,' Margaret commanded. 'Now.'

Pamela picked up the handcuffs and locked one around her left wrist. She looked at Margaret before taking the next, irrevocable step.

'Go on,' Margaret said. 'Hands behind your back, of course.'

Pamela brought her arms behind her and locked her wrists together with the handcuffs. Margaret smiled briefly and replaced the control box in her handbag.

Unable to lean back because of the handcuffs, Pamela perched on the edge of the seat, leaning against the side of the car to keep herself from falling over on the turns. Like Margaret, she was silent, but, unlike her mistress, far from calm. There was no way to predict what Hannelore Bern might do, but it was certain to be unpleasant. Borrow a leaf from Helena's book, she told herself. Transform the pain into sexual pleasure. The pain was almost certain to be sexually oriented so she was fairly confident of her ability to cope. Let it be the whip, she prayed silently to whatever gods were currently not listening on her wavelength.

Margaret grew a small smile, which she directed at Pamela from time to time. 'Don't worry,' she said at one point. 'I will not let Hannelore do anything permanent to you.'

'Nor keep me on a permanent basis?' Pamela enquired anxiously, striving to appear calmer than she felt.

Margaret detected her anxiety at once, and did nothing to allay it. 'I haven't decided,' she said. 'You *have* been rather a lot of trouble lately. I have been invited for tea and a short business discussion. Afterwards, Hannelore would like to have a few words with you. We will have to see what happens then.'

Pamela knew she would not get anything more definite from Margaret while she was in her tormentress mood. She passed the rest of the journey in silent anxiety.

Presently Bruno drew up before the familiar house. He opened the door for his passengers. 'I will call you on the mobile phone when I wish to be picked up,' Margaret told him. He nodded, watching impassively as they climbed the steps. Margaret knocked on the door, but nothing happened for long moments. That did not improve her mood. She began to tap her foot impatiently.

Finally a maid opened the door. Like those in Margaret's house, she wore the uniform: short black dress, apron, black tights and high heels. Unlike Margaret's staff, she did not wear leg-irons routinely around the house. But Pamela, her powers of observation sharpened by the proximity of danger, saw that this was not because Hannelore Bern trusted her servants more than her German counterpart did. She noticed a leather collar around the maid's neck, almost hidden by the high neck of her dress.

Pamela guessed that it was an electric torture device similar to the one she wore. She felt a thrill of excitement as she imagined where the maid's dildoes might be lodged.

Margaret swept into the hall. 'Where is Frau Bern?' she demanded.

The maid dropped her a curtsey and pointed to the double doors on the left side of the entrance hall. Margaret nodded curtly and signalled Pamela to follow her.

Without stopping to knock Margaret opened one of the doors and stepped into the room. Pamela caught a glimpse of Hannelore Bern, seated languidly in an armchair, her long legs crossed. What happened next was not very clear. Pamela, still out in the hall, had an impression of quick movement off to one side as the door slammed in her face.

Handcuffed, she stood outside the door listening to the noises from the sitting room. She heard an irregular series of thumps, and Margaret's voice raised in anger. 'What are you doing? Take your hands off . . .!' Her protests were cut off abruptly. From the strident but muffled grunts that followed, Pamela inferred the application of a gag. Nothing else, she knew, would silence Margaret so effectively when she was working herself into a state of righteous indignation.

Her first instinct was to flee. But there was no place to go. She was in the citadel of her putative enemy. Her hands were cuffed behind her back, putting her at a further disadvantage. Her mistress, to whom she looked for protection, was presumably now a prisoner in that same citadel, and Pamela guessed that it would not take Hannelore long to discover the control box in Margaret's handbag – nor to work out how to use it.

Nor did it. The muffled thumps and grunts continued as Margaret protested her treatment at whatever hands were meting it out. But as Pamela hesitated, Hannelore found the box, and pressed the button. Pamela shrieked in surprise, her knees buckling as the electricity coursed through her body. She fell to her knees. However, her scream must have startled Hannelore, for the burning in her anus and around her scrotum stopped abruptly, leaving her breathless and weak.

The door opened and Pamela faced her erstwhile mistress. Hannelore smiled unpleasantly when she saw Pamela on her knees. 'Welcome back,' she said ironically. 'Do come in.'

Pamela began to struggle to her feet, but Hannelore pushed her back down. 'Enter my presence on your knees,' she ordered.

It sounded like a line from a bad movie, but it was meant seriously. Hannelore showed the control box to Pamela. 'I am in charge now,' she said. She watched with satisfaction as Pamela shuffled into the sitting room on her knees.

To one side, Margaret, handcuffed and gagged, was being stripped naked. Slowly, because she still struggled. Hannelore's servants had got her skirt and high heels off, rendering themselves less prone to painful kicks from their furious prisoner. She still lashed out with her stockinged feet, but much less effectively. Her mood was not improved by the sight of Pamela on her knees before their captor. She glared at them both.

Hannelore left Pamela in her attitude of submission and strode across to confront Margaret. She picked up a whip en route, motioning to her two servants to stand aside. It was a long thin whip with a wooden handle that would be very painful to the victim. If wielded by a determined and experienced user (and Hannelore was both), it might well break the skin and draw blood.

Pamela doubted if Margaret had felt the whip since her first visit to Bacton. She hadn't liked the experience much then, and was even less likely to relish it now, at the hands of her rival and in full view of her kneeling slave.

Hannelore lashed Margaret across the stomach and upper thighs, the lash making a dull sound as it struck her slip. Margaret grunted at each blow, but the main effect was to infuriate her further. Her face reddened as she tried to expel the gag to remonstrate with her tormentress. Had her hands been free, the remonstrance would have been more physical than verbal.

Hannelore struck Margaret several more times over her clothing without producing the desired effect. She shifted her aim, curling the thong around Margaret's knees. She jerked the whip, pulling her victim's legs out from under her and sending her crashing to the thickly carpeted floor with a thump.

Winded and momentarily stunned, Margaret lay in an untidy heap, giving Hannelore's slaves the opportunity to subdue her more thoroughly. Hannelore herself sat astride her fallen rival while exhorting her slaves to bring something with which to hobble Margaret. As it happened, there was rope at hand. Pamela would have been surprised if there had not been. Very quickly the slaves stilled Margaret's kicking legs and tied a loop around each of her ankles, leaving little slack between them.

Hobbled, the leopardess was now unable to use her feet to any effect. The slaves, at Hannelore's bidding, lifted Margaret to her feet, where she stood glaring helplessly at her captors.

Pointing to Pamela, Hannelore ordered her minions to hobble her as well. They did so swiftly and efficiently.

With both her captives effectively immobilised, Hannelore returned to the highly congenial – to her – task of stripping Margaret. She called for a pair of shears, with which she set about cutting off the rest of her captive's clothing. It was a practical, if destructive, method of separating her from her clothes without having to separate her hands and feet.

The jacket took some time, as it was made of fairly substantial material and had to be cut down the back from collar to waist, and then up along each sleeve to free it from Margaret's arms. The blouse, thinner, took less time. Margaret fought these indignities, but could not prevent them.

Standing before her captors in nothing but her underwear, her long hair straggling over her face, Margaret was still unbowed. Her shoulders shook with the intensity of her rage.

Hannelore handed the shears to one of her slaves and stood back the better to appreciate the disrobing of her rival. The slip was easy. The slaves cut the shoulder straps and allowed the silken garment to slither to the floor, where it lay around her ankles like a second set of hobbles. Her matching bra, pants and suspenders were a light powder blue today, sheer and silky and expensive. Shiny blue opaque stockings emphasised the firmness of her long rounded legs. From across the floor Pamela admired them on her knees.

Seeing Margaret and Hannelore together, Pamela found it impossible not to compare them. Both were undeniably beautiful, mature women with full breasts and long full legs, not at all like the stick-insect figures that dominated the fashion catwalks. Both were dangerous, which made them – to Pamela – more beautiful. Both had long blonde manes falling below their shoulders, more hair than most women would bother with, Hannelore's slightly longer than Margaret's. Hannelore was also slightly taller.

If she had to make a choice, though, it would have to be Margaret. Better the devil you know best, she thought. And Margaret had promised to treat Richard and Ingrid and Helena – though not Pamela, she hoped – differently in the future. Hannelore was unlikely to make any such promises.

Pamela's favourite dominatrix stood at bay before her captors, looking wildly beautiful in her déshabillé and helplessness. Though still technically clothed, she looked more erotic in her sheer underwear than if she were completely nude. The bra cupped her full breasts and thrust them upwards invitingly, her nipples clearly visible through the tight sheer cups, slightly flattened by the silky material.

The effect of this spectacle underlined the double view of Pamela and Richard. He saw a beautiful woman in her underwear, inviting in her helplessness, stirring his cock and tightening his stomach with desire. Pamela saw the same woman helpless like herself, inviting her to identify with her, become like her.

Hannelore picked up the whip once more. It struck Margaret's barely protected body with the sharp crack of leather on flesh. Angry red lines appeared on the fine skin as Hannelore lashed her captive in earnest, the whip rising and falling all over Margaret's body.

Hannelore lashed Margaret's breasts, causing them to bob up and down under the force of the blows. Margaret grunted in pain, the sound muffled by her gag. The red marks, seen through the sheer material, looked more erotic than those on her bare skin, Pamela/Richard thought. The dildo in her anus, and the ring around her scrotum, sent powerful messages to Pamela's belly and crotch as she watched the whipping of her mistress.

Margaret stood erect and proud beneath the rain of blows. Although it was obvious that she was in pain, she did not shrink from her tormentress. The result was a comprehensive whipping, with Hannelore paying particular attention to Margaret's breasts, offered up by the sheer bra. As the lash struck her sensitive nipples, she strove to look impassive.

Not altogether successfully. Pamela, watching on her knees from across the room, saw the flush that heralded Margaret's arousal creeping into her face and down her neck. Because of the red whip-marks, Pamela could not tell if the flush had spread as far down as her tormented

213

breasts, but she saw that they rose and fell agitatedly with her ragged breathing.

Hannelore noticed her victim's agitation as well, and interpreted the signs correctly. 'Look,' she cried delightedly, 'she is getting excited.'

Margaret looked daggers at her tormentress, but there was no denying the accuracy of her diagnosis. Nor any way to escape what came next.

Hannelore dropped the whip and advanced to cup Margaret's breasts. Margaret retreated, moving carefully because of the hobbles. Hannelore cornered her victim against the sofa and squeezed both of her breasts.

Margaret tried to tear away by twisting her shoulders, but Hannelore hung on. With her fingers she teased the swollen, reddened nipples. A sound halfway between a groan and a sob emerged from behind the gag. Margaret's face was now fiery with humiliation and the arousal she could no longer conceal or resist.

Neither could Hannelore conceal her glee at having penetrated her rival's defences. She kneaded Margaret's taut nipples between thumbs and forefingers, studying her captive's face to gauge her response.

Pamela saw the unmistakable shudder as Margaret came. She heard her moan of pleasure, even muffled by the gag. Hannelore no doubt felt the shudder as well at the moment of Margaret's climax. She continued to torment her captive, driving her to yet another orgasm when she suddenly leaned closer to bite an engorged nipple through the sheer fabric of the bra. Margaret groaned deep in her throat, her shoulders shaking and her hips thrusting as if to welcome a cock that was not there.

Pamela would gladly have supplied the cock, the instrument in question swelling, pressing against her belly and the tight corselet. She squirmed excitedly causing the erect cock to slide against the slick nylon of her tights. Unnoticed by Margaret and Hannelore, she began to work herself towards one of those messy accidents which her mistress deplored. Hannelore would probably disapprove as well. Defying two dominatrices with one orgasm, she thought, that idea exciting her still more.

Margaret's mingled pleasure and distress as she was made to come by her rival and in the presence of her kneeling slave only increased Pamela's excitement. She watched avidly as the drama unfolded before her.

Hannelore slid a hand under the waistband of Margaret's pants, stroking her mons veneris and slipping a finger into her cunt. Margaret, touched intimately, groaned helplessly. Hannelore withdrew her finger and sniffed it daintily. With a broad smile she held it under Margaret's nose. Margaret twisted her head away, unwilling to smell the evidence of her arousal. Hannelore released Margaret's nipple and twined her hand in Margaret's long hair, forcing her to hold her head still while the finger was thrust once more under her nose. Margaret's face reddened as she smelled herself. For good measure, Hannelore once again sniffed her own finger, nodding in satisfaction.

She stepped away from Margaret and retrieved the whip. Eyeing Margaret's crotch, she took aim. Margaret, divining her intent, clamped her thighs tightly together, shaking her head wildly and making protesting noises through her gag.

'Open your legs, Margaret,' Hannelore commanded.

Margaret bit down simultaneously on her gag and her determination. She shook her head once more. She glanced across the room and saw Pamela watching her. She also noticed the signs of her arousal, and the small movements that betrayed her goal. Margaret glared at her.

Pamela guessed that she would be whipped later for her temerity, but she was past caring. Silently, she too willed Margaret to spread her legs and expose her cunt to

215

the whip. She shivered at the memory of the pussy-whip on her own body, between her legs. She shivered at the memory of the electric torture. She shivered as she felt the dildo inside her and the ring around her scrotum. But mostly she shivered with excitement at the prospect of Margaret being whipped on her cunt, and the orgasm they would both enjoy if only the damned woman would relax and enjoy what couldn't be avoided.

Margaret, being Margaret, of course, could not relax. Relaxation meant submission, a lesson she had not yet learned well enough. Pamela sometimes despaired of her mistress. It isn't that hard, she screamed silently across the room. Just look at me. Do what I do.

Margaret kept her legs closed. There was no convenient way just then for Hannelore to get her to spread them. The hobbles did not help either. Hannelore returned to the attack on Margaret's breasts, lashing them from all angles, making the full globes bounce, drawing lines of fire across her swollen nipples.

Under the fresh onslaught Margaret moaned again. She came suddenly, her knees half buckling and her hips thrusting. Red of face, she gasped for air as another orgasm swept over and through her. She struggled to stay erect, bracing herself against the wall behind her with her manacled hands. They slid on the smooth wallpaper, forcing Margaret to spread her legs to keep from falling.

Quick as a striking snake Hannelore swung the whip up between Margaret's parted thighs, a sharp crack signalling the impact on her cunt.

Margaret jerked erect with a strangled cry. Hannelore struck her again before she could recover her balance and her closed-leg stance. The second blow to her exposed cunt undid her. She lost control, her hips pumping madly and her breasts rising and falling with her efforts to breathe. Her legs parted even further as the wave of mingled pain and ecstasy swamped her wil to resist. Hannelore struck her repeatedly, drawing loud moans from her captive as she came repeatedly.

When Hannelore shifted her attention back to Margaret's breasts, she shook her head wildly and moaned, thrusting her hips forward and bending her knees in an attempt to open her legs still further. Hannelore needed no second invitation. She swung the whip up between Margaret's straining thighs again and again. Margaret moaned as each blow struck her exposed cunt.

Pamela, seeing her surrender and hearing her cries of ecstasy, redoubled her own efforts, pumping with her hips and causing her turgid cock to slide against the smooth material that confined it. And she came too, her own cries of pleasure rivalling Margaret's. The warm semen spurted inside the tight corselet, spreading on her belly and down her thighs, staining her tights and even soaking through her skirt. Through it all Pamela kept her gaze on Margaret's shuddering body, her own pleasure augmented by that of her mistress.

Hannelore tore her eyes away from Margaret's surrender long enough to see the cause of the noises from behind her. She smiled broadly, congratulating herself for having brought them both to orgasm without allowing them to touch one another.

Pamela, shuddering in the aftermath of her orgasm, sank back on her heels, the slave in the presence of her mistress. But a very satisfied slave.

Margaret allowed herself to slide down the wall, coming to rest on the floor with her legs straight out in front of her. Her hair was wildly dishevelled, loose upon her shoulders, half covering one side of her face. Her sheer bra and pants were darkened with sweat, and there were dark patches on her stockings. Having lost all dignity and control seemed unimportant to her just then. No doubt she would recover dignity and hauteur soon enough, but now she slumped uncaring before her rival and in the presence of her kneeling slave.

Pamela rested as best she could, kneeling still with her bottom resting on her heels. Like Margaret, she was recovering from the recent storm.

As Margaret began to take an interest in her surroundings once again, she looked up and saw Hannelore's smile of triumph. Looked quickly away. Caught sight of Pamela. Glared at her. She flushed and tried to rise. The handcuffs and hobbles prevented her.

Hannelore, seeing her struggles, suggested that she might better achieve a kneeling position. Like Pamela, for example.

Margaret glared at her too.

Catching Margaret's eye, Pamela gave her a long look which, she hoped, would reassure her beleaguered mistress of her continued devotion.

Margaret nodded minutely in response.

Hannelore noticed the attempts at communication. She evidently disapproved. She picked up Pamela's control box and held the button down.

Pamela was totally unprepared for this fresh assault on her body. She felt as if her arms and legs and torso were on fire. She sank to the floor, where she lay jerking and rolling and catching her breath.

She awoke alone. No Hannelore; no Margaret; no other slaves. Pamela felt as if she had been abandoned in the house of her enemy. Where was Margaret? Hobbled and handcuffed still, she lay on her side as she had fallen, taking stock of her aching body. She would have liked to rub the affected parts. Or better, to have someone else rub them.

In her convulsions she had kicked one high-heeled shoe across the room. She could see it lying under a chair. The damp patch of semen in her crotch had cooled, become sticky. The smell of it brought back the image of Margaret's helplessness, and of her own orgasm as she had watched her mistress come. Mutual orgasm, she thought. Most satisfying, even when the two persons were separated by half the room. Perhaps that was why Hannelore had punished her with the electric shock. Had Margaret been in control, she might very well have done the same thing. The two were alike in many ways.

Pamela lay quietly. There was nothing else to do. Sooner or later someone would come for her. She did not think she would like what would happen then.

It was later, rather than sooner, that she heard the door open. Footsteps approached across the carpet. Hannelore, looking fresh and rested, looked down at her.

'We need to have a talk,' she said. 'Alone. Do you think you can get back on your knees?'

Pamela struggled to rise. In the end Hannelore helped her into the kneeling position.

'Better,' she declared. 'It makes it easier to see one another's faces, and establishes a pecking order.'

'Where is Margaret?' Pamela demanded. 'What have you done to her?'

'Nothing more serious than what you have already seen. I thought she needed further subduing, so there was a bit more of the whip, and a bit of what you English call so quaintly "the other". She seemed to enjoy that, at least in the end, when she couldn't help herself. She can be so stubborn.'

'Unlike you?'

'You are not in a good position to provoke me.'

'What are you doing to her?' Pamela asked again.

'Why are you so concerned about Margaret Wagner? She gave you to me, so she can't think that much of you. She brought you here today intending to let me torture you. You don't owe her anything.' Hannelore paused, struck by a new thought. 'Perhaps you are in love with her. Many slaves fall in love with their mistresses. Has she let you screw her yet? Is that it?' she asked contemptuously, 'Yes. I can see that it is.' The thought did not please her.

Pamela braced herself for another shock.

Hannelore spoke again. 'You are nothing to her. That's why she sent you to me in the first place.'

'Things have . . . changed . . . since then,' Pamela said.

'Things never change with Margaret Wagner.'

Pamela did not reply. 'Why did you want to talk to me?' she asked instead.

'I think you know why.'

'I can think of two reasons,' Pamela said. 'Either you want me to leave Margaret and stay here, or you want me to give you the video tape I made when I left here. Perhaps both.'

'Don't flatter yourself,' Hannelore replied, too quickly. 'I have many more like you, men and women, who will do anything I ask, even if I ask them to put on the clothes and manners of the opposite sex. And some of them are rather better at it than you. What makes you think I want you?'

'I am the only one I know who has successfully defied you. And that piqued your interest. Revenge cannot be discounted either.'

'And you are once again in my power.' She brandished the control box. 'I can do anything I want with you.'

Pamela nodded.

'Well, are you gong to give me the video tape?'

'No.'

'Then we will have to persuade you, won't we?' Hannelore said. 'What do you think I should do first? The whip? Do you have any preferences?'

'As you said, you can do what you like. I can't stop you, but you won't change my mind.' Pamela spoke with a certainty based on experience. She had been shocked. She probably would be again. But there was only so much agony she could endure before she passed out. The whip Hannelore had used on Margaret lay nearby, but that would bring as much pleasure as pain. She knew that Hannelore would not commit murder, so she knew that she had already suffered the worst that could be done to her.

'Why are you being so stubborn?'

'Because I can't trust you to let us go again once you have what you want. And in any case, I couldn't give you the tape even if I wanted to. It's safe back in England.'

'I can make you tell me where it is.'

'I don't think so.'

Hannelore's patience ran out. She pushed the button, sending the current surging once more through Pamela's body.

Pamela jerked and twisted, sinking to the floor once again. She fought her handcuffs. Her hobbled legs kicked out wildly, sending her other shoe flying to join the first. And the torture went on. In her shame and submission Pamela wet herself, the warm stream soaking into her tights and corselet and dress and running to the floor. She felt the contents of her bowels trying to force their way past the stabbing plug in her anus.

The sensation ended as abruptly as it had begun, leaving Pamela still conscious but shaken. Her wet clothing clung to her body, and she thought inanely that it would serve Hannelore right if her carpet was stained.

'The tape,' Hannelore demanded.

Pamela shook her head weakly. 'No.'

The shock struck again, and Pamela jerked and writhed and twisted at the feet of her tormentress.

She had no idea how many times Hannelore repeated the process. It could have been dozens of times. Each time Hannelore repeated her demand, and each time met the same refusal, until Pamela was too weak to respond. Only then did Hannelore stop, leaving Pamela alone again in a wet, smelly heap on the floor.

Another eternity of dazed semi-consciousness passed before she heard footsteps again. She braced herself for a resumption of the torture. When it didn't come, she raised her head cautiously. Two pairs of feet stood nearby. One pair in high heels, the other in stockinged feet, wearing rope hobbles. Hannelore and Margaret, of course. Pamela rolled on to her side and looked up at the women.

'While you were resting, I had another idea. Since you seem immune to pain, I thought I would see how you react to pain inflicted on her.' Hannelore gestured in Margaret's direction.

Pamela's glance shifted to look at her mistress. Margaret still wore her sheer pants and bra and stockings. She also wore a nearly complete set of stripes, criss-crossing her body from ankles to shoulders. Pamela guessed that her rear elevation was similarly marked. Her wrists were still handcuffed behind her back. She wore her gag now with a weary resignation.

'We have been working hard on your precious mistress while you were resting,' Hannelore informed Pamela. 'She enjoyed some of it, and some of it was . . . not so enjoyable. No doubt she will tell you all about when you two are tucked up in bed.' She made a face. 'But for now, I will give you the outline, since she is so reticent.

'As you can see, she is now wired up very much as you are. Come closer, Margaret. Let Pamela admire your new things.'

As she spoke Hannelore jerked her captive nearer by a short leather strap fastened to a collar which, Pamela saw, matched her own. Margaret was about to feel what she had felt earlier. A stab of sympathy shot through her as she imagined the imperious woman suffering the same agony.

Margaret showed no sign of fear. Part of her public image, Pamela knew, like her resistance to sexual arousal and her denial of her body's needs – until Hannelore had broken through her defences and forced her to admit them. Pamela herself had never denied her sexual needs, nor seen any need to. That was why Pamela was Pamela, and Margaret, Margaret. And why, when Margaret had finally broken, the sight had aroused Pamela so strongly.

Hannelore broke in upon her reveries once more. 'I am sure Margaret would like to show you her new ornaments but, as she cannot, I invite your attention to them in her stead. Going from neck to crotch, we have the electronic dog collar which supplies the power to, er, move her so profoundly. From there, we move to her proud breasts. You will notice the lovely gold caps over her nipples, and the wires leading from the collar down to them.'

The thin wires led from Margaret's collar, down over the upper slopes of her breasts to her nipple shields. From there they led down the lower slopes of her breasts, held snugly against the flesh by the sheer cups of her bra. The wires were gathered together where they emerged, leading down her flat stomach to her crotch, where they disappeared into her pubic hair and down between her legs.

Hannelore turned Margaret around to show her from the back. Her back and bottom, her thighs and calves, all bore the red stripes of the whipping she had undergone. But, more importantly, Pamela saw the wires that emerged from between her arse-cheeks and ran up her back to her collar, completing the circuit of pain.

'Nice long thick dildoes in there,' Hannelore indicated Margaret's crotch, 'all wired to her collar for maximum effect.'

Margaret's hands twisted nervously in her handcuffs, but she gave no other sign of the anxiety she must be feeling.

Hannelore thrust Margaret to her knees, facing Pamela. She looped the strap from Margaret's collar through Pamela's and knotted it. They were left facing one another from a distance of less than a foot.

Pamela, looking steadily into Margaret's deep blue eyes, said softly, 'Don't worry. I'm with you.'

Margaret nodded minutely, acknowledging the new bond between them. And so they kneeled, touching only in spirit, helpless to avoid what was going to happen to them.

Hannelore spoke scornfully. 'I think it will be more effective to allow you to see each other's suffering since there seems to be this close bond between you. I will, er, turn you on alternately.' She smiled at the pun, but the humour was lost on her two captives. 'You can stop me at any time by giving me what I want.'

Margaret looked at Pamela and shook her head, which Pamela took to mean, don't give her what she wants. Pamela nodded her understanding.

'Margaret first,' Hannelore announced. 'Some friendly persuasion applied to her breasts and nipples will allow her to make up for your head start, Pamela.'

Margaret stiffened in anticipation. Then the current arched her back, thrusting her tormented breasts forwards and upwards as if she were offering them to her torturess.

Her gag reduced the scream to a loud grunt.

Hannelore held the button down, prolonging the torture and seeming to enjoy Margaret's shame hugely. Margaret fought the hobbles and handcuffs, panting. She twisted spasmodically, almost toppling them both as the strap between their collars came taut.

Pamela braced herself to prevent Margaret from pulling her over as she struggled. Somehow she managed to keep them both upright. Hannelore had said she was only going to shock Margaret's breasts.

How would she react when their captor sent the current through her cunt and anus? Suppose she shocked Margaret at all points simultaneously? Pamela was suddenly glad she didn't have breasts.

When at last the torture stopped all of Margaret's tense muscles relaxed. Her nostrils flared as she drew air into her starved lungs. There were tears in the corners of her eyes.

As Pamela watched in astonishment, they overflowed and ran down her cheeks, leaving wet tracks. She had never expected to see the ice maiden cry. Impulsively, moved by the obvious suffering of her hitherto stern and unbending mistress, Pamela leaned forward to kiss her eyes and cheeks.

'Touching,' Hannelore Bern sneered.

Margaret jerked back as if the kiss had burned her.

Instinct, thought Pamela. Never show emotion, which Margaret equated with weakness – especially to one's captor or before one's slave. She would have to learn differently from Richard and Ingrid and Helena. She had a long way to go, Pamela thought, smiling at Margaret despite the rebuff.

After a moment Margaret smiled tentatively back, acknowledging the bond of shared suffering. The smile was for Pamela alone. It was a brief reward, cut short by the renewed application of electricity to Pamela's body.

She cried out in her turn, her body convulsed as Margaret's had been. She was lost in the torment that stabbed through her. When it ended at last, she too slumped, leaning against Margaret.

And so their ordeal continued, Hannelore switching from one to the other. Pamela watched in fascinated exhaustion as Margaret was shocked once more. Hannelore seemed determined to break Margaret. She held the button down for a very long time, a last effort to wring from her captive what she wanted.

Margaret jerked and twisted wildly as the current surged through her body, her cunt and anus and breasts and wildly flailing legs. She toppled over, pulling Pamela with her. Margaret bucked and writhed in agony, her screams muffled by the gag but loud in the ears of her slave.

Helpless, Pamela was forced to watch the torture of her mistress. She felt Margaret's body go slack as she passed out, the wild screams dying away. She saw Margaret wet herself, the sudden flood from between her legs staining her pants and stockings and the carpet beneath her. And, although she could not see it, Pamela knew that Margaret had emptied her bowels too. Sisters (of a sort) in suffering, she thought.

When she saw that Margaret was unconscious, Hannelore mockingly asked Pamela, 'Shall I make you pass out too? Would you enjoy that?'

'You know, of course,' Pamela managed to say, 'that some people would pay good money to be treated like this?'

Hannelore looked angrily at her. She seemed about to carry out her threat but, in the end, perhaps admitting that she could not force Pamela to relinquish the video, she did not. She turned and left the room.

Pamela shifted so that she lay beside Margaret, closer physically than she had been for a long time. There was only the matter of the handcuffs and the hobbles they both wore to prevent the physical union her cock ached for. And her tight panty corselet and her tights, and Margaret's pants, and the dildo in her cunt. Pamela reluctantly settled for worming her way closely alongside, warming her mistress's body with her own. Maybe, when all this was over, the leopardess of Soltau would remember it with gratitude and a whip.

When Margaret woke, she groaned in disgust at her state, but there was nothing she could do about it. Seeing Pamela's proximity, she tried at first to move away, but then thought better of it, or of Pamela. She smiled briefly and allowed the intimacy to continue.

'I didn't give her the tape,' Pamela said.

Margaret smiled again. She said something through the gag that sounded like, 'Well done.'

They lay quietly together. When the slaves came for them, Pamela's head lay on Margaret's breasts.

The slaves removed their hobbles but not their handcuffs. One of them unfastened the strap joining their collars before helping them to their feet. Hannelore being absent, the slaves felt freer with the two captives. They introduced themselves as Traudl and Ulrike. Ulrike collected the control boxes.

Pamela saw that they too wore collars. 'How are they controlled?' she asked.

Traudl explained that there were panels with numbered buttons at strategic places around the house – rather like a modern version of the nineteenth-century bell system. Hannelore, she added, carried a smaller version when she knew beforehand which slave she wanted.

Pamela thanked her for the explanation. Margaret, characteristically, bristled.

The two young women conducted the captives towards the showers in the slave quarters in one wing of the house.

Pamela remembered the quarters from her earlier sojourn.

Margaret was experiencing them for the first time. Having slaves, and keeping them in separate quarters, was familiar enough to her. Being conducted to those quarters in handcuffs was not so familiar. She did not relish her treatment but, since Hannelore's girls had not removed her gag, she could only express her outrage by body language.

Which she did, stalking down the hall with her head high, ignoring the urine and faeces running down her stockings – and the rude comments of Hannelore's girls.

Traudl remembered Richard from his earlier 'visit', she said. She promised to tell the other girls that he was here.

Margaret, overhearing, turned back to glare at Pamela. Pamela looked back innocently, shrugging her shoulders: I can't do anything about that.

Margaret squared her shoulders and straightened her spine indignantly. Traudl pressed the button on Margaret's control box. Her hauteur vanished in an instant. She stumbled to one knee as the current surged through her. She groaned. A further leak from between her thighs ran down over her stockings.

Having established the pecking order, Traudl released the button and the two girls helped a subdued Margaret back to her feet.

Nevertheless they took no chances with her. In the shower room, with the fiendish devices removed, Ulrike selected several thick nylon tie-wraps from the supply kept there. She fastened one around each of Margaret's elbows, pulling them snug and snipping off the excess. She joined the elbows with a third tie-wrap, pulling them tightly behind her and causing Margaret's breasts to thrust out exaggeratedly. Only then did she unlock the handcuffs, replacing them with yet another tie-wrap around Margaret's wrists. She pulled them tightly together.

Pamela watched the securing of her mistress closely. She saw the red bands on Margaret's wrists where she had fought her handcuffs. Her own, she guessed, were the same. They felt raw beneath the steel bands.

Traudl and Ulrike made rude remarks about Margaret's jutting breasts, touching the gold nipple shields and pinching her skin. They were greatly amused, Margaret less so. Eventually tiring of their sport, they stripped her naked, carefully undoing the straps of the her bra and removing it intact.

'We could have cut it off,' Traudl told her. Margaret was not placated.

They removed her collar and the gold caps over her erect nipples. The girls laughed, touching and pinching them. Margaret scowled. They removed her sheer pants and drew the dildoes from her cunt and anus. Margaret shuddered as they slid out of her, then gave herself a shake, as if to say, there, that's over.

The two girls turned their attention to Pamela. Traudl unlocked her handcuffs and collar and invited her to get undressed.

'Why are you letting her go free?' Margaret asked in chagrin.

'Because we can,' Ulrike replied. 'And because we think you need a visit from Richard quite as much as you both need a shower.'

Margaret gasped and reddened, struggling briefly against the tie-wraps. Finally she watched mesmerised as Pamela shed her clothes and Richard emerged like a moth from the cocoon. She looked at his erection. 'No, Pamela,' she said, as much plea as command.

'It looks like Richard to me,' Ulrike said. 'I wish we were not wearing these damned chastity belts.'

Pamela was gone. Richard looked at Margaret. She reddened and stepped backwards until she came up against the wall. Her eyes were rivetted on his cock, which pointed challengingly at her. She shook her head again.

She reddened further when he moved towards her. 'Let's have a shower,' he said. 'We can negotiate the terms of entry later.'

He turned on the water and began to wash Margaret thoroughly. She looked at him, her eyes huge with appeal. He jerked his head towards the two watching girls. 'Later,' he mouthed.

When they were both clean, he shut off the water and dried Margaret. The girls led them to a room.

229

'Frau Bern has assigned this room to you,' Ulrike said. To Margaret she said, 'You are lucky she did not order you put in solitary confinement.' She indicated Richard's erection with a grin. 'I hope you enjoy your stay with us.'

The door closed with a loud click from the lock. There was no handle or keyhole on the inside.

'Well,' he said to Margaret, 'at last we're alone. Are you ready to tell me what this is all about? Did you expect Hannelore to take you prisoner too?'

Pointing over her shoulder with her chin, Margaret indicated the tie-wraps holding her at wrists and elbows. 'Take these off me.' When he did nothing, she added a reluctant, 'Please,' with an anxious look at his cock.

He shook his head. 'What we will do is this, Margaret. We will go to the bed and I will lie down on my back. You will straddle me while I guide this –' indicating his cock '– inside you. Then you will ease down until you are fully penetrated, and we will have a little talk before I fuck you. Or we can do it the other way around: I fuck you first, and we talk afterwards. But either way you are going to tell me what today was all about. And either way you are going to be fucked.'

'And if I do not wish to talk, or to be . . . fucked? What then, Pamela?'

'Richard,' he corrected her. 'And you have no choice.'

Margaret bridled at his tone. Her head came up and her eyes flashed. 'I do not wish to be fucked, but I may tell you about today if you free me.'

He shook his head. 'Which shall we do first?' he asked again.

'Why are you doing this to me?' she asked pleadingly.

'Because I can. And because I want you now.'

'You . . . want me?'

For answer he steered her to the bed. Her resistance crumpled, and she allowed herself to be led.

He lay down and reached up to steady her with his hands on her waist as she straddled him. 'Lower,' he said as he guided his cock into her. She was wet and parted despite her earlier show of reluctance. He slid inside as she lowered herself on to him. She smelled delightfully of soap and water and eagerness.

'Oh!' she said. 'Oh!' Her body shuddered and she clamped his cock with her vaginal muscles.

'Now, Margaret, if you're seated comfortably, we will begin. These stripes, for instance.' He traced the red marks that criss-crossed her nipples and areolae. With her wrists and elbows tied behind her back her full breasts were prominently presented.

Margaret gasped and shuddered at the touch. He felt her tighten once more around his cock. She lifted herself up and settled down again with a moan.

'Pay attention, Margaret,' Richard told her. He cupped her outthrust breasts in his palms and pinched her nipple between thumb and forefinger. 'Did you come here expecting Hannelore to do this to you?'

'Oh, God! Richard, I am going to come!' Her voice rose as he caressed her.

'Self-control, Margaret. Remember?' He released her engorged nipples and traced the marks on her stomach and belly. He stopped just short of the point where they were joined.

Margaret looked desperately at him. Her face was contorted as she teetered on the brink of orgasm.

'Well? Did you expect this?' he asked again.

'You're a devil!' she burst out. 'For God's sake, let me come! Please!'

'Hold still, Margaret. Answer the question.'

She struggled to raise herself up the pole inside her. Richard held her down as she twisted and moaned. Her vaginal muscles clenched and relaxed as she tried to come without being able to move.

She moaned. Her voice rose in a shriek as he moved inside her. She looked wildly at him as he lay still again. 'Oh, God! Don't stop now!' she pleaded.

'So why do you think she did it?' he persisted, trapping her waist with his hands as she tried to thrust herself up and down on his cock.

'Please don't do this to me! Finish me off! I'm burning up!'

Her could feel her tight muscles clamped around him, and she was indeed hot, if not exactly about to suffer spontaneous combustion. 'Will you answer me afterwards?'

'Oh, God! Yes! Anything. Just let me finish!'

'Anything.' A large cheque indeed, if he could cash it. But this interrogation-by-fornication and interrupted foreplay was alien to him. Margaret was expert at it. It was a large part of her hold over him and Helena and Pamela. He released her waist.

Margaret at once lifted herself up, and slid back down his cock with a sigh, twisting her hips as she moved, faster and faster, her breath rasping in her throat and her eyes wild.

In order to prevent himself from coming at once he cupped her frantically bobbing breasts and pinched the nipples once again. Margaret came at once, moaning, her internal muscles clamping him. He saw her stomach and belly tighten as her orgasm tore through her.

'Oh, God, oh, God, oh, God, oh, God!' Margaret was frantic, as wild as he had ever seen her. And she made him come anyway, shuddering as she shuddered, the hot spasms running through him as he emptied himself into the frantic woman on top of him.

Margaret screamed in release as she felt him come, her hips corkscrewing and thrusting wildly. She moaned and shuddered for a long time after he had finished.

Margaret took a long time to come down. He lay beneath her, his hands loosely around her waist, still buried in her. She lay on top of him. Her breasts were flattened against his chest, the nipples hard and tight. From time to time she shuddered and moaned with the aftershocks of her orgasm.

Eventually she struggled upright, still straddling him. When Richard made as if to withdraw, she shook her head. 'I want you to stay inside me if you can. I may need more of the same in a short while.' With the ghost of a smile she added, 'And I will talk more freely at cockpoint.'

'Shall I untie you?'

'No. Let me think I am your captive for now. Interrogate me roughly. I find the experience ... invigorating.'

Richard would not have used that exact word, but he understood her mood perfectly. His own pleasure lay that way too. It was interesting to find the same chord in Margaret, even if it took something like the ordeal they had shared that day to bring it to the surface.

Eventually it was time to talk. Still impaled on his cock, Margaret straightened her legs and settled down with a sigh. 'Hold me,' she said softly.

Richard slid his arms around her at waist and shoulders, holding her warm fragrant body on top of his.

Margaret lay her head on his shoulder and turned her face to him. Richard felt her soft feathery breath on his neck. Her hair spread across his face, creating a private space in which they could lie and whisper to one another.

'I did not expect Hannelore to do what she did,' Margaret began, 'but it was always a possibility. We are very much alike, you know. I have often thought about what I would do if she walked into my house alone. And obviously she had thought about the same thing. So when I brought Pamela to her, she did what I might have done. Will do, one day.' Margaret spoke without rancour.

'Does this mean your business relationship is over?'

'Oh, no. Not at all. We are competitors, but we sometimes work together. That will go on. The business

233

of making money, which is both hers and mine, goes on. What we do on a . . . more personal level . . . well, that is between us.'

'And what about . . . Pamela? Did you bring her here to be tortured?'

'Not exactly, although I knew that that too was possible. Probable,' she amended. 'I would have done the same thing if the roles had been reversed.' Margaret paused, her breath soft and warm against the side of his neck. 'It was really a sort of test for Pamela. I wanted to see where her loyalties lay. How far I could trust her – before I entrusted myself entirely to the three of you.'

'You're ruthless.'

'Well, yes, I suppose so. But isn't that what you all like in me? What you all want me to be with you, whenever I am not swooning with desire, or demanding punishment at your hands rather than submit to your base passions?' There was a chuckle in her voice as she delivered herself of these theatrical cliches.

'Don't forget,' she went on, 'that today was a test for me, too, albeit an unexpected one. I have not had my pain threshold tried so severely for ages. I like to think I did as well as Pamela did.'

'Did you plan to give Pamela to Hannelore again?'

'Of course not. I am fond of her. But Pamela had to believe that she might become a gift in order to pass the test. Tell her so the next time you see her.'

'You're a devil, you know.'

'Ah, but I am *your* devil. Does the Grand Inquisitor have any more questions?'

'I suppose not,' he replied.

'And did I pass his test? Will he perhaps put me to the sword again? It certainly feels as if he wants to.'

So they began the pleasant process of arousal once again. The sword did not outwear the sheath for a long time.

* * *

In the morning Ulrike woke them. She snipped the tie-wraps that held Margaret's wrists and elbows behind her back and summoned them to a conference with Hannelore.

'Only to be expected,' Margaret said, stretching her cramped shoulder muscles. 'She needs to know how we will respond to yesterday's entertainment. She is not really worried about a lawsuit, but we may harbour ill feelings. Can you imagine going before a court and asking for damages for yesterday? I shudder to think of the news stories.'

Richard agreed. If the world ever got to know what they did for pleasure, it would almost certainly try to stop them. 'But what are you going to do about – or to – Hannelore?'

'Nothing right now,' Margaret replied. 'Later I will invite her to my house on some pretext – perhaps on a real business matter. And she will come, even knowing she will probably have to pay for yesterday in some non-lethal and extra-financial way. She will see it as a challenge. But if I did something right away, the tit-for-tat nature of the transaction would be too obvious. And I need some time to think of some suitable programme – something original for her entertainment.' Margaret smiled in anticipation as she dressed in the clothes provided by Hannelore.

To Richard the clothes looked plain: ordinary bra and pants, opaque, non-revealing, not arousing like yesterday's. The dull brown tights and low-heeled shoes, the shapeless blue dress, were not flattering. When he remarked on it, Margaret smiled again.

'When one wishes to subdue a peacock,' she observed dryly, 'it is sometimes advantageous to mute the colours.'

'The thoughts of Chairman Wagner.' He laughed.

'Chairwoman Wagner,' she corrected with a laugh. 'Or didn't you notice the difference last night?' She indicated the clothes provided for him: Pamela's outfit from the day before, cleaned and pressed and neatly folded. 'She is putting you in your place too.'

He agreed. 'But I don't think I want that. It might be counter-productive, as they used to say. Don't you think so?'

'That depends on the result you want to produce,' Margaret replied. 'If you do as she wishes, she will think you are subdued and acquiescent. Are you?'

'That depends on who is doing the subduing.'

'Me or her, you mean?'

'Yes.'

'And which do you prefer?' Margaret asked archly.

'Better the devil you know than the one you don't.'

The indirect reply pleased Margaret, where a more direct declaration of loyalty or affection – or even love, in view of the previous night – might have embarrassed.

'What effect *do* you want to produce?' she asked.

After a moment he replied, 'Penis envy.'

Margaret laughed aloud. 'And do you expect her to fall to her knees at the sight of your cock and worship it?'

'Not exactly, though it might be nice. I suppose I just want her to see I have one. And, who knows,' he said airily, 'the rest might be wanting one too.'

Margaret looked oddly at him, her expression halfway between a grin and a frown, like a chameleon placed on a colour it couldn't quite manage. Finally she asked, 'What are you going to do?'

'Go naked but with a gun, I suppose. Nothing like showing off to create envy in others.' He grinned.

Margaret's handbag had been returned with the clothes. She rummaged inside and produced the key to his cock-ring. 'Best have this off, then,' she said. 'Never go into battle with your gun on safety.'

The ring loosened and slipped to the floor, leaving him feeling oddly naked.

Margaret kneeled to pick it up, brushing against his cock, which was showing signs of interest, though whether for battle or something else was unclear. Margaret took him into her mouth. He felt her lips around the shaft, caressing it, making it hard and tight. She withdrew until it pointed threateningly at her, then planted a kiss on the head before once more taking it inside her mouth. She cupped his balls with one hand.

Richard was speechless with surprise. Automatically, he put both hands on her head, as he did when Helena took him into her mouth. But this was Margaret, who would not take kindly to guidance. So he merely rested his hands on her head.

She looked up at him, widened her eyes and rolled them. 'Mm,' she moaned. Then she bit him.

'Ow!' he cried, trying to move his cock out of danger. Margaret held him for long moments with her teeth. Then she stood up, smiling sardonically.

'Don't think that yesterday and last night have tamed me. The leopardess of Soltau still has teeth.'

'So I see,' he said ruefully. 'Where did you hear that expression?'

'Walls have ears,' she said cryptically.

'And do these?' He gestured at the walls of their cell.

Margaret stiffened in alarm. 'Do they?'

'I don't know. Probably. Eyes too.'

She glanced wildly around, seeking hidden microphones and video cameras.

'You won't see them,' he told her. 'They're probably in the light fixtures. Disguised, at any rate.' Her alarm amused him, making partial amends for the bite. 'Are you worried about the general public seeing your fair bod in flagrante? Or sucking my cock?'

'I was not sucking!' she cried.

He shrugged. 'That's how it will look on tape.'

She swept the room once more with her eyes, and then brought them to bear on him. 'You knew all about

237

this,' she accused him. 'You deliberately set out to humiliate me!'

'What's humiliating about sucking a man's cock?'

Margaret looked daggers at him. 'Now Hannelore can hold this over my head, and threaten *me* with exposure! Damn you both!'

'Threaten to expose you to whom? And anyway, she can't do that. We have the video of her and your namesake Gretchen as a counter-threat. Mutual deterrence, wouldn't you say?'

'*You* have the tape.'

'*We* have the tape,' he replied. 'One for all and all for one, remember? Don't worry.'

Margaret looked faintly relieved, but clearly she did not like relying on someone else for help – especially not this kind of help. Not sure it would be forthcoming, Richard thought, after a lifetime of self-reliance.

But at last she came to a decision. She stripped off the drab clothing. Richard stared at her, partly in admiration as she laid her body bare, and partly in amazement. She was really a most extraordinary woman.

'Peacocks,' she said, 'cannot always be subdued. They may also counter-attack.' She folded the dress and laid it on the chair. 'How do we let Hannelore know that we are ready?'

'*She* will let *us* know when *she* is ready. You'd do the same thing in her place. Be patient. Come back to the bed and make animal noises with me.'

Margaret looked wildly around, conscious of being under observation. She shook her head vigorously. He didn't press her, knowing she was not very pressable.

She perched on the edge of a chair, looking both agitated and impatient. Sitting naked in a bedroom with a naked man was not her custom – unless he was safely chained and she wished to tease him with the unattainable.

They waited for a long time, Margaret's tension mounting dangerously.

238

Richard relaxed on the bed, pointing at the ceiling. 'Sure you don't want to come sit on this? It'll pass the time, and it's a great tranquilliser.'

Ulrike chose that moment to interrupt. Richard sighed in resignation. Margaret looked relieved.

Their nudity alarmed her. 'Why are you not ready? Frau Bern is waiting for you.' It was clear from her agitation that keeping Frau Bern waiting might be dangerous.

'We *are* dressed,' Margaret told her. 'Take us to your leader.' She signalled Richard to take Pamela's clothes along. 'That will save her a shopping trip. You know how she hates to shop for clothes.'

Hannelore Bern received them in the same room in which she had tortured them the day before. She sat at ease in an armchair, dressed, Richard thought, to overawe. Her expression when she saw her visitors was comical. Round one to us, he thought.

Hannelore recovered quickly, but she did not ask them to be seated. She intended to dominate the proceedings.

Richard caught Margaret's eye, inclining his head towards the sofa. They sat side by side, allied against Hannelore, who gave them a furious look. They waited for their hostess (as Margaret had called her ironically) to make the first move.

She was clearly disconcerted by their appearance, clearing her throat twice without speaking. Finally she said, 'You look rested, but I have no idea how you managed that.'

Neither made any comment, though Margaret reddened at this confirmation of the video cameras.

'Have you changed your mind about giving the tape to me? You know that I can expose you to ridicule simply by showing the tape.'

Margaret spoke. 'I don't think that would be very wise. We would be forced to release our own video of sports day at the bank. There would be red faces all round, don't you think?' she asked, appropriating Richard's argument without a blush.

'Yours would be redder!' Hannelore said shrilly.

'I doubt that, but you can test the reaction from our colleagues at any time. We would, of course, run our own audience-reaction studies too, and let the faces redden as they will.'

Hannelore turned to Richard. 'Pamela, you have the tape. Give it to me.'

'It's Richard, not Pamela. And no, I won't give you the tape. You can see why. Don't make the same mistake Margaret made,' he said, ignoring the angry noises from beside him. 'You can't continue to force people to do your will forever, unless you're minded to kill a few dissenters *pour encourager les autres*. We all know you won't do that, so we are at a stalemate. Mutual deterrence, as they used to say. Shall we make a video non-exhibition pact?'

Margaret nodded her approval.

Faced with a united front, Hannelore sat silently for a long time. Finally she said, 'You will not show the video?'

They shook their heads.

'Very well, then. I agree.'

Margaret smiled. 'I believe we have reached a satisfactory conclusion. Therefore we would like some suitable clothes. There must be something for Richard to wear. Trousers and shirt and shoes at least. And something tasteful for me. Oh, and please telephone my chauffeur to pick us up.'

Hannelore nodded reluctantly and pressed a button on the control box. Very soon Traudl appeared with flushed face and agitated bosom.

'You buzzed, Madam?'

Hannelore nodded and gave her the necessary instructions.

Margaret spoke *sotto voce* to Richard. 'Peacocks, pree-sennt feathers!'

He smiled. This was more like the old Margaret. The steel was back in her backbone. He was feeling rather steely too, cockwise. Margaret noticed but said nothing.

Hannelore noticed as well. She stared at his erection. Like Margaret, she would never ask for sex. It had to sneak up on her. One day it might.

'Penis envy,' Margaret said, loudly enough for Hannelore to hear.

Hannelore flushed and jerked her gaze away. The silence stretched uncomfortably until Traudl summoned them to the dressing room. Richard smiled and waved a cheerful farewell, but Hannelore did not say goodbye.

On the drive back to Zurich Margaret was mainly silent, though she smiled occasionally, once or twice at Richard. At the hotel she went straight to her room. If she felt self-conscious about being seen taking a man with her, she gave no sign.

The purchases from the day before had been sent up. Margaret went directly to the pile of boxes and bags. She opened the packages from the dress shop, laying the assortment of lingerie and corsetry out for inspection.

'Take those clothes off at once, Pamela,' she ordered. 'You know how I detest transvestites.'

Richard was glad to see Margaret back in command. After excusing himself, he went to the bathroom to shower and change. As he took off his trousers, he discovered a small jeweller's box in the pocket. It contained Margaret's nipple shields and the pins for fixing them in place. One day soon, he thought with a smile.

Epilogue

Richard came home to a quiet house. But it didn't feel empty, even though there was no sign of Helena. The warm drowsy air of spring filled the rooms as he searched for her, or for some explanation of her absence. He went silently through the silent house, not wishing to disturb the atmosphere by calling out. In the bedroom, he saw at once the woman bound to the bed on her back. She was naked save for stockings and suspenders and high heels. She wore a tight-fitting rubber hood and gag, hiding her face and head. Her long blonde hair trailed over her shoulders from beneath the hood, and her pubic hair was a crisp blonde between her widely spread legs. Over her nipples she wore golden shields, held in place by gold pins. On the chair by the bureau a leopard print dress had been carelessly flung.

NEXUS NEW BOOKS

To be published in May

INNOCENT
Aishling Morgan

Innocent tells the story of the young and faithful lady's maid Cianna and her haughty mistress Sulitea. Shipwrecked in the kingdom of Alteron, Cianna must wrestle other women for the entertainment of the masses. But as the fur flies in her world of gladiatorial combat, the distinction between her bizarre sport and her life is confusingly and thrillingly blurred. A filthy gothic fantasy tale from the author of *Pleasure Toy*.

ISBN 0 352 33699 4

UNIFORM DOLL
Penny Birch

Jade is usually a confident young lesbian, very aware of what she wants, and what she doesn't. Unfortunately her taste for being bullied can very easily get out of hand, and when she decides to compete with her filthy uncle Rupert in collecting the uniforms of sex partners, it quickly does. What starts out as a playful if provocative hobby leads to her finding herself obliged to accommodate men as well as women, and ending up in a seriously sticky mess – literally.

ISBN 0 352 33698 6

ONE WEEK IN THE PRIVATE HOUSE
Esme Ombreux

Jem is a petite, flame-haired, blue-eyed businesswoman. Lucy, tall, blonde and athletic, is a detective inspector. Julia is the slim, dark, bored wife of a financial speculator. Each arrives separately in the strange, ritualistic, disciplined domain known as the Private House. Once they meet, nothing in the House will be the same again – nothing, that is, except the strict regime of obedience and sexuality. A Nexus Classic.

ISBN 0 352 33706 0

To be published in June

RITUAL STRIPES
Tara Black

Mesmerised by the punk diva in a Seattle club, Cate Carpenter stumbles into a world of erotic cruelty. Thrilling unexpectedly to their use of instruments of chastisement, she gains admittance to an SM club linked to an ancient fertility rite. However, once recruited to work in their library of arcane fetish erotica, Cate makes enemies of everyone with her ruthless manoeuvrings and vicious canings. With the boot on the other foot, Cate must learn to temper her impulses, and come to understand that a true domina will seek out, from time to time, the pain that she inflicts on others. An arousing look at SM politics!

ISBN 0 352 33701 X

PALE PLEASURES
Wendy Swanscombe

Three sisters, Anna, Beth and Gwen Camberwell, are willingly imprisoned in the German schloss of their master, Herr Abraham Bärengelt, who is obsessed with the alabaster whiteness of their skin. They endure the most extreme torments and tribulations therein as the half-mad, half-genius Bärengelt gives free rein to his twisted imagination. Arcane, inventive erotica from the author of *Beast*.

ISBN 0 352 33702 8

AMANDA IN THE PRIVATE HOUSE
Esme Ombreux

Drawn from her sheltered life when her housekeeper Tess goes missing, Amanda goes to France in an attempt to find her. During the search Amanda meets Michael, an artist with bizarre tastes who awakens in her a taste for the shameful delights of discipline and introduces her to a secret society of hedonistic perverts who share her unusual desires. Amanda revels in her newfound sexual freedom, voluntarily submitting to extreme indignities of punishment and humiliation, but does not realise until too late the full extent of the society's depraved and perverted plans. Can Tess and Michael save her from the ultimate degradation the society has in store? A Nexus Classic.

ISBN 0 352 33705 2

If you would like more information about Nexus titles, please visit our website at www.nexus-books.co.uk, or send a stamped addressed envelope to:

Nexus, Thames Wharf Studios,
Rainville Road, London W6 9HA

NEXUS BACKLIST

This information is correct at time of printing. For up-to-date information, please visit our website at www.nexus-books.co.uk

All books are priced at £5.99 unless another price is given.

Nexus books with a contemporary setting

ACCIDENTS WILL HAPPEN	Lucy Golden ISBN 0 352 33596 3	☐
ANGEL	Lindsay Gordon ISBN 0 352 33590 4	☐
BEAST	Wendy Swanscombe ISBN 0 352 33649 8	☐
THE BLACK FLAME	Lisette Ashton ISBN 0 352 33668 4	☐
THE BLACK MASQUE	Lisette Ashton ISBN 0 352 33372 3	☐
BROUGHT TO HEEL	Arabella Knight ISBN 0 352 33508 4	☐
CAGED!	Yolanda Celbridge ISBN 0 352 33650 1	☐
CANDY IN CAPTIVITY	Arabella Knight ISBN 0 352 33495 9	☐
CAPTIVES OF THE PRIVATE HOUSE	Esme Ombreux ISBN 0 352 33619 6	☐
DANCE OF SUBMISSION	Lisette Ashton ISBN 0 352 33450 9	☐
DARK DELIGHTS	Maria del Rey ISBN 0 352 33276 X	☐
DIRTY LAUNDRY £6.99	Penny Birch ISBN 0 352 33680 3	☐
DISCIPLES OF SHAME	Stephanie Calvin ISBN 0 352 33343 X	☐

DISCIPLINED SKIN	Wendy Swanscombe ISBN 0 352 33541 6	☐
DISPLAYS OF EXPERIENCE	Lucy Golden ISBN 0 352 33505 X	☐
DISPLAYS OF INNOCENTS £6.99	Lucy Golden ISBN 0 352 33679 X	☐
DISPLAYS OF PENITENCE £6.99	Lucy Golden ISBN 0 352 33646 3	☐
DRAWN TO DISCIPLINE	Tara Black ISBN 0 352 33626 9	☐
AN EDUCATION IN THE PRIVATE HOUSE	Esme Ombreux ISBN 0 352 33525 4	☐
EMMA'S SECRET DOMINATION	Hilary James ISBN 0 352 33226 3	☐
GISELLE	Jean Aveline ISBN 0 352 33440 1	☐
GROOMING LUCY	Yvonne Marshall ISBN 0 352 33529 7	☐
HEART OF DESIRE	Maria del Rey ISBN 0 352 32900 9	☐
HIS MISTRESS'S VOICE	G. C. Scott ISBN 0 352 33425 8	☐
IN FOR A PENNY	Penny Birch ISBN 0 352 33449 5	☐
INTIMATE INSTRUCTION	Arabella Knight ISBN 0 352 33618 8	☐
THE LAST STRAW	Christina Shelly ISBN 0 352 33643 9	☐
LESSONS IN OBEDIENCE	Lucy Golden ISBN 0 352 33550 5	☐
MASTER OF CASTLELEIGH	Jacqueline Bellevois ISBN 0 352 33644 7	☐
NURSES ENSLAVED	Yolanda Celbridge ISBN 0 352 33601 3	☐
ONE WEEK IN THE PRIVATE HOUSE	Esme Ombreux ISBN 0 352 32788 X	☐
THE ORDER	Nadine Somers ISBN 0 352 33460 6	☐

THE PALACE OF EROS £4.99	Delver Maddingley ISBN 0 352 32921 1	☐
PEACHES AND CREAM £6.99	Aishling Morgan ISBN 0 352 33672 2	☐
PEEPING AT PAMELA	Yolanda Celbridge ISBN 0 352 33538 6	☐
PENNY PIECES	Penny Birch ISBN 0 352 33631 5	☐
PET TRAINING IN THE PRIVATE HOUSE	Esme Ombreux ISBN 0 352 33655 2	☐
REGIME £6.99	Penny Birch ISBN 0 352 33666 8	☐
SEE-THROUGH	Lindsay Gordon ISBN 0 352 33656 0	☐
SKIN SLAVE	Yolanda Celbridge ISBN 0 352 33507 6	☐
SLAVE ACTS £6.99	Jennifer Jane Pope ISBN 0 352 33665 X	☐
THE SLAVE AUCTION	Lisette Ashton ISBN 0 352 33481 9	☐
SLAVE EXODUS	Jennifer Jane Pope ISBN 0 352 33551 3	☐
SLAVE GENESIS	Jennifer Jane Pope ISBN 0 352 33503 3	☐
SLAVE MINES OF TORMUNIL £6.99	Aran Ashe ISBN 0 352 33695 1	☐
SLAVE REVELATIONS	Jennifer Jane Pope ISBN 0 352 33627 7	☐
SLAVE SENTENCE	Lisette Ashton ISBN 0 352 33494 0	☐
SOLDIER GIRLS	Yolanda Celbridge ISBN 0 352 33586 6	☐
THE SUBMISSION GALLERY	Lindsay Gordon ISBN 0 352 33370 7	☐
SURRENDER	Laura Bowen ISBN 0 352 33524 6	☐
TAKING PAINS TO PLEASE	Arabella Knight ISBN 0 352 33369 3	☐

THE TAMING OF TRUDI	Yolanda Celbridge	☐
£6.99	ISBN 0 352 33673 0	
TEASING CHARLOTTE	Yvonne Marshall	☐
£6.99	ISBN 0 352 33681 1	
TEMPER TANTRUMS	Penny Birch	☐
	ISBN 0 352 33647 1	
TIE AND TEASE	Penny Birch	☐
	ISBN 0 352 33591 2	
TIGHT WHITE COTTON	Penny Birch	☐
	ISBN 0 352 33537 8	
THE TORTURE CHAMBER	Lisette Ashton	☐
	ISBN 0 352 33530 0	
THE YOUNG WIFE	Stephanie Calvin	☐
	ISBN 0 352 33502 5	
WHIP HAND	G. C. Scott	☐
£6.99	ISBN 0 352 33694 3	
WHIPPING BOY	G. C. Scott	☐
	ISBN 0 352 33595 5	

Nexus books with Ancient and Fantasy settings

CAPTIVE	Aishling Morgan	☐
	ISBN 0 352 33585 8	
DEEP BLUE	Aishling Morgan	☐
	ISBN 0 352 33600 5	
MAIDEN	Aishling Morgan	☐
	ISBN 0 352 33466 5	
NYMPHS OF DIONYSUS	Susan Tinoff	☐
£4.99	ISBN 0 352 33150 X	
PLEASURE TOY	Aishling Morgan	☐
	ISBN 0 352 33634 X	
THE SLAVE OF LIDIR	Aran Ashe	☐
	ISBN 0 352 33504 1	
TIGER, TIGER	Aishling Morgan	☐
	ISBN 0 352 33455 X	

Period

CONFESSION OF AN ENGLISH SLAVE	Yolanda Celbridge ISBN 0 352 33433 9	☐
THE MASTER OF CASTLELEIGH	Jacqueline Bellevois ISBN 0 352 32644 7	☐
PURITY	Aishling Morgan ISBN 0 352 33510 6	☐

Samplers and collections

NEW EROTICA 3	Various ISBN 0 352 33142 9	☐
NEW EROTICA 5	Various ISBN 0 352 33540 8	☐
EROTICON 1	Various ISBN 0 352 33593 9	☐
EROTICON 2	Various ISBN 0 352 33594 7	☐
EROTICON 3	Various ISBN 0 352 33597 1	☐
EROTICON 4	Various ISBN 0 352 33602 1	☐
THE NEXUS LETTERS	Various ISBN 0 352 33621 8	☐

Nexus Classics

A new imprint dedicated to putting the finest works of erotic fiction back in print.

AGONY AUNT	G.C. Scott ISBN 0 352 33353 7	☐
BAD PENNY	Penny Birch ISBN 0 352 33661 7	☐
BRAT £6.99	Penny Birch ISBN 0 352 33674 9	☐
DARK DELIGHTS £6.99	Maria del Rey ISBN 0 352 33667 6	☐
DARK DESIRES	Maria del Rey ISBN 0 352 33648 X	☐
DIFFERENT STROKES	Sarah Veitch ISBN 0 352 33531 9	☐

EDEN UNVEILED   Maria del Rey   ☐
                                    ISBN 0 352 33542 4

HIS MISTRESS'S VOICE   G. C. Scott   ☐
                                    ISBN 0 352 33425 8

THE INDIGNITIES OF ISABELLE   Penny Birch writing   ☐
£6.99   as Cruella
                                    ISBN 0 352 33696 X

LETTERS TO CHLOE   Stefan Gerrard   ☐
                                    ISBN 0 352 33632 3

LINGERING LESSONS   Sarah Veitch   ☐
                                    ISBN 0 352 33539 4

OBSESSION   Maria del Rey   ☐
                                    ISBN 0 352 33375 8

PARADISE BAY   Maria del Rey   ☐
                                    ISBN 0 352 33645 5

PENNY IN HARNESS   Penny Birch   ☐
                                    ISBN 0 352 33651 X

THE PLEASURE PRINCIPLE   Maria del Rey   ☐
                                    ISBN 0 352 33482 7

PLEASURE ISLAND   Aran Ashe   ☐
                                    ISBN 0 352 33628 5

SERVING TIME   Sarah Veitch   ☐
                                    ISBN 0 352 33509 2

A TASTE OF AMBER   Penny Birch   ☐
                                    ISBN 0 352 33654 4

- - - - - - ✂ -

Please send me the books I have ticked above.

Name   ....

Address   ....

            ....

            ....

            .... Post code....................

Send to: **Cash Sales, Nexus Books, Thames Wharf Studios, Rainville Road, London W6 9HA**

US customers: for prices and details of how to order books for delivery by mail, call 1-800-343-4499.

Please enclose a cheque or postal order, made payable to **Nexus Books Ltd**, to the value of the books you have ordered plus postage and packing costs as follows:

UK and BFPO – £1.00 for the first book, 50p for each subsequent book.

Overseas (including Republic of Ireland) – £2.00 for the first book, £1.00 for each subsequent book.

If you would prefer to pay by VISA, ACCESS/MASTERCARD, AMEX, DINERS CLUB or SWITCH, please write your card number and expiry date here:

....

Please allow up to 28 days for delivery.

Signature ....

Our privacy policy.

We will not disclose information you supply us to any other parties. We will not disclose any information which identifies you personally to any person without your express consent.

From time to time we may send out information about Nexus books and special offers. Please tick here if you do *not* wish to receive Nexus information. ☐

- - - - - - ✂ -